THE ORPHAN'S PROMISE

LINDSEY HUTCHINSON

Boldwood

First published in Great Britain in 2025 by Boldwood Books Ltd.

Copyright © Lindsey Hutchinson, 2025

Cover Design by Head Design Ltd.

Cover Images: Shutterstock, iStock and Head Design Ltd.

The moral right of Lindsey Hutchinson to be identified as the author of this work has been asserted in accordance with the Copyright, Designs and Patents Act 1988.

All rights reserved. No part of this book may be reproduced in any form or by any electronic or mechanical means, including information storage and retrieval systems, without written permission from the author, except for the use of brief quotations in a book review. This book is a work of fiction and, except in the case of historical fact, any resemblance to actual persons, living or dead, is purely coincidental.

Every effort has been made to obtain the necessary permissions with reference to copyright material, both illustrative and quoted. We apologise for any omissions in this respect and will be pleased to make the appropriate acknowledgements in any future edition.

A CIP catalogue record for this book is available from the British Library.

Paperback ISBN 978-1-83518-920-7

Large Print ISBN 978-1-83518-919-1

Hardback ISBN 978-1-83518-918-4

Ebook ISBN 978-1-83518-921-4

Kindle ISBN 978-1-83518-922-1

Audio CD ISBN 978-1-83518-913-9

MP3 CD ISBN 978-1-83518-914-6

Digital audio download ISBN 978-1-83518-916-0

This book is printed on certified sustainable paper. Boldwood Books is dedicated to putting sustainability at the heart of our business. For more information please visit https://www.boldwoodbooks.com/about-us/sustainability/

Boldwood Books Ltd, 23 Bowerdean Street, London, SW6 3TN

www.boldwoodbooks.com

1

BIRMINGHAM, 1888–89

'I've told you before, Aunt Win – I don't wish to marry!' Rose said harshly.

The sharp slap to Rose's cheek resounded around the bedroom.

'Now look what you made me do!' Win's voice quavered as she stepped away from her niece.

Rose's hand went to her stinging face as she glared her anger at her mother's sister. Rose was feeling pressured yet again regarding marriage. She didn't want to wed until she found just the right man, but Win was adamant that a wedding should take place – and soon. Unable to understand the urgency, Rose's pulse began to rise in anger.

'As I've explained to you countless times, if you don't wed soon you will find yourself a spinster!' Win replied.

Like you! Rose thought but wisely kept this to herself as she dressed for yet another dreary dinner party.

Rose Hamilton was, at nineteen years old, a beautiful young woman with hair so dark it appeared black. Her blue eyes held a violet hue when she became angry or excited. She lived in a large house in Birmingham with her maternal aunt, Winifred Jacobs, known to all as Win. She had been here since her parents, Miles and Jenny Hamilton, had died of fever whilst abroad many years ago. Rose was well educated and had no trace of a Birmingham accent; she would be a fine catch for any man in search of a wife.

Moving to the mirror on her dressing table, Rose deftly pinned her teardrop hat in place with a long pearl-headed hatpin.

'Hurry up, Rose, we mustn't be late!' Win flung over her shoulder as she left Rose's bedroom.

Staring at the image looking back at her from the mirror, Rose sighed. 'Why do you insist on trying to marry me off, Aunt?' she whispered.

Opening a tiny pot, she dabbed a little rouge to her lips, then smoothed her finger over each cheek to give her a fresh look. Getting to her feet, she checked her side-button boots were clean, then ran her hands over her skirt. Walking over to the long dress mirror in the corner of her room, she gazed at her full reflection.

'I hate this dress,' came another whisper, 'it's so childish.' Buttoned to the neck with long sleeves, the white cotton skirt ended at her boots with a huge ruffle hem.

'Rose!'

Hearing the call, she sighed again and strode from her room, along the landing and descended the sweeping staircase to the hall where Win was waiting.

'Do come along, you know how I despise being late!' Win said as they stepped out into the last of the sun's rays. 'It's still so hot,' she went on as she climbed into the waiting cab which had been heralded by Jackson, the butler.

'I love the summer,' Rose muttered as she followed her aunt.

As they settled and the carriage moved off, Win asked, 'Where's your parasol?'

'I forgot it,' Rose answered sheepishly.

'Oh, really! It simply won't do, Rose!'

Rose shrugged and looked out of the window.

'I do declare these streets get grubbier by the day,' Win said as the cab took them from the outskirts into the town, before veering off again to the wealthier areas. 'Now remember – behave yourself. The Wellinghams are well-respected pillars of the community, and this is a perfect opportunity for us to find you a decent husband.'

Rose nodded but kept her eyes on the busy streets, watching folk beavering about their business. She wondered where they were all going and what they would do when they got there. Women with gaggles of children pushing their way through the crowds, men in dirty clothes heading home from work, and beggars sitting on the street corners. Rose noticed a busker and chimney sweep stop to exchange a word as the cab slowed, having been caught in the traffic of carts and carriages. They lurched as the vehicle gathered speed once more, moving down a street of grimy buildings standing cheek by jowl in the bustling town.

As they travelled, Rose thought about the place she'd lived in all of her young life. She recalled from her studies that Birmingham boasted Bingley Exhibition Centre, opened in 1850. In 1853 the Mint was first contracted to produce coins of one pound sterling. The year 1859 saw the School of Music formed and in 1861 a bylaw required all new houses to be connected to the sewers. There was a central library, fire stations and law courts, police stations and cable trams. It had its first electricity supply in 1882 but many places still relied upon gas lighting. There was also a telephone exchange, museums, theatres and an art gallery. Everything one could wish for, but Rose had seen barely anything of her hometown.

The scenery began to change to more open spaces and large houses set back off the road. Screens of trees kept some residences hidden from view, while others had long gravel driveways.

The cab turned a corner and into one of these drives lined each side with poplar trees. It drew to a halt at the end in front of a huge mansion. Win and Rose alighted and were greeted by a butler who glanced at their invitation card before leading them inside.

Mr and Mrs Wellingham were waiting in the spacious hall to welcome their guests. A maid offered a tray of glasses of wine, which Rose was denied. Another maid produced a tray of homemade lemonade, giving Rose a sympathetic look. Rose was introduced to the hosts before being dragged away by her aunt.

The guests were led into the drawing room by yet another maid to make space for others arriving. Win escorted Rose around the room, exchanging a word here and there with the higher echelons of society.

Rose smiled sweetly in all the right places but said little. She watched her aunt playing the lady bountiful as she explained how she had taken in her niece after the death of her parents. Rose grimaced inwardly as people congratulated Win on such a selfless act. They had absolutely no idea how much Rose missed her mother and father, and what she wouldn't give to have them back with her. It was true Rose lived in relative luxury, but the one thing she craved was the one thing she didn't have – love.

Sipping her drink, Rose's attention wandered as she glanced around the room. Mostly it was filled with older couples talking quietly. There was no one of her own age and Rose sighed; why was she here? She knew Win was on the lookout for a discerning fellow who would make Rose a good husband, but *they're all old!* she thought.

Suddenly Rose felt her arm being grabbed.

'Rose, that gentleman standing by the fireplace is the one who wishes to negotiate for your hand,' Win said quietly.

Rose followed Win's line of sight and frowned. 'Aunt Win, please tell me you're joking! He must be a hundred if he's a day!' In truth the gentleman was probably in his fifties. He was short of stature with a balding head. Small eyes nestled in a rounded face, giving him a pig-like look.

'Don't be so rude, girl! He's a very wealthy man; owns a string of businesses, I believe.'

Rose looked at his attire which, although clean, was not new. She thought if he was so rich he should have at least bought a new suit.

'I don't care if he owns the town, I'm not marrying him!' Rose looked away as the short balding man glanced in her direction.

A moment later, the butler rang a hand bell. 'Ladies and gentlemen, dinner is served.'

Slowly everyone moved to the massive dining room and found their seats.

'Oh, no!' Rose whispered to herself. She was sitting right next to the little man she and Win had been discussing. A feeling of foreboding settled on her as she went to take her seat.

2

'May I?' the man asked as he stood behind Rose's chair. Inclining her head, she gasped as he rammed the chair into the back of her legs, causing her to drop heavily onto the thick padding. She smiled her thanks as he sat down and shook out his napkin which he tucked into his neckwear.

Wine glasses were filled, except Rose's, and the first course arrived – French onion soup. Low conversation buzzed around the table and Rose winced as her suitor slurped his soup noisily.

'My name is Ray Johnstone,' he mumbled.

'Rose Hamilton,' she replied after dabbing her mouth with the napkin lifted from her lap.

'Oh, I know who you are, m'dear. That's why I'm here, to talk to your aunt.'

'Mr Johnstone, may I suggest you don't bother.' Rose allowed the maid to remove her bowl and curled her lip as Ray drank the dregs from his before relinquishing it.

'Why not?' he asked abruptly.

Rose watched red wine being poured and tapped her glass for it to be filled. The butler looked down at her and she grinned.

With a smirk of his own, he obeyed her silent instruction. Turning back to Ray, she said, 'I don't wish to be married – to you or anyone else.'

Johnstone blew out his cheeks and shot a sour look at Win sitting across and a few seats down from him. Rose allowed herself a small smile, feeling rather better now she'd got this off her chest.

The roast beef dinner and sorbet to follow was enjoyed in peace by Rose. Johnstone didn't speak to her again, much to her relief.

Later, the ladies took coffee in the drawing room whilst the men enjoyed brandy and cigars in the parlour.

'Mr Johnstone will be...' Win began.

'He won't, Aunt. I told him straight away he was wasting his time.'

Win's face was a picture of shock. Her greying hair drawn back severely into a bun at the nape of her neck did nothing to soften her features. She was a thin lady who ate like a little bird, her pinched face almost always frowning. 'Why, Rose? Why do you insist on making me look a fool?'

'That's not my intention, Aunt, but you just won't accept that I don't want a husband.' The frustration in Rose's voice was evident.

Just then, they were interrupted by a lady Rose didn't know who wanted to speak with Win. Rose took advantage of this intervention to find the privy. A maid directed her upstairs and Rose thought, *how lovely, an indoor bathroom!*

Returning to the drawing room, Rose sauntered towards the French windows which stood open, allowing a cool breeze to carry the fragrance of flowers into the stuffy room.

'Miss Hamilton, if I'm not mistaken.' The deep voice took Rose by surprise.

Turning towards the speaker, she nodded. The man was in his middle to late thirties, she guessed, and was very handsome. His dark hair had begun to grey at the temples, giving him a distinguished air. Brown eyes looked into hers and Rose felt a blush rise to her cheeks.

'May I introduce myself? My name is Charles Dean.'

'Pleased to meet you, Mr Dean,' Rose replied shyly.

'I don't know about you, but I find these occasions rather a bore,' he whispered.

Rose grinned. 'I came with my Aunt Win.'

'Ah, yes. Miss Jacobs.'

'Do you know her?' Rose asked.

'I do know her.'

'Oh dear, that sounds ominous.'

'Not at all, but it's clear what she's here for. I would guess she's in search of a suitable husband – for you.'

'I'm afraid so.' Rose lowered her eyes so he would not see the sadness she was sure they held.

'Has she succeeded?' Charles asked.

'She had thought Mr Johnstone but I quashed his intentions at dinner.'

Charles's booming laughter rang out, drawing eyes their way. 'Good for you. I don't think he's the man who would make you happy.'

'Neither do I. He slurps his soup!'

Again Charles laughed and Rose began to relax and enjoy his company. Charles, she noted, was older than herself and full of confidence, which she had to admit she liked. He was terribly handsome too and she couldn't help but look into his eyes when he spoke. He made her feel shy and daring at the same time and her heart began to beat a little faster as he stared at her.

'Ladies and gentlemen, please take your seats in the music room,' the butler called out.

'Oh, no, another hour at least of listening to a lady singing her heart out, but sounding like a cat with its tail caught under a door!'

Rose giggled as she followed the others to find a seat.

A man in a tailcoat stood by the piano next to a woman in a voluminous pink dress.

'Reminds me of a blancmange,' the whisper came in Rose's ear and she smiled at Charles before he moved away from her.

The duo were introduced and before long Charles's prediction proved correct. The singer was not opera trained but gave it her all, straining to reach the high notes which was painful to the ears.

Rose felt eyes on her and turned her head to see Charles watching her. He grimaced at the singing and Rose could barely contain her smile. She had to look away from him before she burst out laughing.

Everyone sighed with relief when the singer and pianist took their final bow.

Rose ambled out into the gardens, which were bedecked with lanterns, although it was still quite light. She breathed in the warm summer air as she strolled along the gravel pathway.

'We meet again,' Charles said as he caught up with her.

'Mr Dean, did you enjoy the entertainment?' Rose asked, a little tongue in cheek.

'Is that what it's called? Good grief, I thought it more like Kilkenny cats fighting!' Rose cast a glance around, fearful of being overheard. 'My apologies, I only meant to make you smile. It can't be much fun for you being dragged along to these evenings.'

'It's not so bad, at least I enjoy a good dinner,' Rose quipped.

It seemed the more they talked, the more her own confidence was building.

Laughing, he asked, 'So tell me, Miss Hamilton, when do you think it likely your aunt will find you a husband?'

'Never, Mr Dean.'

'Oh, and why is that?'

'Because life has too much to offer to be shackled to a sink and a husband who wishes to rule over his lady. I'm not looking to be married now – if ever.' Seeing his eyebrows rise and his mouth open, she went on, 'You have made me smile, the look on your face is priceless.'

3

'Rose? Rose! There you are, it's time we were leaving.' Win bustled towards her niece who was still chatting with Charles Dean.

'Aunt Win, may I introduce...' Rose began.

'Charles,' Win cut across sharply.

'Winifred. I see time has not improved your temperament.'

Rose frowned, then she recalled Charles saying he knew her aunt.

'Nor your roguish ways,' Win snapped back. 'Excuse us, we're leaving.' Grabbing Rose's arm, she dragged the girl away.

'Goodnight, Mr Dean,' Rose called.

'Goodnight, Miss Hamilton, no doubt we shall meet again.'

I do hope so, Rose thought as she was hurried to the hallway to give thanks to their hosts. She smiled inwardly as she thought about how easy Charles was to talk to. He listened to what she had to say without shouting her down, and his handsome look was a definite bonus. His eyes crinkled and sparkled when he laughed, and his teeth were white and perfect. Rose's pulse sped up as she considered... could he be the man for her?

Outside the line of cabs moved forward as each was taken and moved off. Win shoved Rose into one and called out their destination.

'So you know Mr Dean, it would seem,' Rose commented as the cab pulled away.

'Oh, yes, I know Charles of old, and I warn you he can be a cad!'

'I liked him, he made me laugh.'

Win harrumphed. 'You stay away from that one, my girl.'

'That could be difficult if you keep taking me to these dinners and balls,' Rose said.

'Don't be obtuse, Rose, you know exactly what I mean.'

Rose sighed and said no more. She was enjoying thinking about the handsome Charles Dean.

When they arrived home, they were greeted by Jackson, the butler, who paid the cabbie while Rose went indoors. Win followed, saying, 'I was very disappointed in you this evening. We were there to find you a husband!'

'No, Aunt Win, *you* were there for that reason, I was not. *I do not want to wed!* It doesn't matter how often you pursue this endeavour, Aunt, I'm not interested!' Rose strode up the stairs to her bedroom where a slam of the door put the full stop on the conversation. Sitting on the bed, Rose's clenched fists slammed down onto her thighs in utter frustration. She breathed deeply through her nose as she tried to calm herself. When would Win understand how she was feeling?

Jackson slipped away to the kitchen.

Neither of the women had noticed Katy Slater, the maid, hiding in the shadows. Clearing her throat, Katy stepped into the light from the hall gas lamps. 'Can I get you anything, madam?'

'No, Katy, I'm going to bed.'

Katy bobbed a knee and scuttled down the few steps to the kitchen.

'They're back then?' Mary Winters asked. Mary had been the cook at the Hamiltons' residence for years. She and Jackson had been employed by Win when she had taken Rose in. A widow, Mary had been happy watching Rose grow into a lovely young woman. She had also been devastated by the news of the Hamiltons' deaths. Mary was as round as she was high with silver-white hair and twinkling blue eyes. She had lost her husband in a pit accident ten years into their marriage, and Mary had not looked at another man since.

'Ar, and the missus ain't happy,' Katy replied.

'She never is. Put the kettle to boil, there's a good girl.' Mary watched the young maid go about her business. Katy was an orphan with virtually no education. She couldn't read or write very well, but she was a demon with figures. No one knew why but Katy could work sums in her head quick as a flash. The girl was stick thin, no matter that she ate mountains of food; she often laughed, despite having a haunted look about her at times. Mary loved her like she was her own.

'There you go, Mrs Winters. Can I have a biscuit, please?' Katy asked.

'Course you can, lovey; I don't know where you put all that food, you must have hollow legs!' Mary replied with a warm smile.

Katy giggled as she dug a hand into the jar. 'In the mouth and round the gums, look out belly, here it comes.' Then she bit into the confection as Mary laughed loudly.

'I wonder why the missus wants to marry off Miss Rose so badly?' Mary mused.

'I don't know. She don't have to wed if'n she don't want to, does she?'

'I wouldn't have thought so. There's more to this than meets the eye if you ask me.'

'I d'aint ask you,' Katy answered innocently.

'It's just a saying, sweetheart,' Mary explained. Inside, Mary had her own suspicions as to the missus's reasons but she kept them to herself – for now, at least.

'Oh.' Katy eyed the jar, willing another biscuit to leap out and into her fingers.

'How do you fancy a sausage sandwich?' Mary asked.

'Ooh, yes, please!' Katy jumped to her feet. 'I'll get 'em off the cold slab.'

Mary smiled as she placed the frying pan on the hotplate of the range and scraped some pork dripping into it. Her mind, however, then turned to Rose once more as she cooked their supper. The more she thought about it, the more she was convinced she was right and the time would come when she would have to speak to someone about it.

'Gossiping again, Mrs Winters?' Jackson's deep voice made Mary jump as he came through from the butler's pantry.

'Must you go sneaking around? You nearly gave me a heart attack!'

'My apologies, I'm sure.'

'Do you want some supper?' Despite Jackson being the butler, he was also Mary's friend and she liked him enormously. They often chatted when everyone else was in bed and he didn't take umbrage when she was occasionally sharp with him.

'Thank you, no. I think I'll head up now. Goodnight.' With that, Jackson left the kitchen.

'Was that Mr Jackson?' Katy asked as she passed over the sausages.

'Yes, he's gone to bed,' Mary replied, dropping the sausages into the pan.

'You know I do like him. He's like a father figure to me,' Katy said, which brought a smile to Mary's lips.

'Something smells good.'

Cook and maid started at the sound of Rose's voice. Mary wasn't sure that Rose would join them that night as she usually did, and was glad when the girl walked into the kitchen.

'Would you like to join us, Miss Rose?' Mary asked.

'If there's enough, yes, please.'

'I'll make a fresh pot of tea,' Katy said as Rose sat at the table.

'How was your evening?' Mary asked.

'Oh, you know, same as ever.' Rose went on to tell them all about Ray Johnstone as well as Charles Dean. She was perfectly comfortable talking to the staff in this way, they were her only friends, after all. After the death of her parents, Rose had become even closer to Mary. She looked on the older woman as a surrogate mother, someone who would listen to her problems without making any judgement. Mary could always be relied upon to provide sound advice as well as a shoulder to cry on.

'That Charlie Dean sounds like fun,' Katy said between bites of her sandwich.

'Mr Dean was funny, I have to admit, but Aunt Win said I should stay away from him.'

'Why?' Mary asked, feeling a little uncomfortable. She knew the reason but felt it was not her place to speak out. Mary was aware that Charles Dean and Win Jacobs had been quite close at one time, and she worried this could be the reason for Win's behaviour.

'I have no idea. It appears they know each other and Aunt Win thinks he's a cad.'

'Sounds like a bit of jealousy,' Katy put in.

'Just eat your supper, lass, while you're talking you're missing a bite.' Mary's reprimand was so mild Katy never even noticed it.

'I suppose I could ask him how he knows my aunt if I should ever see him again,' Rose said, then popped the last of her food into her mouth.

'That'll rile the missus if you do,' Mary warned.

'Everything annoys her these days,' Rose agreed. 'Thank you for supper, I'll sleep better now.' After saying goodnight, Rose left them to go to her bed.

'I'll wash the plates and pans,' Katy offered.

'Bugger it, leave them for the morning,' Mary said as she got wearily to her feet.

'That ain't like you,' Katy said with a worried frown.

'I'm getting old, I think. Come on, let's go to our own beds, the morning will be here soon enough.'

4

Rose thought about the conversation she'd had with Mary as she lay in bed, and wondered again about why her aunt was so set against Charles Dean. Rose considered him a thoroughly nice man, not that she'd had much to do with men in general, but at least he had a sense of humour.

Watching the silvery beams of moonlight chase the shadows into the corners of her room, Rose hoped she and Mr Dean *would* meet again because she really quite liked him. Something about the man made her feel safe in his company, and she was sure he liked her too. Again, she dared to wonder if a relationship with Charles Dean wasn't wholly out of the question.

The following morning, over breakfast, Rose wanted to bring up the subject of Charles Dean again, but decided against it as Aunt Win seemed in no mood for tittle-tattle.

'When you have finished, we are going into town. I think it is about time to refresh your wardrobe.' Win cast a glance at Jackson, who stood silently at the side of the room. He nodded.

Rose glanced up from her boiled egg, saying, 'Thank you, Aunt, maybe I could have something a little more grown-up this time. I am no longer a child, after all.' A feeling of excitement washed over her until Win spoke again, dashing all hopes of a little independence being allowed.

'I realise that. However, prim and proper is the way to go if you want to attract a husband.' Win spoke without taking her eyes off her teacup.

Rose sighed loudly and pushed her plate away.

'Not hungry?' Win asked, eyeing the half-eaten food.

'Not any more. Excuse me.' Rose stood and walked from the dining room. Ascending the stairs, she collected her straw boater, bag and parasol before returning to the hall to pin her hat in place.

Katy came up from the kitchen to collect the plates and asked, 'You going out, Miss Rose?'

'Apparently we are going shopping,' Rose replied with a roll of her eyes.

'Ah, well, good luck.' The maid wiggled her eyebrows and smirked, making Rose smile.

'Watch where you're going!' Win snapped as she walked straight into the maid.

'Sorry, madam.' Katy stuck out her tongue behind Win's back and Rose turned away before she laughed out loud. It was behaviour that Katy should have been reprimanded for, but Rose loved her dearly and would never say a word which would get the girl in trouble.

As she adjusted her hat in the hall mirror, the butler appeared.

'Hail a cab, Jackson,' Win instructed.

With a nod, Jackson walked down the drive and looked around. Seeing a cab waiting along the street, he waved his arm but the cabbie didn't notice. Jackson rammed his fingers in his mouth and whistled loudly. That got the cabbie's attention; he waved in return and clucked to his horse.

On the doorstep, Win muttered, 'I really must do something about that maid, she's so clumsy.'

Rose shivered to think her aunt might sack the young girl. 'She means well, Aunt,' she said quietly as they watched Jackson return, the cab following along behind.

Rose climbed aboard and waited while Win gave the cabbie a list of names of the shops they might visit. Win was just about inside when the cab lurched forward. She stumbled before landing heavily on the seat. 'Stupid man!' she muttered. Looking at her niece, she went on, 'We have a number of occasions coming up, all of which could be of benefit. That is why we are shopping today. We have to get you seen in all the right circles if we are to be successful in our quest.'

'*Your* quest,' Rose said, not deigning to look at Win. Instead she stared out of the window at the ladies in their fine clothes, wishing she could wear the same. She noticed also the poorer women in their drab skirts and blouses as they hurried towards the market in search of a bargain. The dirty buildings stood cheek by jowl with men hanging about on street corners, all hoping to be given a day's work. The pavements were crammed with people all seeming to have somewhere to go. Women with gaggles of children hanging onto their skirts rushed along, dashing across the road between the traffic. Carts and wagons clogged the highways as they crawled towards their destinations, and Rose felt exhilarated by the hustle and bustle of the town.

The cab slowed then halted and Win got out, telling the cabbie to wait. Rose followed her into the very large shop, its windows displaying beautiful clothes which could be found indoors. A red suit with black brocade caught her eye, the skirt falling gracefully to the floor and the jacket nipped into the waist, and Rose sighed with longing.

'Miss Jacobs, how nice to see you again,' the modiste gushed.

'We have functions to attend so I need my niece to be outfitted appropriately,' Win replied as she marched across to the sitting room.

'Of course. Are we talking balls?'

Win raised an eyebrow before saying, 'Yes, as well as soirées and tea parties.' She dropped onto a highly padded chaise longue.

The modiste clapped her hands twice and two young ladies came running. After quiet instructions, the girls disappeared then returned carrying arms full of dresses. Each one was held up for Win to inspect, a nod telling them which ones Rose was to try on.

Rose's heart fell as she eyed the garments. Long sleeves, high necks and all in dark colours. 'I'd like something a little brighter,' she said.

'We can make them in any colour or material you wish,' the modiste answered.

'There's nothing wrong with grey or brown, Rose, at least they are respectable,' Win snapped. 'Now, try those and let me see.'

Rose dutifully did as she was told, despite feeling wretched about the drab colours. Win was sipping coffee when she returned wearing a dark green dress which buttoned at the front to the neck, almost choking her. The leg o' mutton sleeves billowed out like sails on a boat.

'Turn around. Yes, I like it.' Win nodded as Rose faced her once more.

'I'm not wearing this!' Rose protested.

'Rose!' Win was aghast at the outburst.

'It's too old for me, Aunt,' Rose said.

'I'm inclined to agree,' the modiste put in quietly. 'Maybe we could try something more suited to her age.' Rose gave the woman a grateful smile, at least someone was on her side.

Rose strode away back to the changing room before Win could answer. Next she tried on a ball gown in lemon tulle. The neckline was cut dangerously low and the capped sleeves rested delicately on her shoulders. Nipped in to the waist, the layers of the skirt fanned out, ending at her shoes. 'Aunt Win will hate this,' Rose said as she looked at herself in the long mirror, 'but I *love* it!'

Rose swept into the viewing room and spun around. 'This is perfect!'

'No! No! It's far too risqué!' Win was horrified at the amount of flesh on show. 'Take it off this instant!'

'It is the height of fashion at the moment...' the modiste began, but at a look from Win she closed her mouth with a snap.

'If the bodice was – higher, and the sleeves were... I'm really not sure at all,' Win said as she tilted her head to the side.

'Please, Aunt Win!' Rose begged. 'I'm sure all the girls will be dressed similarly.'

'Hmm.' Win thought about it and she couldn't argue with the statement. If allowing Rose some leeway on the clothes front would bag her a husband then it would be worth it. 'All right, but not lemon.'

'Thank you!' Rose dashed off to the changing room, followed closely by the modiste.

'So what colour is it to be?'

Rose whispered, 'Red, bright red!' She laughed at the look of shock on the other woman's face.

5

'Your aunt will have a fit if we deliver a red dress!' the modiste said, wringing her hands.

'She won't know until it's too late. Please do this for me. You saw the green dress she wanted – I'm nineteen, not ninety!'

'I understand that but – red? She won't pay for it when she sees it and we will lose money on it,' she said, wiping a sheen of sweat from her brow with a handkerchief pulled from her pocket.

'I will buy it myself. Have it delivered to the house by way of Mary in the kitchen. I will ensure she has the money ready for you. I'd best have one made in blue too so Aunt Win won't question it.' Rose was a little concerned about what Win would say, but the powerful feeling of rebellion was on her and she would not deny it.

'Very well, on your head be it. Now let's try some more before she comes looking for us,' the modiste whispered conspiratorially.

Rose received a monthly allowance but had spent very little over the years. Of course she'd bought cosmetics and the like but

Win still paid for her clothes, which was why Rose couldn't really complain.

After a couple of hours, aunt and niece left with nothing more having been said about the ball gown. Rose was delighted at the change in Win regarding the purchasing of garments, having given her niece far more choice for herself.

'Thank you, Aunt,' Rose said in the cab on their way home, patting the boxes next to her; the other dresses being made to measure.

'On reflection, I realised that you *are* no longer a child and you must start to take on some responsibility. Choosing your own wardrobe, I thought, would be a good start.'

Rose smiled but inwardly shuddered. She knew that when Win discovered the colour of the ball gown, all this new-found responsibility would be snatched away again. Red was not a colour prim and proper ladies wore, it was more synonymous with the ladies of the night. Rose was aware of this but the feeling of devilment had run away with her, and now with excitement building, she was actually looking forward to the upcoming ball.

'Tomorrow evening we will be attending a soirée at the Glendenings'. Everyone who is anyone will be there.'

'Including Mr Dean?' Rose asked.

Win bristled. 'I expect so, he appears to be everywhere of late.'

This seemed the perfect opportunity to ask the question which Rose wanted the answer to. 'Why don't you like him, Aunt?'

'The man is not the sort you should associate with, Rose, trust me on this.'

'I thought he was rather nice.'

'So does everyone in the beginning. He can be charming on

the surface but beneath he is a rake. I don't want you to have anything to do with him, is that clear?'

'Yes, Aunt,' Rose mumbled but her brain was asking, *what if he talks to me again? I can hardly see how I could avoid conversation then without appearing rude.* She felt again the rebellious spirit rise in her like a racehorse wanting to gallop and she smiled, knowing she would allow it its head.

Once home, Rose took her packages straight to her room where she hung up her new dresses. She sat on the bed to admire them but it was the ball gown she wanted to wear and couldn't wait for it to be delivered. All she had to do was get to it before Win did; she would have to watch out for it arriving.

Going downstairs, Rose went to the kitchen.

'Hello, Miss Rose, did you have a lovely shopping trip?' Mary asked.

'Yes, thank you. By the way, Mary, I'm expecting a package sometime soon and I'd be grateful if you would take it in and pay for it if I leave you the money.'

'O' course I will, Miss Rose, but can I ask – why me?'

'It's – a surprise, and I don't think Aunt Win will approve one little bit. Now is there any chance of a cup of tea?'

'Right away, Katy will bring it to the sitting room.'

Giving her thanks, Rose left the kitchen.

'What was all that about?' Jackson asked.

'I ain't got a clue,' Mary answered. Rolling out the pastry for the pie she was making, Mary's thoughts turned again to Win and Charles Dean. The two had attended school together and had become very close. Everyone, including Win, had thought they would marry when they were old enough, but Charles had other ideas. Win had been devastated when Charles had assured her it was not his intention to wed her. After a blazing argument,

Charles and Win had become estranged; Win had never forgiven him. It was the talk of the town for a long time.

Now it seemed Charles was showing an interest in Win's niece. Despite being eager to marry the girl off, there was no way on God's green earth Win would allow Charles Dean to court Rose. How could she when she still had feelings for the man herself?

'I'll take this tea up,' Katy said, breaking into Mary's thoughts.

'Thanks,' Mary replied as she placed the finished pie in the range to bake.

In the sitting room, Win was replying to correspondence and Rose was looking out of the French windows at the garden. She watched the birds tapping their beaks on the grass, searching for a tasty worm before hopping to another area.

'Thank you, Katy,' Win said as the tray was laid on the table. The maid bobbed a knee and left the room quietly. Win moved from her escritoire to pour the refreshments, and Rose joined her.

'Will you tell me about the soirée, Aunt?' Rose asked.

'Oh, it will be dinner first, usually very good. The Glendenings' cook is a marvel. Then drinks in the drawing room before retiring to the music room where the entertainment will be held. Probably a singer, as is usual at these functions.' Rose nodded and sipped her tea. 'I just hope it's not opera, I can't bear a caterwauling woman,' Win went on.

'Is it only ever singers?'

'Normally, yes, but not always. Some hosts book a magician or a comedian but it's rare in our circles.'

Aunt Win, you are a snob! Rose thought. One-upmanship was very important to Win, as Rose had learned over the years of living with her; Win definitely saw herself as one of the higher echelon of society.

Finishing her drink, Win returned to her little writing desk and Rose went outside to enjoy the dying rays of the sun.

Sitting on a bench beneath a huge oak tree, she watched the squirrels scampering and envied them their freedom. Birds twittered high in the canopy and insects buzzed lazily past. In the distance, a church clock struck five times, denoting the hour. Rose closed her eyes, luxuriating in the heat of the sun on her face, for which Win would undoubtedly berate her. Pale skin was considered to be beautiful but Rose didn't care at that moment. She felt her skin prickle, and breathed in the warm summer air which carried the fragrance of honeysuckle and jasmine. A rustle in the grass had her open one eye to see a vole disappear into the undergrowth. With a smile she closed the eye again, perfectly at peace in her surroundings.

6

Having moved from her desk, Win stood behind the long drape and watched her niece. She was beautiful, no one could deny that, and in a couple of years would become a very wealthy woman in her own right unless...

Retaking her seat, Win's thoughts travelled back in time. Many years ago, Win had agreed to care for Rose whilst her sister, Jenny, and her husband, Miles, travelled to Africa. Rose was still in school and needed to finish her education so had remained behind. But whilst there, Miles and Jenny had contracted a fever – some sort of dysentery from what Win was told. After a short but disabling illness, both had succumbed and died. A missionary had written to Win informing her of her sister's demise, having found the necessary information amongst the Hamiltons' belongings. Both had been given a Christian burial, she was assured.

Once a suitable mourning period had elapsed, Win had received a letter from a solicitor who requested a meeting. He had heard the news of the deaths and needed to share the details of Miles's will.

Win had attended that meeting while Rose was at school and was astounded when learning the contents of the will. Rose would inherit everything on her twenty-first birthday; Miles's substantial fortune, the family home as well as the house Win lived in which also belonged to Miles. However, there was a clause in the will which Win had clung to for dear life. Should Rose marry *before* her twenty-first birthday then everything would go to Win. She had no idea why Miles had written this into his last will and testament other than trying to keep the money and property in the family. When a woman married, all that she owned then came to her husband automatically. Miles had clearly thought that Rose would know her own mind at twenty-one years of age, but maybe not before then.

Whatever the reasoning, Win *had* to get Rose married off soon, otherwise she could find herself penniless and out on the street. Up until now, Win and Rose had lived comfortably due to a housekeeping account set up at the bank by Miles before he left the country. There was enough to see Win to the end of her days, but would that change when Rose took her inheritance? Win didn't know and she had no intention of finding out. She had just over eighteen months now to get that girl wed and she would do all she could to ensure it happened. Win was set to become the wealthiest woman in Birmingham, maybe even the country. And what of Rose, what would happen to her if she was unhappy in her marriage?

'Tough,' Win murmured, totally absorbed in her daydreaming. Once her niece was off her hands, Win would not spare her another thought.

Glancing again at the invitations on her desk, Win knew she was in a race against the clock. Somehow she had to find a suitor who Rose would not reject out of hand, which was easier said than done. Eighteen months was the blink of an eye in the great scheme of things, and Win knew that once Rose accepted a proposal there would have to be an engagement period. It would have to be short and the wedding very soon afterwards, otherwise time would run out.

Picking up the card from the Glendenings, Win prayed this would be the occasion where Rose would meet her future husband. If not...? Win hastily returned to completing her acceptances to forthcoming functions.

* * *

The following evening, Rose dressed in one of her new dresses. White cotton with a thin blue vertical stripe, it was gathered at the back to rest on a small bustle. Delicate white shoes peeped from beneath the hem and as she buttoned up the bodice, Rose smiled. At last she felt like a grown-up. Sitting at her dressing table, she touched rouge to her cheeks and lips before brushing her long dark hair. It shone like a raven's wing in the sunshine coming through the window, but being left worn loose labelled her as still being a child. Grabbing pins, she worked to pile it high on her head and, looking at her reflection, she gasped. A young woman stared back at her and Rose's smile broadened. A tiny hat and the transformation was complete.

Going to the long mirror, she checked her look again and, feeling satisfied, she left her room, descended the stairs to where Win was waiting.

'Rose, you look very nice but you know you should have left your hair down. It lets people know you are unattached.'

'I prefer it like this.'

'Cab's here, madam,' Jackson called out.

'Well, there's no time to change it now. Come on before we're late!' Win pushed Rose out of the front door and into the waiting cab. As it pulled away, she said, 'Now you mind you behave yourself. There are two gentlemen who could be interested in making you into a wife.'

'Aunt, how many times do we have to go through this?'

'Rose, I will brook no argument from you. How do you think your parents would feel...?'

'They won't, they're gone!' Rose snapped, feeling more and more exasperated.

'Yes, they are, and you are now my ward, my responsibility. I want to honour my promise to them to ensure you are well taken care of once I'm no longer here.' Win saw her words had hit the mark as Rose lowered her eyes. Forcing a catch in her voice, she went on, 'So now you understand?'

Rose was sure her parents would want her to marry well, but surely they wouldn't have forced her into a marriage she didn't want? She felt the pressure Win exerted over her but then she considered her own feelings on the matter. 'Yes, but Aunt, what about what I want? I'm too young to be thinking of marriage.'

'Rose, girls far younger than you are being wed. If you're not careful, all the eligible bachelors will have been taken.'

Rose rested the back of her head on the high seat of the cab. How could she make her aunt understand? If she couldn't marry for love, then she would remain single. She didn't want to be joined to a man who was old enough to be her grandfather, and she said so.

'Then let's look for someone younger – nearer your age,' Win answered.

'Where? Everyone at these parties are older people!'

'Maybe, but a lot have sons, Rose.'

'I suppose so.' Rose nodded but she was still unsure as despondency settled on her.

'All right, we're here. Remember what I said and do try to enjoy yourself.'

7

Alighting from the cab, they were greeted by a butler who led them into the drawing room. Rose glanced around the room at the furniture which was highly polished and worth a fortune. Ladies were sitting talking, their men discussing business by the huge fireplace, drinks in hand.

'Ah, Win – and Rose, how lovely you look,' Mrs Glendening called as she strode towards them.

Rose smiled then sighed as Win was dragged away by the hostess towards a group of women. Left alone, Rose sauntered across the room, heading for the glass doors open to the garden. As she went, she looked at the portraits hung on the walls; clearly the Glendenings' ancestors. Stepping out onto the well-kept lawn, Rose instantly felt more comfortable. She found a bench and sat down, seeing the grass spread out to cover the large garden. Lanterns hung from tree branches and stood like tiny guards along the pathways. These would be lit later when the sun sank below the horizon. She could still hear the low buzz of conversation broken by the occasional high-pitched woman's laugh.

What am I doing here? she asked herself. *I'd much rather be at home sharing supper with my friends Katy, Mary and Jackson.*

A deep voice startled her and she looked up into the brown eyes of Charles Dean.

'Miss Hamilton, I do declare!'

'Mr Dean.'

'What happened to your pigtails?'

Rose patted her hair, saying, 'Please don't tease me, Mr Dean.'

'My apologies. May I say you look radiant this evening.' Charles pointed to the bench and at Rose's nod he sat next to her and saw the blush rise to her cheeks. 'Are you enjoying yourself?'

'I was glad to be invited.'

'Miss Hamilton, I do believe you have just fibbed.'

Rose lowered her eyes guiltily.

'It might not be as bad as you imagine – although I doubt it.'

Rose laughed.

'That's better, I like to see you smile.'

'I was just wondering why I bother to attend these...'

'Because Win drags you along; because she's determined to find you a beau.'

'How do you know my aunt, Mr Dean?'

'We went to school together,' he answered without hesitation.

'I see. She doesn't seem to care for you overmuch. Oh, I'm sorry! I shouldn't have said that, please forgive me.' Rose's fingers fumbled in her lap.

'If you thought it, why not say it? It's true, after all,' Charles admitted. Just then, the dinner gong sounded and Charles stood, holding out a hand to help Rose to her feet. 'I hope it's not beef again,' he sighed, causing Rose to grin.

Together they went indoors to find their seats in the dining room. Rose was placed directly opposite Charles and smiled when he wiggled his eyebrows, clearly pleased with the arrangement.

Looking down the long table, she saw Win sitting to the right of Mrs Glendening in pride of place. *She'll love that*, Rose thought.

Wine was brought and poured, but again not for Rose. A frown of irritation creased her forehead but was soon replaced by a smile as Charles leaned across the table and swapped his full glass for her empty one and winked in response to her surprise. Duck pâté was served and chatter began. Each time Rose looked up from her plate, she could feel Charles watching her and her heart hammered. Was she simply nervous or was this something more?

An elderly gentleman next to her asked her name and she replied; protocol observed, he went back to his food.

Drawn to Charles yet again, she saw him tilt his head towards the older man she had spoken to and he shook his head with a grin. He was teasing her again and Rose couldn't help the corners of her mouth turning up, which she covered with her napkin.

Starter plates were whisked away before being replaced by a fish course which Rose declined. She hated fish so sipped her wine instead. She noted Charles also waved the course away. Was it because she had or did he not eat fish either? She found out when he grimaced across the table at her.

Next came the main course of roast pork with all the trimmings and Rose tucked in. A selection of cheeses with homemade biscuits rounded off the meal and again Rose shook her head. She couldn't manage another bite.

After a while, the host stood, tapping his glass with a spoon. 'Brandy and cigars in the drawing room, gentlemen. Ladies, coffee will be brought to the sitting room.'

The scrape of chairs on the parquet flooring had Rose wince before she followed the line of women.

The Orphan's Promise

Rose was dutifully chatting with the ladies in the sitting room but felt stifled. She wanted nothing more than to escape the confines of the stuffy room and wander out into the fresh air. Finding herself alone again, she took her chance and slipped out into the garden.

'Miss.' The gardener acknowledged her presence as he lit the lanterns, giving the whole area a fairy-like quality. Rose smiled and meandered along the stepping stones set into the gravel path. The sun had set and very slowly darkness was descending. The perfume from the roses wafted on a zephyr and birds argued over roosting places.

'Beautiful, isn't it?'

Rose knew the voice even before she turned. Charles, had he sought her out? She hoped so and the thought again brought a flush to her cheeks.

'Yes, it was rather hot indoors,' she replied.

Running a finger between collar and neck, he said, 'I know what you mean. Did you enjoy your wine?'

'I did, it was very gallant of you.'

'I couldn't see you without, in fact, if I had my way you would have everything you ever wanted.'

Rose blushed fiercely, hoping the twilight hid her burning face. She felt the fire in her blood as it rushed around her body, increasing her pulse to a frightening rate. She felt the butterflies in her stomach and laid a hand there, hoping to settle them. Her breast rose and fell with deep breaths as she tried to bring her emotions under control.

A gong rang out, summoning the guests to attend the evening's entertainment.

'It will take a lifetime to get to know you at this rate,' Charles said with a beaming smile.

'Perhaps we should go in.' Rose stepped smartly back towards the sitting room, her heart beating like a drum.

In the music room, Rose took her seat next to Win, but was instantly aware of Charles positioning himself a few chairs away. He nodded to her and she nodded back before Win tapped her arm. Win gave Charles a look that could sour milk but he just grinned back cheekily before looking away.

8

Three young men entered to applause from the gathering. One sat at the piano, another lifted a violin and the third took up an accordion. After a moment of tuning the music began, and before long everyone's feet tapped along to the bouncy rhythms. People clapped along and everyone joined in singing the most popular songs. The applause almost raised the roof as the musicians took a final bow. Rose had thoroughly enjoyed the performance and, she noted, even Win had taken pleasure in it.

Returning to the sitting room, Rose immediately sought sanctuary in the garden. The fresh breeze kissed her glowing skin and she inhaled deeply. Walking to the bench, she sat enjoying the subdued light from the lanterns. She was humming quietly to herself, watching the lights sway gently on the tree boughs.

'I thought I might find you here,' Charles said as he stepped towards her.

'Then you were correct,' Rose said.

'May I?' When Rose inclined her head, he sat down next to her. 'Did you enjoy the music?'

'Oh, yes! It was delightful.'

'I agree, it made me want to dance at times.'

Rose nodded. 'I couldn't keep my toes still.'

'Miss Hamilton...'

At that very moment, Win came rushing towards them. 'Rose! Whatever are you doing?'

'I was talking with Mr Dean,' Rose answered innocently.

'Were you indeed? Back in the house this instant!' Win stood ramrod straight as Rose dutifully obeyed her instruction. Waiting by the doors, Rose listened intently. 'I don't know what your game is, Charles Dean, but it stops right now!' Win snapped.

'I was merely talking to a bored young woman,' he answered.

'Is that so? Well, in future you stay away from my niece!' Win was shaking with anger.

'That could prove difficult, Win, if we frequent the same functions.'

'I'm warning you, Charles...!'

Rose glanced from one to the other as the argument raged on, albeit quietly. She was confused and desperately wanted to know why Win was being so rude to the man she had begun to have feelings for.

'What, Win? What will you do?' Now Charles's voice held a tinge of anger too.

'You can't have her, Charles. I'll see you in hell before I'll let that happen!' Win marched away, leaving Charles with a smirk on his face.

'We will see, Win Jacobs,' he muttered.

Rose quickly moved into the room rather than be caught eavesdropping. Whatever was going on between Charles Dean and her aunt, Rose was determined to find out. Seeing the look on Win's face, she thought, *not a conversation for tonight though*.

'There you are, Win,' a woman said, 'now bring Rose to afternoon tea tomorrow. Then she can meet my son, Rodney.'

'Thank you, Frances, we'll be there at four o'clock.'

'Splendid!' The woman disappeared into the crowd.

'It would have been nice for someone to ask me,' Rose mumbled.

'Don't be so childish, Rose, this is about…'

'I know, finding me a husband!' Rose answered sharply.

'Come along, it's time we left, you're clearly overtired,' Win said, taking Rose's elbow and steering her forward to give their thanks and say their goodnights.

Rose glanced around and smiled as her eyes found Charles leaning against a doorjamb watching her. He raised his glass in a toast to her before she was hauled away to the waiting cab.

Climbing aboard, they settled into the darkness. 'I don't want you seeing Charles Dean again, Rose. I understand he will be in attendance at parties, etc., but you are *not* to be alone with him!'

'We were only talking, Aunt,' Rose whispered, feeling more and more frustrated at having no explanation.

'Rose, obey me on this!'

'Why?' Rose asked, desperate to get to the bottom of the whole debacle.

'Because… just do it and don't ask questions! Now, we will not speak of it again!'

In fact, not another word was exchanged about anything all the way home. Rose was daydreaming about the handsome Charles and Win was fuming at the man's audacity.

Rose went straight to her bedroom once they arrived; Jackson being left to pay the cabbie and lock up. Taking down her hair, Rose then undressed and threw on her nightdress. She washed her face in the bowl on the stand in the corner, the water from the jug cool on her skin.

A quiet tap on the door before it opened saw Katy enter with a tray. 'We thought you might like a cuppa before bed, Miss Rose,' the maid whispered.

'Thank you, Katy, I was about to come down.'

'How was the missus tonight?' Katy dared to ask.

Rose blew out her cheeks with a huge sigh.

'Oh, that good?'

Rose laughed. 'Why do you call her the missus when she's not married?'

'Dunno, really. Anybody ranking higher than me is a missus, I suppose.'

'Katy, you are a tonic.'

'Ain't I just? See you in the morning.' Katy slipped silently from the room, leaving Rose with a smile on her face as she sipped her tea.

* * *

The following morning, over the breakfast table, Win spoke from behind her newspaper. 'We are to be at Frances Green's house at four o'clock for tea.'

'Yes, Aunt.'

'There you will meet Rodney and – you will be nice to him.'

'Yes, Aunt.' Rose got to her feet and stopped when Win asked, 'Not hungry again?'

'No, Aunt.' *How does she do that?* Rose thought as she walked from the dining room. *Her eyes never left the newspaper.* Going to the kitchen, she got her answer.

'She's got eyes up her arse has the missus,' Katy said.

'Katy!' Mary said.

'It's all right, Mary, I was wondering.'

'I hear you'm out for afternoon tea today.'

'Yes, Mrs Green's. I'm to meet her son, Rodney.'

Katy burst out laughing. 'Rodney, who names their kid Rodney?'

'Mrs Green, evidently,' Rose replied. All three shared a titter which halted abruptly as Jackson walked in.

'Katy!' Win's voice sailed into the kitchen. Katy rolled her eyes and ran up the steps into the hall, followed closely by Jackson.

Alone with her friend, Rose took her chance. 'While I remember, this is the money for my package. When it comes, can Katy sneak it into my room?' Mary nodded.

After a few moments, Katy skipped back to the kitchen. 'Missus is out shopping, and she'll be back for lunch.'

'Right, Katy, make tea. Now, Miss Rose, tell us all about your evening,' Mary said, settling onto a hard chair.

'Mrs Winters, it's really none of our business,' Jackson said as he entered.

'How else am I to know what the other cooks are serving up, Mr Jackson?' Mary asked pointedly.

With a sigh, the butler retired to his pantry to go over the accounts.

Rose described the food, saying it was nice but not as good as one of Mary's roasts. She told of the musicians, then went on to relate the contretemps between Win and Charles.

'I wish I knew why she dislikes him so much. He's so very nice and he does make me laugh,' Rose said.

'Probably summat and nothing,' Mary replied, 'I wouldn't worry about it.'

'I expect you're right,' Rose said, getting to her feet. 'I'll be in the garden.'

Mary watched her go and a feeling of foreboding settled on

her. Young Rose was developing feelings for Charles Dean if she wasn't mistaken, and Mary worried for her. Win would never allow the two to become an item, no matter how much she wanted Rose wed. *There'll be ructions there before too long*, Mary thought, *and Rose will be the one who gets hurt.*

9

Win arrived home, having bought herself a new hat, a large flowered creation with a huge feather on the side. She and Rose ate lunch silently then Rose went to her room to rest before readying herself for their outing.

Dressed in a cream skirt and blouse, Rose brushed out her hair, leaving it loose about her shoulders. Parasol in hand, she descended the stairs and waited in the hall. Win appeared in a brown skirt and jacket, the monstrosity of a hat pinned to her hair.

Walking out of the house to the cab heralded by Jackson, they climbed aboard.

'Remember what I said, be nice to Rodney.'

Rose nodded as Katy's words making fun of the name came back to her.

The streets were busy with people bustling about in the sunshine. Hawkers called out as they held up cheap toys from a tray hanging around their necks. Sweeps were up to their eyes in soot from clearing chimneys before fires would be burning night and day in the colder months. Cable tram wheels squealed as they stopped to disgorge their passengers.

Win took a delicate fob watch on a gold chain from her pocket. She checked the time then replaced it.

'Are we late?' Rose asked.

'No, we'll be fine.'

Rose went back to gazing out of the window. A window cleaner was at the top of his ladder, sloshing water on the glass panes. Folk passing by avoided walking beneath it for fear of attracting bad luck. She liked watching everyday folk going about their business and envied them their freedom. She knew their lives were hard, trying to earn a living and keeping their families fed, but at least they didn't have to answer to anyone, unlike herself.

Eventually the cab drew into a short drive and halted. Win got out, telling the cabbie to wait, they would be about an hour, she said. Rose alighted and followed her to the front door where Win hammered on the knocker. It was Mrs Green herself who answered and ushered them inside. The house wasn't as grand as the others they had been to but it was nicely laid out.

'Come through, we'll have tea in the garden as it's such a nice day.' Tables and chairs were set out on the lawn and a young man came to greet them. *This must be Rodney*, Rose thought.

After introductions, Rose was proved correct and she sat to accept tea from their hostess. She eyed Rodney from beneath her lashes and inwardly sighed. Only in his twenties, he was already going bald and he guffawed rather than laughed. He had a prominent nose and a weak chin. He was not what one would call a man's man, seemingly more at home in the company of women. Rose could never imagine herself married to this man, not after meeting the charming Charles Dean. She said little and ate sparingly of the sandwiches and cake. She sighed with relief when it was time to go.

'I'll expect to hear from you,' Frances Green said, seeing her guests out.

'Indeed,' Win replied, saying no more until the cab was underway once more. 'Rodney seemed a nice young man, don't you think?'

'No.' Rose's answer was short and sharp.

'Rose, you really must make an effort.'

'Why?'

'You know why!' Win's temper was mounting.

Rose stared out of the window, which enraged Win all the more.

'Look at me!' Win spat. Rose did as she was bid. 'Rodney is no oil painting, I grant you, and his family are not terribly well-off, but...'

'But my dowry would help enormously!' Rose was angry now too.

'For God's sake, Rose!' Win was certain Rose had no idea about her inheritance, which would make her a very wealthy woman, and she intended to keep it that way.

'No more tea parties, Aunt. I'll attend what you have already accepted but after that – no more!'

'Rose! I'm only thinking of you. I want you to be settled when...'

'When you die, yes, I know. What about my feelings, though, Aunt? I could never live with a man like Rodney!'

'Maybe he's not for you,' Win said, seeing Rose meant every word she said.

'He's *definitely* not for me! Now can we please drop this? I don't wish to discuss it any further.'

Win's lips drew into a tight thin line as she tapped a finger on her bag. A glance from Rose halted the annoying sound and silence reigned for the rest of the journey.

No sooner had the cab stopped outside their house than Rose jumped out and strode indoors. Passing Jackson in the hall, she ran upstairs to her room.

'Tea in the sitting room,' Win ordered as she walked in.

The butler walked off and as Katy prepared the tray he told Mary of the frosty atmosphere.

'Afternoon tea wasn't a success then by the sounds of it,' Mary mumbled.

Katy delivered the refreshments and back in the kitchen she said, 'I wonder what the missus has done this time to have Miss Rose so riled up.'

'God only knows, but if she carries on like this there's gonna be one almighty row.' Mary sat at the table while Katy poured for them all.

'I don't half feel sorry for Miss Rose. Even a blind man can see she ain't happy.'

'I know, Katy, but there's nowt we can do except pick her up each time she gets knocked down.'

'She ain't been, has she? By a cart or what?' Katy asked worriedly.

Jackson sighed loudly and Mary replied, 'No, love, what I mean is we just have to show her we love her even if that aunt of hers doesn't.'

'Oh, right, yes.' Katy smiled, relieved Miss Rose hadn't actually suffered an injury.

'I daresay we'll find out soon enough what's upset that lovely girl,' Mary said.

'Indeed, Mrs Winters,' Jackson concurred as he sipped his tea.

Mary thought about the situation, and she knew there was

more to it. The hurry to get Rose wed – why? Once Rose was gone, would Jackson, Katy and herself be kept on or would they be booted out too? Questions with no answers filled her mind. Somebody needed to find out what was going on – and soon, because poor Rose was the only one who was suffering.

10

Win and Rose sat at the dinner table that evening and once served their meal, Win said, 'Jackson, please remind Mrs Winters that the ladies will be coming tomorrow to play cards.'

'Very good, madam.' Jackson hooked a finger to Katy, who bobbed her knee then scurried back to the kitchen with the message.

'Bloody hell, I'd forgotten about that!' Mary said as she plonked herself at the table.

'I expect the missus will be pissed again,' Katy commented.

'Careful what you say, lovey, we don't want her to overhear,' Mary warned. 'I think you're right though, that woman does like a drink.'

'You know what's odd though?' Katy murmured.

'What?'

'Well, she has a brandy every night before bed, but only one. Then each month the card players takes it in turn to be the hostess. The missus never comes back worse for wear, she's only like that when they come here.'

'You're right, pet, I didn't realise that until you said it. Maybe she's just showing off that she can afford to buy expensive alcohol.'

Katy nodded. 'I'll wash the glasses later and get the booze decantered.'

Mary smiled. 'Decanted,' she corrected.

'Ar, whatever. I suppose I'll have to undress her and put her to bed – again.'

'You're a good girl, Katy,' Mary praised.

'I won't be if she sicks up on me one more time though!'

'She's a very unhappy lady, Katy.'

'Why? She's got a lovely house and...'

Mary didn't hear any more as a thought struck her like a bolt out of the blue. Was this Win's house? Mary racked her brains, trying to recall things said many years ago. She remembered that this house belonged to Rose's father. He had given Win leave to live in it so she could be near her sister, his wife. The question now was, had he signed it over to Win, or did it still belong to the Hamiltons, in other words – Rose? It seemed unlikely that Miles Hamilton would give away a big house, even to his sister-in-law. Mary pondered this as she drank her tea. How could she find out? The answer to that was – she couldn't. Mary also knew that it would eat away at her until she discovered the truth; because she had an awful feeling it was tied to Rose being married off.

'What sandwiches are you doing for tomorrow?' Katy's words brought Mary's attention back to the present.

'Salmon and cucumber and cheese and chutney. Queen cakes and Gypsy tart.'

'Ooh, lovely. The missus will be pleased with that. You want another cuppa?'

Mary nodded, her mind wandering again to her thoughts of earlier. Maybe she could have a quiet word with Rose. If she sent Katy to the market while the card games were being played, that would be the perfect time. Jackson would be busy keeping the drinks flowing so he would be out of the way too, otherwise he'd be telling her to keep her nose out of upstairs business.

Miss Rose usually came to say goodnight to them so she could arrange something then. She'd send Katy to the pantry for the biscuits and whisper her request to see Rose privately tomorrow afternoon. With a nod, Mary was happy with her plan. Now she had to hope it worked.

It was around ten o'clock that night when Rose popped into the kitchen.

'Cup of cocoa before bed, Miss Rose?' Mary asked.

'Yes, please,' Rose replied.

'I'll get the milk,' Katy said and went to the scullery to ladle milk from the churn into a pan.

'Miss Rose, I have to see you privately tomorrow afternoon while the games are on,' Mary whispered urgently. 'I'll send Katy on an errand. It's important.'

'All right, Mary, I'll join you as soon as Aunt Win's ladies arrive.' Rose saw Mary nod, heaving a sigh of relief.

'Can we have biscuits with this?' Katy asked on her return with the milk.

'You can and there's chocolate cake on the cold slab as well,' Mary said with a chuckle as Katy clapped her hands. 'Take some to Mr Jackson in his pantry.'

After saying goodnight, Rose went to bed, puzzled by Mary's mysterious request. She'd said it was important and clearly it was – to her. Rose prayed Mary had not decided to quit her job after so many years of excellent service. Besides, Rose saw her as a mother figure and would be lost without her.

Rose didn't sleep well that night and in the morning she felt tired and listless. After tea and toast, she took a walk around the garden in the hope it would inject some life into her. It seemed the sun was having a lazy morning too as it didn't show its face until quite late. Again she wondered what Mary wanted to speak to her about.

Going back indoors, she knew the cook would be busy preparing refreshments for the gathering of card players, but she strolled into the kitchen regardless. Sitting at the table, she watched Katy pouring alcohol into cut-glass decanters, sherry in one and whisky in another. Her eyes then turned to Mary cutting little sandwiches and placing them on doily-lined plates. Three-tiered cake stands held small Queen cakes and fancy biscuits.

'You all right, Miss Rose?' Mary asked.

Rose nodded. 'Yes, I'm just a little tired today.'

'I'm going to the market later, you should come with me, the walk might do you good,' Katy called over her shoulder.

Mary shot Rose a pleading glance for her to refuse. 'Thanks, Katy, but I think I'll have a rest on my bed.' Mary sighed with relief.

Between them, cook and maid transported plates, cutlery, napkins, food and drink to the sitting room where a gate-leg table had been opened out and covered with a white cloth. Jackson supervised what should go where and checked all the glasses were sparkling clean.

Early afternoon saw the guests arrive and shown to where Win was waiting for them. Once they were settled with the butler in attendance, Katy left for the market with a shopping list and some money.

'Now then,' Mary whispered. 'I need to talk to you about this house.' Relating everything she could remember, Mary sat back, waiting for Rose's reaction.

11

'So you think this place could belong to me?' Rose asked. She was shocked at the idea of owning the house and despite her surprise at Mary mentioning it, she was glad she had.

'I'd bet my savings on it,' Mary answered.

'How could I find out?'

'Well, there has to be a set of deeds somewhere, and I'm guessing wherever they are there will be a copy of your father's last will and testament.'

'How will that prove anything?' Rose asked, not seeing the connection.

'In his will your father will have stated who gets what, so there's your proof of ownership.'

'I could just ask Aunt Win,' Rose offered.

'You could, but are you sure she'd tell you the truth? I ain't calling her a liar, but...'

'She might worry I would ask her to leave.' Rose completed the cook's sentence.

Mary nodded. 'I'm surprised you weren't at the reading of the will.'

'I would have been at school.'

'I know but an hour off wouldn't have hurt your studies none.'

Rose frowned. Mary was right, she should have accompanied Win and been a party to hearing her father's wishes. 'I wonder where Win keeps these documents.'

'They could be with the solicitor still, but it's my guess they're in this house somewhere. Win would have them where you can't find them if our thinking is correct,' Mary said.

'Then I should try to discover them. That way we'll know for sure.' Getting to her feet, Rose gave Mary a hug. 'Thank you for caring so much.'

'Just don't let the missus catch you searching, because if she gets wind of what you're up to she could shift those papers where you'll never find them. Take my advice – be discreet.'

'If Aunt Win needs me I'll be in the attic having a clear out of all the junk,' Rose said with a grin.

'Good place to start,' Mary chuckled.

Rose skipped from the kitchen and ran up the stairs, then up another flight to the door of the attic. Pushing it open, she stepped inside. The sun shone through the window, highlighting the many cobwebs, and Rose gave a little shiver. It was creepy up there and cold too.

In the corner was her rocking horse and she walked over to stroke its mane. Memories flooded her mind of when her father held her on its seat and rocked her gently. Next to it sat an old chest, the lid of which was covered in dust. She lifted it to reveal her dolls, some made of wood, others of clay. Bringing them out, she smiled as she recalled the pretend tea parties they'd attended. Checking the chest, which held nothing more, she replaced the dolls and closed the lid, the dust flying into the air as she did so.

There were boxes of teddy bears and dolls' clothes, miniature porcelain tea plates, cups and saucers as well as a selection of brightly coloured balls. A doll's perambulator stood unused for many years with its sheets and blankets lovingly made by her mother. Rose held them, a tear in her eye.

Then she remembered why she was up there and set about checking every box. Old clothes in some, shoes and boots in another but no paperwork of any sort.

Feeling disappointed, she brushed the dust from her hands and left the attic, pulling the door shut behind her. Returning to the kitchen, she saw Katy was back. Mary looked up as she entered and raised her eyebrows. Rose gave a tiny shake of her head and saw Mary screw up her mouth.

'Cuppa, Miss Rose?' Katy asked.

'Yes, please, Katy.' As the maid went to fill the kettle from the standpipe in the garden, Rose whispered, 'Nothing. I'll have to look elsewhere.'

Mary nodded and Katy reappeared.

'I've saved us some salmon sandwiches, ladies, so we can have a party of our own,' Mary said.

Katy placed the kettle on the hotplate and sat down, waiting for her food. Before long, they were tucking in and chatting like the old friends they were.

* * *

Upstairs in the sitting room, Win was being bombarded with questions as she tried to concentrate on her cards. *Had she found a suitor for Rose yet? Why was Rose so disinclined to wed?*

Win ate sparingly but drank plenty and slowly she felt her senses leaving her. Her speech became slurred and she kept dropping her cards. She cursed as she bent to retrieve them and her guests realised it was time they left.

Eventually Win was alone, sprawled out on a sofa, snoring loudly, Jackson having seen the guests out.

Katy had seen the ladies leave and discovered the missus out for the count. Coming back to the kitchen, she said, 'Mr Jackson is just bringing the alcohol down. Her ladyship is drunk as a lord, there ain't no way we can get her to bed. She'll 'ave a stinker of a headache when she wakes up.'

'Another foul mood then,' Rose muttered.

'Just stay out of her way until she starts to feel better,' Mary advised. 'She'll take herself up to bed when she's ready, but I suspect she'll sleep for a good while yet.'

Rose instantly picked up on the hidden suggestion Mary was making. 'I think I'll take advantage of the peace and quiet then,' she said and seeing Mary's nod she left the kitchen.

Passing Jackson in the hall, Rose raced up the stairs and ran into Win's room, looking around. Where would she hide the papers? Rose tried the bedside cabinet first, being careful not to disturb anything that Win would notice. Finding nothing, she searched the wardrobe; again she drew a blank. Finally she dipped into Win's top drawer in the chest. Beneath silk underwear she found what she was looking for. Pulling out the papers and bank book, she read them quickly and gasped. Taking a moment to scan the contents again, she replaced them, ensuring everything was as she found it.

Slipping from the room, she closed the door and went to her own bedroom. Sitting on the bed, Rose stared into space, trying to digest what she'd read.

12

That evening, as she sat alone in the dining room, Rose heard Win negotiating the stairs with a lot of moaning. She picked at her food, having very little appetite.

Jackson cleared her plate away, asking, 'Can I get you anything else, Miss Rose?'

'No, thank you.'

The butler took the half-eaten food back to the kitchen. When Mary saw the plate, she wondered if Rose's search had been successful, and that's why she was off her food. Minutes later, Rose joined them, saying, 'Aunt Win has just dragged herself to bed.'

Mary raised her eyebrows and caught the barely perceptible nod from Rose in reply. *So I was right, she's found them!*

Rose shared tea with the butler, cook and maid before she went to her bedroom. She lay on the bed thinking about the will and trying to comprehend the meaning behind the words. Everything would go to Aunt Win if Rose married before her twenty-first birthday – but why? Regardless, it strengthened her resolve to remain single, and now she knew why Win was so desperate for a wedding to take place before then.

The house she lived in belonged to her too, which Win had said nothing about. Her parents' house still stood, probably rented out for an exorbitant amount. *That's my money; that house is mine too*, she thought. *The question now is what do I do about it?*

Rose considered her options. She could confront Win about her discovery, which would inevitably lead to a dreadful argument. Win would accuse her of snooping, which she had been, of course, but what then? Residing under the same roof could be unbearable, with resentment on both sides. Rose didn't think for a minute that her aunt would move out. She'd tried too hard to inherit the house and money, and she wouldn't give up now. On the other hand, Rose could say nothing to Win, but that would mean continuing to meet prospective husbands. Although Rose had said there would be no more, she knew Win would ignore that. She would have to as she had too much to lose otherwise. As the thoughts chased each other through her mind, Rose's anger built inside her. She was upset but more she was furious with her aunt at keeping such secrets. She and Win were blood relatives; how could she do this to her? The conclusion she came to was – greed. Win just wanted the money and to hell with her niece!

As the moon peeped from behind a cloud, Rose climbed off the bed. She tiptoed down the stairs, across the hall towards the kitchen to make herself a hot drink. She saw a light on and realised someone was still up. She hoped it wasn't her aunt, and was relieved to see Mary making a pot of tea.

'I thought you'd be down at some point,' the cook said.

'Oh, Mary! You won't believe what I have to tell you!' Rose took a seat.

'Right, let's have it, but quietly – just in case.'

Rose related all she could remember from the paperwork and

bank book and when she had finished Mary's mouth was hanging open. 'Well, I knew about the house but the will – and you being wed – why?'

'I don't know, Mary, and probably never will now that my father is dead.'

'What will you do?'

Rose shook her head. 'I have no idea other than to say I'm determined now to remain single.'

'I can't say I blame you on that score. Maybe you should think on it for a while, things might be clearer once the shock wears off.' It was sound advice but even Mary didn't believe her own words. It was a very difficult position to be in, and she didn't envy the girl having to make a decision one way or the other. She watched Rose leave the kitchen and disappear into the darkness of the hall. It was time for her to be in bed too but Mary lingered a while longer, her mind going over yet again what Rose had told her.

Finally, a thought gave her some comfort, enough to get some sleep anyway – Rose needed to consult a solicitor. Turning off the gas lamps, Mary wound her way up the back stairs in the dark. She needed no light, having trod this way thousands of times over the years. Entering her room, she smiled. Katy, bless her, had lit the lamp.

* * *

The following morning, Mary served breakfast in the dining room, much to Jackson's disgust. 'Katy is brewing fresh tea, and I didn't want this to get cold,' she said in answer to Win's question of why the cook was above stairs. Catching Rose's eye, Mary lifted an eyebrow.

Rose nodded, saying, 'Mrs Winters, I'd like to take a picnic to the park later.' Win was absorbed in the newspaper, clearly not listening to the exchange.

'I'll prepare something nice for you, Miss Rose.' Mary went to do just that and an hour later Rose entered the kitchen holding a book.

'I thought I'd read and take advantage of the good weather,' Rose said.

'Here's a little picnic for you as requested. Sandwiches, cake, fruit and lemonade,' Mary said. 'I need to visit the butcher to place an order so if you don't mind I'll walk with you.'

'Katy could go for you,' Jackson volunteered the maid without consulting her.

'Thanks, but I need some exercise and fresh air. I'm cooped up in this kitchen night and day. Katy love, you can start the missus's lunch while I'm out.'

'All right.' Katy beamed at being given such a big responsibility.

Shortly afterwards, Mary and Rose strolled down the drive. 'Where are we going?' Rose asked.

'To find a solicitor so I hope you've got some money with you.'

Rose tapped her drawstring bag. 'May I ask why?'

'It's my thinking he could shed some light on the contents of your father's will.'

'Oh, Mary, what a good idea!'

Striding out, the two entered the town, checking the nameplates on each property as they passed by.

'This ain't no good, we could walk for hours and not find one,' Mary grumbled.

'Wait here a moment,' Rose said and stepped lightly towards a gentleman and his lady. 'Excuse me, sir, but I wondered if you would be kind enough to direct me to a solicitor's office.'

'Certainly, m'dear. Watts & Watts can be found on Steelhouse Lane just before you reach the Victoria Law Courts.'

'I appreciate your help, thank you.' Rose smiled sweetly as the gent tipped his top hat. Returning to Mary, she said, 'We need a cab.' Looking around, she waved an arm and a cabbie waved back before moving towards them.

Rose gave the address and she and Mary climbed aboard, both eager to possibly have their questions answered.

13

The cab stopped and the two women alighted. Rose requested the cabbie wait; he agreed with a nod. Going inside the office, Rose asked to see a solicitor.

'Do you have an appointment?' the haughty secretary asked.

'No.'

'Then I'm afraid...'

'This office comes highly recommended and is well-known for providing an excellent service,' Rose interrupted. 'I'm sure Messrs Watts & Watts would not wish their reputation to be sullied because an appointment was not made.'

'Please... I'll see what I can do.' The secretary scuttled off through a door and a moment later called Rose and Mary to follow her.

'Come in, ladies, please take a seat.' The young man sitting behind his desk had a kindly face. 'What can I do for you on this fine day? Oh, forgive me, my name is John Watts.'

'Rose Hamilton and this is my friend, Mary Winters.'

'Delighted to meet you both.'

'Mr Watts, I come seeking advice on my father's will,' Rose explained.

'I see. Do you have it with you?' he asked.

'No, it's rather complicated.' Rose felt her resolve draining away. Maybe this wasn't such a good idea after all.

'Perhaps you should tell Mr Watts everything, Rose,' Mary said gently. Taking a deep breath, Rose did exactly that.

John Watts listened carefully, nodding and making notes as she spoke. When she had finished, he sat back in his chair. 'So you want to know...?'

'Where I stand legally,' Rose cut across. 'I don't understand why my father made the decision he did regarding my getting married.'

'Let me see if I can explain. As the law stands, you have the right, as a single person, to own property in your own name. If you were to marry, you would be bound by what is called coverture. This doctrine treats a married couple as one economic unit.' Seeing Rose frown, he went on. 'Your husband would have control over your property, your assets, e.g. money, and even you and any children you might have.'

'Bloody hell!' Mary gasped.

Watts held up a hand. 'However, the Married Women's Act of 1870 states that any wages or property earned through her own work or inherited would be regarded as her separate property.' Rose and Mary exchanged a glance. 'In 1882 the Married Women's *Property* Act extended this to all property regardless of its source. It would also be protected from your husband's creditors.'

'Then I can claim my inheritance from my aunt?'

'Yes, strictly speaking, but from what you've told me I think it unlikely she will give it up so easily. She could contest it in court.'

'The law is on my side – you just said so!' Rose exclaimed.

'Indeed it is, Miss Hamilton, but this Act is still in its infancy, only seven years old. What if the judge is an old fuddy-duddy who still clings to the coverture ideas? He could rule against you.'

'Wouldn't he be breaking the law though?'

Watts nodded. 'Yes, but would you be prepared to fight his ruling through the courts? It would take every penny you have.'

'Mr Watts, what can I do?' Rose asked, feeling wretched.

'Firstly you need to procure the will, deeds, bank book, receipts, letters – anything you can find and bring them to me. My apologies, if you wish to hire me as your lawyer, that is.'

Rose looked at Mary, who nodded, saying, 'We can't do this on our own, sweetheart.'

'Then yes, please, Mr Watts,' Rose said.

'Good. Now, as I said, I'll need any paperwork relating to the will and your father's solicitor, the house you reside in and the one you grew up in, as well as any notifications from the bank regarding incomings and outgoings. Can you find out the name of the solicitor who drew up your father's will?'

'My aunt has it though.' Rose was feeling overwhelmed by it all and began to fret.

'Any solicitor worth his salt will have a copy in his archives. I can obtain a copy from them. I assure you it won't be a problem.'

'I'll do what I can,' Rose said.

'One more thing, you need to know whose name is on the bank book.'

'Thank you, Mr Watts, I'll be in touch as soon as I can.' Rose stood to leave.

'Oh, and Miss Hamilton, take my advice and don't wed until all this has been settled.' Rose laughed as they shook hands.

Climbing into the carriage, Rose breathed a sigh of relief then said as the cab moved off, 'Mary, I didn't pay him!'

'He'll bill you for it, don't worry,' Mary assured her.

'This was such a good idea, Mary, thank you.'

'Right, we have some planning to do.'

'How do you mean?' Rose asked.

'You searching for the information Mr Watts wants!'

'Oh, yes, of course.'

'We can't let the missus know, or Katy for that matter. She's a lovely kid, is Katy, but a little young and I don't think we could trust her to keep her mouth shut, she gets too excited.'

'I have to agree, but I love her dearly,' Rose said.

'Me an' all but she don't think before speaking. Then there's Jackson, we have to be very careful because he's as sharp as a tack.'

Pulling up by the park, they alighted. Rose paid the fare and they strolled through the gates and along the path. Finding a bench, they sat to share the picnic and exchange ideas about the best way to retrieve the information from the documents.

'Miss Rose, I'd best get to the butcher and order the meat for the week.'

'I'll come with you.' The two women walked briskly from the park, each lost in their own thoughts.

When they arrived home, a screech echoed across the hall. 'Rose! Where *have* you been?'

Rolling her eyes, Rose walked to the sitting room, leaving Mary to go to the kitchen. 'I've been to the park,' Rose answered as she entered to see Win at her desk. *I could search there too when I get the chance*, Rose thought, eyeing the paper in Win's hand. There could be more papers from the bank in the desk.

'You really must let me know when you're going out!' Win snapped.

'Why? There was nothing for me to do here.'

'I could have made arrangements...'

'Then you really must let me know when you do.' Rose

echoed her aunt's words, feeling very much more confident since her meeting with John Watts.

'What has got into you, Rose? Sarcasm is the lowest form of wit.'

Rose sighed audibly. 'What did you want, Aunt?'

'Nothing specifically, I was wondering where you were. Anyway, it's time for lunch.'

'I've eaten.' Seeing the questioning look, Rose added, 'I had a picnic as I said this morning but clearly you weren't listening.' Standing up to her aunt gave Rose a feeling of confidence and it was heady to say the least. Her back straightened just a little more and her head lifted, daring Win to challenge her again.

The movement was not lost on Win as she said, 'I see,' before striding from the room to eat her food alone.

Rose glanced at the desk then at the door. Would there be time for a quick search? Shaking her head, she decided against rifling through the papers for anything Mr Watts might find useful, it was too risky. She would bide her time, there would be a better opportunity.

Going to the dining room, Rose sat down. 'I've changed my mind, the food smells delicious.'

Jackson went to the kitchen and returned with Katy in tow. The maid grinned as she quickly set another place. Miss Rose knew she had cooked all by herself and had complimented her by partaking of the lunch. Katy was delighted.

14

With food finished, Rose walked out into the garden. Sitting on the warm grass, she picked absent-mindedly at the blades as her thoughts swirled.

She had to find the opportunity to go snooping again so Mr Watts could have the information he needed. There was the red ball gown to smuggle into the house without Win finding out. She didn't want her aunt to see it until it the night of the ball, by which time it would be too late to do anything about it.

This led her to wonder if Charles Dean would be attending and if so, what he would think of her dress. Perhaps he would be as shocked as Aunt Win. Rose didn't care, she was going to wear it regardless of the outraged stares and mutterings it would raise. She smiled to herself as an image of Charles rose in her mind, he really was a very handsome man. If he attended the upcoming ball, would he sign her dance card? Dressed in bright red, Rose considered the possibility of having no signatures at all.

'Rose, do get up off the ground, for goodness' sake!' Win's voice came at her like a thunderclap, making her jump to her feet. 'Can't you at least act like a lady?' Rose drew in a breath to answer but she didn't get the chance. 'I hope you haven't forgotten it's the ball this Saturday.'

'No, Aunt, I'm actually looking forward to it.'

Win narrowed her eyes in suspicion but said only, 'Good, I'm glad.' She walked away, wondering at the change in her niece, hoping it had nothing to do with Charles Dean. Sitting at her small desk, Win's thoughts stayed on the man she had loved almost all of her life. She felt the stab of pain again as she remembered hearing Charles tell her he had no intention of making her his wife. Naturally she had laughed it off, telling everyone that she and Charles were only good friends anyway, but beneath her bravado Win had been heartbroken.

As the years passed, her heart cracked a little more each time they met at the many functions held in the town. The one saving grace was that Charles had not wed either and Win had harboured the belief that there might still be a chance for her. Until, that is, Rose appeared on the scene. In Win's haste to get Rose seen at society parties, it had never occurred to her that she had unwittingly placed temptation before Charles. Now she had an extra task – endeavour to keep that man away from her niece.

Rose walked into the kitchen where Mary said, 'Oh, Miss Rose, your package has arrived. Katy has put it on your bed. The other came by way of the front door.'

'Thank you.' Rose dashed off to inspect her new ball gowns. Running up the stairs, Rose went to her room and locked the door behind her. She opened the box excitedly and gasped. Pulling out the gown, she held it against her and looked in the long mirror. Laying the dress on the bed, she stripped off her clothes to try on her new acquisition. It fit perfectly, the bodice cut low and nipped in sharply at the waist. The full skirt held a sheen as the light caught it and the capped sleeves rested elegantly on her shoulders. Delighted, she swished around the room before sitting on her bed. Did she dare wear it? Bright red, it screamed lower-class attire; perfect for the street walkers patrolling the streets after dark.

Taking it off, she hung it in the wardrobe before trying on the blue one, then as she dressed once more, she wondered how she could keep it a secret until they arrived at the ball. Then she recalled the chest in the attic, the one containing old clothes. Maybe she could find something in there to cover it.

Unlocking the door, Rose rushed up the back stairs yet again. She went straight to the chest and began pulling out the dusty garments. With a smile, she held up a full-length lightweight coat. In cream cotton, it would be perfect, with more than enough material to cover her dress.

Taking it downstairs to the kitchen, she held it up for Mary and Katy to see.

'Where on earth did you find that old thing?' Mary asked.

'In the attic and I wondered if Katy could clean it up for me. I'll need it for Saturday.'

'I remember your mother wearing it,' Mary said a little sadly.

'All the more reason for me to use it,' Rose said.

'I'll do what I can, Miss Rose, but it ain't the fashion no more,' Katy added, taking the garment into the scullery to begin cleaning it.

'What are you up to?' Mary asked. 'First the mysterious package and now your mother's coat...'

'I have to cover my dress until I get to the ball.'

'Why?'

'Because... it's red!'

Mary's mouth fell open as she sat heavily onto a kitchen chair. Finding her tongue, she said, 'The missus will have apoplexy! Miss Rose, you can't...'

'I can and I will. Mary, I have to do this. I must get out from under Aunt Win's yoke.'

'Yes but... red! You'll be an outcast, folk will ostracise you! No more parties...'

'Exactly! It was all I could think of to stop Aunt Win and her matchmaking plans.'

Mary nodded as the penny dropped. 'So no more trying to find you a beau.'

'No one will be interested, Mary, they won't want their son wed to a...' Rose searched for the right word.

'Tart,' Mary supplied.

Rose's mouth dropped open but then she realised Mary was right in her choice of the word. 'Well... I suppose, but at least my inheritance will be safe.'

'You crafty madam!' A warm smile spread across Mary's face.

'Now you understand.'

'You realise that it will be the talk of the town for years to come. It will win you no friends.'

'Mary, you, Jackson and Katy are my only friends now, why would I want more?'

'As long as you know folk will whisper about you behind your back,' Mary warned.

'I don't care. All I know is if I shy away now, I will have another eighteen months of being paraded like cattle in front of prospective suitors.'

'I can't deny that. If you're hell bent on doing this then just prepare yourself for people to turn their backs on you – quite possibly literally.'

Neither of the women noticed Jackson listening to their conversation from the doorway to his pantry.

15

'There you go, I've sponged it down as best as I can,' Katy said as she returned, coat in hand.

'Thank you, Katy, you've made a good job of it too. I'll go and hang it up.' Rose took the garment and left the kitchen.

'You all right, Mrs Winters? You look a bit tired,' Katy said.

'Yes, I'm fine, for the moment anyway.'

'Right, I'll get on with peeling the spuds.'

Mary nodded but her mind was on the reaction of the attendees at the upcoming ball, and Win Jacobs. Rose was inviting trouble if she wore that dress, but she was a headstrong young woman. Mary couldn't help but wonder if their visit to the solicitor had boosted Rose's confidence and whether that was such a good thing. Then again, the gown had been ordered before that; clearly Rose had been thinking this through for some time. *Maybe I should try to talk her out of wearing the dress, it would save her a lot of heartache in the future.*

Mary determined she would talk to Rose the next time she had the chance. That opportunity arose that night. The summer heat made sleep virtually impossible and Rose went down to the kitchen for a cool drink. Mary was still up and had propped the back door open for a welcome breeze. 'Can't sleep either?' she asked.

'No, I'm so hot.'

'Lemonade is on the cold slab, I'll get...'

'I'll do it, you just rest.' Rose took a glass to the scullery and filled it to the brim.

'I'm glad you've come down, Miss Rose, because I want to talk to you.'

Rose drank half of her drink and placed the glass on the table before sitting down.

'Listen to me now before you say anything. I know and I understand what your plan is by wearing that frock but...' Seeing Rose about to speak, Mary held up a hand to forestall her. 'By doing that you will hurt not only yourself and the missus, but Katy and me an' all.' Rose frowned but held her tongue. 'You see, none of the cooks from the other big houses will have anything to do with us. We wouldn't be able to hold our heads up in the town again with below-stairs staff.'

'Oh, Mary!'

'I know it's selfish but I've known those women for years.'

'I didn't even think of that, Mary. I'm so sorry.' Rose felt wretched that her own selfishness had over-ridden any thought for anyone else.

'Of course it's your decision, I just thought I'd mention it.'

'Thank you. I don't know what I'd do without you, Mary. It's a good job I had a blue gown made as well.'

'So you'll be in blue on Saturday then?' Mary asked, needing confirmation.

'Yes.' Rose got to her feet and on impulse threw her arms around her friend. 'I love you,' she whispered.

'I love you an' all, I always have,' Mary replied, a catch in her voice. 'Go on, get yourself to bed.'

After Rose left the kitchen, Mary drew in a breath and whispered, 'Thank God!' Then Rose's words of love came to her again and she burst into tears. She never thought to hear them and her heart was filled with joy.

Securing the house, Mary went to bed, hoping she could manage a few hours' sleep in the stifling heat. Opening her bedroom door, she smiled. Katy had, as usual, lit the lamp but she had also thrown open the windows.

Climbing into bed in the delightfully cool room, Mary turned off the gas lamp over her bed. Tomorrow she would make Katy her favourite – a chocolate cake – by way of thanks and appreciation.

* * *

After breakfast, Rose went to her room to choose her jewellery and wrap for the ball the following evening. She ran her hand over the beautiful red dress hanging in the wardrobe and sighed. How she would have loved to wear it but she had promised Mary she would not. Pulling out the other gown, she smiled; even this startling royal blue was somewhat risqué. Everyone else, she suspected, would be wearing pale colours; green, pink, baby blue, lemon. Replacing it in the wardrobe, she moved to her dressing table. Opening her jewellery box, she drew out a necklace of fine white stones which fell into a teardrop at her bosom, with earrings to match. Then, from a drawer in the box, she lifted a long string of pearls. With luck, Katy could pin these through her hair which would be piled up in curls. Dainty blue shoes would finish her ensemble nicely along with a silk wrap.

Rose felt the heat rise in her as she thought about Charles

Dean and whether he would be in attendance, she certainly hoped so.

Leaving her room, she skipped down the stairs to be met with, 'Rose, for goodness' sake, walk like a lady!' Win had been crossing the hall at the exact time Rose descended the stairs, feeling full of joy. That one sentence sucked all the happiness out of her. Muttering an apology, Rose stepped out into the garden.

Sitting beneath a tall oak, Rose wondered when she would get the opportunity to again look at her father's will and the bank book. She needed Win to go out to ensure she had enough time to rifle through the drawer in Win's room. As Mary had pointed out, she had to avoid getting caught.

A woodpecker hammered out a steady rhythm on a tree further afield, breaking her train of thought. A cabbage white butterfly landed on her skirt for a few seconds before fluttering away. Birds soared high above her then swooped down and out of sight. She heard the sound of the rag-and-bone man's bugle and the clip-clop of his horse's hooves as they traversed the street. Young children squealed with delight, clearly happy to see the horse and hoping to be allowed to stroke its nose.

Rose thought about what it would be like to have to work for a living, pre-supposing one could get a job in the first place. She'd seen the bread lines in the town where men queued every day in the hope of securing employment. She'd observed the beggars holding out their tin cups pleading for a penny. She'd watched the sweeps cleaning chimneys then going home covered from head to foot in soot. Then her mind turned to the modiste in the dress shop. That would be a nice job – until having to please someone like Win. *I suppose I'm lucky that I don't have to work to put food on the table.* Rose then realised how long her days were when she had to amuse herself. She could only do so much embroidery and read so many books before the pleasure of it was lost. At least she had her friends, albeit they were kitchen staff. Mary and Katy kept her sane when her Aunt Win drove her to distraction.

Getting to her feet, Rose wandered indoors for a cool drink and chat with those dear friends.

16

Saturday morning was clear and bright and Rose found herself looking forward to the ball that evening. Joining Win in the dining room for breakfast, she gave a greeting before going to the sideboard to pile bacon, scrambled egg and toast on her plate, then she took her seat. Jackson poured her tea and she nodded her thanks and began to eat, she was hungry.

'Your dance card is next to your plate, please don't forget it tonight.' Win's voice sailed from behind the newspaper.

'Thank you,' Rose answered between bites.

'Be sure not to upset anyone too. We don't want another episode of you refusing to engage in conversation with would-be suitors.'

Rose closed her eyes tight for a second, feeling her good mood slowly leaving her.

'And don't forget what I told you about a *certain* person should he attend.'

'Yes, Aunt!' Rose snapped as she slammed her cutlery onto her plate.

Win's eyes peeped over the newspaper, one eyebrow raised in question.

'I'm old enough now not to have to be told these things every time we go out,' Rose said by way of explanation.

'Of course you are, I was merely reminding you.'

'Thank you but I don't need your reminders.'

'Tetchy this morning, didn't you sleep well?' Win asked.

'I was perfectly fine until... Oh, never mind!' Snatching up her dance card, Rose strode from the room. Going straight to the kitchen, she plonked herself on a chair with a growl.

'Oh, hey up, the missus been getting at you again?' Mary asked.

'Bloody woman!' Rose muttered, quite forgetting herself for a moment. Mary and Katy stood stock still, midway through their tasks, staring at Rose. 'I'm sorry but she's... I can't do anything right for her!' Rose was exasperated.

'Well, I ain't never heard you cuss like that before,' Mary said.

'Nor me, but it was good.' Katy began to titter and suddenly all three burst out laughing. In her own inimitable way, the maid had eased the tension.

Rose went to her room where she laid the ball gown on the bed. Having a strip wash, including her hair, Rose dressed again and went downstairs. She sat in the garden in the sunshine so the breeze could dry her hair. With eyes closed, she mentally prepared herself for the barrage Win would undoubtedly unleash on her when she appeared in the blue dress. *I swear if she sends me to change, I will – into the red! See how she'd like that!*

Deciding to wander around the garden rather than be scolded for having too much sun on her face, Rose ran her fingers through her long hair, enjoying its silky feel. It wouldn't be long before it was completely dry so Katy could dress it for her later. She hummed a little tune as she admired the flowers in the borders which ran alongside the gravel path. She heard the tiny stones crunch beneath her shoes before moving onto the lawn, her footsteps silent now.

'Miss Rose, the missus wants you,' Katy called out.

'Coming.' With a sigh, Rose walked swiftly into the house and on into the sitting room.

'Ah, there you are. I have to go into town to purchase some new gloves for this evening, is there anything you need?'

'No, thank you, Aunt.'

'Very well, please tell cook I will be back for lunch.'

Rose nodded and left to allow her aunt to complete her errand.

Jackson had hailed a cab and was waiting with the front door open.

In the kitchen, Katy said, 'Gloves in this weather?'

'I agree but all the ladies wear them, they come up the arm and finish above the elbow,' Rose explained.

'I'd sweat like a pig if I had to...' Katy began.

'Katy love, would you fetch the biscuit jar from the pantry?' Mary asked. Watching her go, she quickly turned to Rose, whispering, 'Now's your chance, while your aunt is out.'

'Is that such a good idea?' Jackson asked. The women shot him a look and he went on, 'I know what's going on, I overheard you talking.'

'Mr Jackson, this ain't none of your business,' Mary snapped.

'It isn't yours either, Mrs Winters. I only mention it on the off-chance I might be able to help.'

'It looks like we'll have to tell him,' Mary said.

'Tell who what?' Katy asked as she returned.

With a sigh, Rose swore maid and butler to secrecy before divulging what she knew.

'Bloody hell!' Katy gasped.

'My sentiments exactly, Katy,' Jackson concurred.

'You can't breathe a word of it or we could all find ourselves out on the street,' Rose said anxiously. 'I'm worried for you all being thrown out, but if we stick together we'll come through, I'm sure.'

'I swear,' Jackson said.

'And me – all the bloody time!' Katy's statement made everyone burst out laughing.

All enjoyed homemade biscuits and piping hot tea while Rose was listening for Win's possible return having forgotten something. She lingered a while then when she was confident her aunt had gone, she dashed upstairs and went straight to the underwear drawer in Win's room. She needed the information for Mr Watts but when Rose looked in the drawer she found she was to be thwarted. The documents had gone.

Going to her own room, Rose sat on her bed. Win had moved the papers to God only knew where. Rose wondered why – did Win have suspicions that her niece had searched for them? Thinking back, Rose was certain she had been careful to leave things as she'd found them. Maybe Win swapped the hiding place every so often. Had she been doing this all along, or was it a new thing?

With more questions than answers, Rose went down to the kitchen once more. Mary's eyes found hers and Rose shook her head. Mary frowned and Rose shrugged.

'Any luck?' Jackson asked as Rose sat down.

'No, not this time,' Rose answered.

Trying to take Rose's mind off her quest, Katy asked, 'Are you looking forward to the ball, Miss Rose?'

'I am, Katy. Soirées are a bit stuffy and all pretty much the same, but tonight hopefully I'll get to dance.'

'Your dance card will fill up as soon as you get there,' Mary added.

'We will see, it depends on who will be there, I suppose.'

'P'raps Mr Dean will sign it for you,' Katy mumbled whilst dipping a biscuit in her tea.

'That would be nice, although Aunt Win might not like it much.'

'There ain't nowt she could do about it though. She wouldn't want to cause a scene,' Mary said.

'Well, I'm going into the garden for a while, then I suppose I should go and get ready.'

As Rose stood, Katy said, 'I'll be up as soon as I've finished my tea.'

'No rush, Katy,' Rose said with a smile. 'We have all day.'

'Never mind that, you get up them stairs and help Miss Rose!' Mary scolded but gently.

'It's all right, Mary, there's no hurry. I'll be outside.' Rose walked from the room.

'What do you make of all that, Mr Jackson?' Mary asked.

'I can't be sure, Mrs Winters, but I do wonder if the missus is onto Miss Rose.'

'That's my worry an' all,' Mary mumbled. 'What can we do?'

'Nothing for the present, we just have to wait and see what happens.'

17

On her return from the town, Win was met in the hall by Jackson.

'Tea in the sitting room,' she ordered. Once she was settled comfortably, Win unwrapped her parcel and examined the white silk gloves she had purchased. She placed them on the seat next to her when Katy brought in the tray.

'Where is Rose?'

'She's just gone to her room, madam. She asked me to help her get ready for tonight.'

'Very well, off you go.' Win poured the beverage as her mind revisited her early-morning actions. She had moved her brother-in-law's will, the bank book, and house deeds on a whim. For a reason she couldn't fathom, she'd felt suddenly uncomfortable about where they had lain for years. No one went into her room except Katy, who cleaned in there, and would have no reason to snoop. Besides, Win doubted the girl could even read. Mary never moved from the kitchen and Jackson didn't go upstairs – which left Rose.

With a shake of her head, Win didn't think her niece would dare to pry. Why would she want to? Rose would have no idea about the documents and what they meant. So why the discomfort? Win couldn't deny time was marching on, in fact Rose would turn twenty years old very soon. Maybe this was why Win felt ill at ease, because she had so little time now to see the girl wed or lose everything.

Win moved to her desk and checked again the invitations to be sent out. She had planned a small party for Rose's birthday, just a few people of note; mainly those who had unmarried sons.

Taking the invites to the hall, she placed them on the silver tray on the table for posting. Then she took her gloves to her room.

In the meantime, Katy had climbed the stairs and tapped on Rose's door before entering. Immediately her eyes fell on the blue dress on the bed. 'Oh, Miss Rose, that's beautiful!' she said as she closed the door.

'I know but Aunt Win won't like it.'

'Well, she ain't wearin' it so it don't matter.' Rose smiled. Poor innocent Katy had little idea about dress etiquette and the underlying reasons for not wearing such bold colours. 'Right, let's get your hair sorted first.'

'Can you put this in?' Rose asked, holding up the long string of pearls.

Katy nodded. 'I can and it'll look bostin'!'

The two chattered about who might be attending the ball as Katy brushed Rose's hair. She wove the pearls between curls, pinning them in place, then fastened the necklace and earrings.

'Katy, you are a marvel, thank you.' Rose looked at the fine job Katy had made with her hair then added, 'Now for the gown.'

'Shoes first 'cos I don't think you'll be able to bend down in that frock.'

Rose slipped on her shoes then was fastened into her gown. She checked her look in the long mirror. The same design as the red one, with a tight waist and cut low at the neckline, Rose adjusted the cap sleeves and smiled.

'Bloody beautiful!' Katy gasped. 'Beggin' your pardon, miss.'

'Thank you, Katy, I'm pleased with the overall effect. Now where's my wrap?'

'Here you are.' Katy held out the garment then said, 'Oh, miss, don't forget this!' Picking up the dance card, she tied it securely around Rose's left wrist. 'One more thing.' Grabbing the rouge pot, she opened it, dipped a finger and smoothed gently over Rose's cheeks and lips, blending it in expertly. 'Now you're all set to have a smashing time.'

'Prepare yourself for Aunt Win yelling at me,' Rose warned.

On cue, a shout from the hall said Win was waiting.

'Here we go.' Rose left her room, head held high, and swept down the staircase.

'What in God's name...!' Win yelled on seeing the bright blue gown. Jackson winced as he held the front door open.

Katy ran to the kitchen and ushered Mary into the shadows to see Miss Rose in her new gown. Mary's hand leapt to cover her mouth as she watched.

'Rose, whatever are you thinking? You can't possibly wear that!'

'Aunt Win, in the dress shop you said not lemon. This is not lemon.'

'I can see that, I'm not blind!'

'Well, it's done now and there's no time to change. Besides, the only other ball gown I have is red.' Rose's rebellious spirit rose again in her as she stood ramrod straight, waiting for a challenge that didn't come.

'Red! Oh, I feel faint.' Win grabbed the table for support.

Mary and Katy stifled giggles as they witnessed Rose finally standing up for herself.

'Well, are we going or should we stay home if you are unwell?' Rose asked pointedly.

'We must attend but what people will think when you walk in wearing that...'

Rose cut Win off with, 'I don't care what they think, I like it!' Then, with a quick glance at Jackson, she stepped through the doorway and out to the waiting cab. Jackson lowered his head as Win followed.

Mary and Katy dashed back to the kitchen where they burst out laughing. 'The missus was livid!' Katy said.

'I ain't surprised. That blue is a real eye-opener,' Mary agreed.

'I wonder what the other girls will wear.'

'Probably white, pale pink or lemon,' Mary said before they fell about giggling again.

Then Katy asked, 'Why?' Mary went on to explain how pale colours denoted virginity and bolder colours cast suspicion on the wearer's innocence. 'That's daft,' Katy mumbled.

'I know but it's what the toffs believe.'

'Then I'm glad I ain't a toff. This way I can wear whatever I like.' Katy gave a single nod as she spoke.

'I'd love to be a fly on the wall at that ball tonight,' Mary added.

'Knowing my luck, I'd get splatted!' Katy's statement had them both laughing yet again.

As Jackson joined them, they settled to their meal of potatoes, cabbage and faggots in rich gravy, their discussion centred on Rose and her dress.

18

'How could you do this to me, Rose?' Win growled as the cab rattled along the streets. *I could ask the same of you*, Rose thought as her mind went back to her father's will. 'You should be in white! I can't believe...'

'Aunt, you didn't specify a colour in the shop.'

Win realised the girl was correct but blustered on. 'I considered you old enough to be sensible regarding choosing an appropriate colour!'

'I am and I chose this.' Rose stroked the skirt as she spoke.

'It's not appropriate! It screams hussy!'

'As I said before – it's too late now.' Rose looked out of the window, denoting she was not prepared to discuss it further. *Round one to me*, she thought as the cab wound its way up a long drive and halted in front of what looked like a mansion. However, beneath her bravado she fretted that maybe her aunt was right, and people would judge her harshly for her choice of gown.

Alighting, they strode to the door and were admitted by a waiting footman. The hall floor was a mosaic which any ancient Roman nobleman would have been proud of. To the left was the drawing room and sitting room, both of which had glass doors leading to extensive gardens. On the right was a parlour and music room. The sweeping staircase led to numerous bedrooms and an indoor bathroom. Back stairs took an army of staff to their rooms. The kitchen was below the parlour with a lumber room and scullery. Built on the back of the massive house was Marjorie Huntington-Phillips's pride and joy – her very own ballroom.

The host and hostess greeted them reservedly on seeing Rose's attire. A maid relieved them of their wraps and Win led Rose into the sitting room. Every head turned as they walked in – then the whispering began.

'See how they talk about you?' Win said quietly.

Suddenly Rose didn't feel quite so confident. She hadn't expected the people to be quite so overt in showing their distaste. Her eyes scanned the room for a friendly face but all she saw were frowns.

Win's voice in her ear said, 'I warned you, now on your own head be it.'

Rose turned to her aunt and whispered, 'I'm not the only one who will suffer for this, though, am I? It will reflect badly on you too.'

'Miss Hamilton, how very nice to see you again and looking divine this evening.' Charles Dean's voice boomed out as he crossed the room to shake Rose's hand.

'Thank you, Mr Dean,' Rose responded.

Turning to her aunt, he said simply, 'Win.'

'Charles.'

'I hope you ladies will save me a dance later.'

'I expect Rose's card will fill quickly,' Win answered.

'I don't doubt it,' Charles replied, casting an approving glance over the girl in question.

'Excuse me.' Rose made her escape into the garden where she

drew in a deep breath, feeling safe from the prying eyes. In the corner was a miniature maze for children to play in, and further round was an oversized chess board for adults to play with.

Win moved away to greet others and Charles whipped two glasses of wine from a passing maid's tray. He also made his way outside.

'There you are,' he said, presenting Rose with a glass. 'May I sit?'

'Of course, please do.' Rose accepted the wine and took a sip.

'You look beautiful, the colour of your dress suits your eyes.'

Rose took another sip, delighted by his comment. 'I'm afraid Aunt Win would not agree. She's very cross with me.'

Charles smiled. 'As always, I can't recall the last time I saw her smile.'

'Nor I, it's not something she does any more.'

'You, however, shine like a star when you smile, you light up a room.' Rose blushed fiercely, her eyes dropping to the glass in her hand. 'I apologise, I've embarrassed you. To make up for it, may I sign your dance card?'

'Yes, of course.' Rose held out her wrist and Charles lifted his glass. With a smile she took it from him while he untied the ribbon. Pulling a pen from his pocket, he signed his name, then again and on until the whole card was filled.

'Mr Dean, you can't!' Rose gasped as he retied the card to her wrist. Taking back his glass, he clinked hers, saying, 'I can and I have.'

Rose laughed, feeling so much more at ease here in the garden with this handsome, confident man.

'Dinner first, what will we have, I wonder,' he said.

'I have no idea but I wish it could be faggots like our cook makes.'

Charles's laughter echoed across the expanse of lawn. 'We

shall find out imminently,' he replied as the dinner gong sounded. Getting to his feet, he held out a hand to her.

Rose slipped her hand into his as she stood and a thrill raced through her body. His thumb caressed the back of her hand as they looked into each other's eyes.

'You are so very beautiful, Miss Hamilton,' he whispered, 'the girl with the violet eyes.'

Rose drew in a breath in an effort to still her beating heart. Hooking his arm, he waited. Rose slipped hers through his and together they walked indoors towards the dining room.

Finding their seats, Rose grinned as she saw Charles swap his name card with another a few places down the long mahogany table. He was now sitting directly opposite her.

White wine was poured, including for Rose, and the first course was served. Prawns on a bed of lettuce smothered in a tasty sauce. Low conversation began and a young man sitting next to Rose said, 'I don't like shellfish.'

'Oh dear,' she muttered before tucking in.

The fellow raised a finger to summon an under-footman who was standing by the door. 'Take this away, it's not to my taste.'

The man did as he was bid, returning the dish to the kitchen.

Rose exchanged a glance with Charles, who shook his head in disgust. The young chap could have just left it to be cleared with the empty dishes.

Red wine was now poured and the main course served. Venison with vegetables steamed to perfection, crisp roasted potatoes and a rich onion gravy was served to each guest.

The young man sighed loudly and Rose looked over at him. 'Not to your taste either?' she asked.

'Not really,' he answered as he pushed the food around on his plate.

'You should eat something, it will be a long evening,' Charles suggested.

With a nod, the man made an effort.

The elderly gentleman on Rose's other side made no effort to speak to her, nor Rose to him. Every time she looked up from her plate, she felt Charles's eyes on her. Then, just as she lifted her glass, she felt a nudge to her foot. She shot a look at Charles who grinned and clinked his glass to hers.

She had thought maybe he had caught her unintentionally but his smile told her otherwise. Charles Dean was playing footsie with her under the table! Her eyes flashed a warning but Charles ignored it, again stroking her foot with his. Rose bent her knees further, bringing her feet under her chair. She couldn't help but smile seeing Charles laugh.

Further down the table, Win was watching the pair intently. Whatever was going on there had to be stopped before it got out of hand. Win's attention was drawn away as a woman spoke to her, inviting her to a card afternoon, which she accepted gladly.

Plates were cleared and ice-cream with fresh fruit was served. Rose couldn't eat another thing and leaned back in her chair, watching the man next to her wolf down his sweet. Seeing her not eating hers, he asked, 'Don't you want yours?'

'No, I've had an elegant sufficiency,' she replied. She was shocked when he swapped his empty dish for her full one. Looking at Charles, she saw him shake his head in utter bewilderment. Cheese and biscuits came next, which Rose politely refused; the man next to her piling his plate, much to her amusement.

Throughout the meal, people chatted, and now Rose took the time to glance around. There were a couple of girls her age who were wearing white, and inwardly Rose smiled as she saw them giggling. *Immature young women*, she thought. Then she realised how few people there were considering it was supposed to be a ball. She voiced this quietly to Charles, who said, 'There will be others who will come just for the dancing. Only the most important are invited to dine first.' Rose smiled her thanks.

Charles couldn't take his eyes off her, the candlelight on her dark hair, her skin as smooth as a baby's and those violet eyes sparking like coloured diamonds.

'Brandy and cigars in the drawing room, gentlemen, and for the ladies, coffee in the sitting room,' their host announced.

Rose wasn't surprised when she saw the young man who had sat next to her follow the women rather than the men.

19

As usual, Rose took her coffee outside. She couldn't face the recriminating looks, especially as she knew there would be more when other guests arrived later.

'Hello, I'm Olivia.' The young woman dressed in pale pink had joined Rose in the garden.

'Rose. I'm pleased to meet you.'

'I noticed you when you arrived, but then it's hardly surprising in that colour.'

Rose clenched her teeth at the barely hidden insult. 'That was the idea – to stand out from the norm,' she replied. This evening was going to be fight or flight, and Rose had no intention of running away from anything anyone said.

'You've certainly done that. I can't imagine you'll be doing much dancing.' The spite dripped from Olivia's tongue. 'Of course, all of us young ladies are hoping for at least one turn around the ballroom with that handsome devil, Charles Dean.'

Rose smiled. 'Actually, my dance card is already filled completely. Now, if you will excuse me.' With her nose in the air, Rose walked indoors to set her cup and saucer on a small table.

'Where were you?' Win asked, sidling up to her niece.

'I was in the garden chatting.'

'With whom?'

'A girl called Olivia.'

'Ah, yes, sweet young thing.' Win's eyes scanned the room and she smiled as Olivia entered through the open French windows.

Hardly sweet – poisonous more like! Rose kept her thoughts to herself. If Olivia wanted to be nasty then let her, Rose wasn't that bothered, especially when she glanced at her dance card. *Little Miss Olivia will be green with envy when Charles Dean leads me onto the dance floor.*

'I saw you speaking to Owen Mason at dinner,' Win went on.

'Oh, is that his name?'

'Did he not introduce himself?'

'No, he was very rude about the food,' Rose said. 'Please don't tell me you were thinking of him as a husband for me.'

'His father is very rich, Rose, you would want for nothing. Well, there will be other eligible young men attending if Owen doesn't suit you.'

'He most certainly does not.' Rose heard the musicians tuning up their instruments and she thought, *Now the fun will begin.*

'The dancing is about to begin so get ready to have your card signed,' Win said as she and Rose followed the hostess into the ballroom. Music played as the men joined them and newcomers arrived. The room was filling up quickly.

Rose's eyes searched for Charles but all they found were Olivia and a couple of her friends staring at her. One said something and they all giggled. *Laugh on, ladies, because you won't be laughing when the dancing starts.*

It was hot with so many bodies crammed into the room despite more French windows flung wide open. Small feather fans fluttered as the ladies tried to cool themselves down. The chatter was loud so as to be heard over the music as folk greeted their friends.

'Goodness me, the wealthiest people are all here,' Win said.

Rose nodded, despite not knowing any of them. She did, however, catch the disapproving glances from women newly arrived. *Here we go again*, she thought but kept her head high, determined not to be cowed.

The music stopped and the conductor's voice sailed across the room. 'Ladies and gentlemen, please take your partners for a waltz.' The small orchestra stationed at one end of the room struck up again, and Rose noticed Olivia being led onto the floor by a shy young man. Olivia shot Rose a supercilious smile as they took up their position. She watched as they spun around, weaving confidently between other couples.

Unable to see Charles in the crowd, Rose was about to turn away when he appeared before her. 'My dance, I think?' He held out his hand.

'Charles, what are you doing?' Win asked through clenched teeth.

'Dancing with your niece,' he replied before he whisked Rose expertly into the tide of dancers flowing past a disgruntled Win. They sailed alongside Olivia and her timid partner just long enough for Rose to grin at the girl staring at her in disbelief.

All eyes were on Charles and Rose but the couple didn't notice, they only had eyes for each other. Conversations began about the girl in the blue dress; women slighting her choice of colour, men admiring her beauty and pluck.

'Everyone is watching us,' Rose said.

'I know. The men are wishing they were me,' Charles said with a laugh as he swung her into a spin at the corner.

'The women hate me because of my gown.'

'Ignore them, they're only jealous. Enjoy yourself, Miss

Hamilton, the night has barely begun.' The waltz came to a close and Charles led Rose back to her aunt.

'I know the next dance is with Miss Hamilton but if you'd care to take a turn around the room with me, Win?'

'I would not!' Win snapped.

With a shrug, Charles led Rose out yet again onto the floor. They danced together time after time until Rose said, 'Forgive me but I really must get some air.'

'Of course, may I escort you into the garden?'

Rose nodded and taking his arm they strode outside into the blessed cool of a moonlit night. Lanterns cast little pools of light onto the walkways, and a full moon shed its silvery beams across the extensive lawns. Finding a bench beneath a huge oak, they sat in the shadows of the canopy, a gentle breeze welcome after the stuffiness of the ballroom.

'Aunt Win will have my hide if she catches us out here,' Rose said quietly.

'She takes her role as your guardian very seriously,' he replied.

Rose glanced at him. 'You seem to know a lot about me, Mr Dean.'

'Charles, and yes, I do. I made it my business to find out.'

'Why would you do that?' Rose asked innocently.

'You really don't know, do you? It's because I'm interested in you, Rose; I'm attracted to you.'

Rose felt the heat rise to her cheeks and her bosom rose and fell as she tried to catch her breath. 'I know very little about you, in fact all I *do* know is your name.'

Charles laughed. 'I am unmarried as yet. I have a house in Well Lane just off Allison Street, quite near to the police station. I employ a cook and a maid, both of whom take very good care of me. I inherited a great deal of money from my father which means I don't have to work. However, I'm not one to sit idle, hence my owning a string of narrowboats and barges. Now the tables are turned and you know more about me than I do about you.'

'There's not much to my life, Charles. I'm dragged from pillar to post by Aunt Win while she searches for a husband for me.'

'That sounds very dull.'

'It is,' she replied, lowering her head.

'Then I suggest we spice it up with more dancing, come.' He helped her to her feet and they entered the fray once more.

Rose didn't notice Win standing in the bushes, her dark green dress melting into the shadows.

20

Following indoors, Win watched Rose dancing with the only man she had ever loved. She saw how he looked at her niece, knowing he had never looked at her that way. Jealousy bubbled up inside her, mixing with fury at Charles. She had carried her anger all these years, ever since he had told her they would not be married. Now he had set his sights on Rose, but he would not have the girl. Win had decided long ago that if she could not have Charles Dean then nobody would. Up until recently, Win had not had to worry about Charles wedding another, but Rose was a very real threat. She had to prevent that happening but she was unsure, as yet, how to go about it.

Charles and Rose left the dance floor and walked into the drawing room and over to the punch bowl. Lifting a tiny glass cup from its hook on the side of the large bowl, he filled it with a ladle and handed it to Rose. Then, after filling one for himself, they strolled to sit on a couch.

'People are talking about us,' Rose whispered.

'I know – delicious, isn't it?' he responded before laughing loudly at the shock on her face.

'Rose, there you are, I've been looking everywhere for you,' Win said as she strode towards them.

'Really, Win? I could have sworn I saw you standing outside a little while ago,' Charles said knowingly.

'You must be mistaken, Charles,' Win said but knew he had spotted her watching them. 'Now, Rose, you really must come and circulate.'

'Aunt Win, no one wants to speak to me, and we both know why. At least Charles is gentleman enough to dance with me.'

Charles, now, is it? When did that come about? Win kept her thoughts to herself but said instead, 'Nonsense, girl, stop feeling sorry for yourself and mingle!'

'I'm afraid she can't, Win, as her dance card is full,' Charles put in.

Win grabbed the little card and read his name time after time. 'Really, Charles! This simply won't do!'

'Aunt Win...'

'No, Rose! I will not allow this... this...' Win pointed at them both, 'to go on any longer! You are my ward until you come of age and therefore you will abide by my rules!' Win suddenly realised she'd been shouting and all conversation in the room had halted. She turned slowly to see everyone staring at her. Shoving her nose in the air, she strode from the room. Discussions resumed after a quick glance at the couple on the couch.

'Oh dear, Aunt Win is really angry with me now,' Rose said, feeling she had overstepped the mark and really upset her aunt.

'No, my dear, her ire is directed at me and has been for a very long time. Never mind, let's dance some more.'

Towards the end of the evening, Charles and Rose strolled in the garden again. It was cool and the stars twinkled overhead as the pair traversed the pathway. Charles stopped abruptly and turned to her, saying, 'Rose, all night I've wanted to kiss you.'

'Oh, Charles, I... we can't. If we should be seen...'

'I don't care if we are!'

'That's all right for you to say. I've damaged my reputation enough tonight by wearing this.' Rose picked up her skirt. 'It would be ruined irreparably if we were caught in an embrace.'

'You're right, of course. Forgive me, I should keep my emotions in check.'

Rose nodded, unwilling to tell him she'd had the same feelings. She couldn't afford to encourage him further, because of her aunt for one thing, and for another she couldn't think about a relationship and marriage until she turned twenty-one.

Returning inside, Charles said, 'Here again, Win?'

Win fumed at being seen again despite her best efforts to hide. Striding into the drawing room, she forced a smile when an older woman spoke to her. 'Ah, Win, you really must speak to that gel of yours. That gown... well, need I say more?'

'Rose is a young woman now, Helen, and I do declare I find it difficult. I'm not her mother, after all.'

'No, of course not, but even so... Have words with her before it's too late and her reputation is sullied beyond redemption.' The woman walked away, leaving Win feeling angrier than ever. *The quicker that girl is wed, the happier I'll be.* Grabbing a drink from the punch bowl, Win downed it in one before refilling the cup.

Once her temper had cooled, Win returned to the ballroom. Rose and Charles were dancing and they were talking and laughing. Win felt the pain stab her heart yet again; that could have been her in Charles's arms if only he'd loved her. Win's mind leapt back to that day she and Charles had enjoyed afternoon tea together before taking a walk in the park. They had sat in the empty bandstand, and that was when he told her she shouldn't harbour the hope of them being wed. He explained he had no intention of getting married for a very long time – if at all.

Win had said she would wait until he was ready; that she could never love another. *Win, please try to understand – I don't love you in that way. We are friends but it could never be anything more than that.* He had left her then, sitting alone sobbing her heart out. He had tried his best, she knew, to be gentle but sadness gripped her with an iron fist. She hadn't laughed properly since that day.

'Not dancing, Miss Jacobs?' The voice snapped Win's attention back and she held up her punch cup. 'I was just enjoying the refreshments,' she replied.

With a nod, the man moved on to speak to a colleague.

Chance would be a fine thing, Win thought as she glanced at her empty dance card.

21

The ball had been a huge success and Rose had enjoyed herself enormously. It was not until they got home that Win finally spoke. It was in the hall that Win's anger erupted, taking Jackson by surprise as he closed and locked the door.

'I'm ashamed of you, Rose! Not only did you choose to wear this...' she tugged at the blue dress, 'but you only danced with Charles Dean all night! You gave no one else the opportunity to sign your card. You were out with him in the garden – unchaperoned!'

'You were there, Aunt Win, Charles saw you hiding – watching us,' Rose shot back.

'You should not have been alone with him, Rose, you know that!'

'We were only talking.'

Win sighed loudly. 'You have given completely the wrong impression, don't you understand? No one will want their son to have anything to do with you now!'

'Good! I don't care, I had a wonderful time tonight and you can't spoil that for me!' Rose spun on her heel, held up her skirts and ran up the stairs. She slammed her bedroom door, telling Win she too was very angry.

Jackson had stood by silently in case the missus wanted anything before retiring, but Win ignored him and went to her own room, where she closed the door with a quiet click.

Mary and Katy, hearing the ruckus from the kitchen, listened from the stairs and now returned to the kitchen where Jackson joined them.

'Blimey, they were going at it,' Katy said.

'It's been coming for a while, lovey, and it's my thinking there'll be a lot more yet.' Mary shook her head.

'Miss Rose looked beautiful in her frock though.'

'She did,' the cook agreed, 'although I wasn't sure about the blue at first.'

'Well, I loved it. I hope when she throws it out it comes my way,' Katy said, imagining herself in the gown.

'When would you wear a dress like that?' Jackson asked.

'I don't know but just once I'd like a ball gown,' Katy replied dreamily.

'Me an' all, Katy,' Mary muttered, now lost in the same dream.

'Shall I set the kettle to boil?'

'Better had 'cos I'm guessing Miss Rose will be down in a minute or two,' Mary said as she fetched the cake from the pantry.

True to form, Rose made her appearance after changing her clothes. 'I suppose you heard,' she said as she sat down.

'We couldn't help it,' Katy replied.

'Never mind that, tell us all about your evening.' Mary brushed the argument between aunt and niece aside as tea was poured.

Rose told her friends how much she'd enjoyed herself.

Seeing Katy yawn, Mary sent her to bed. Jackson followed

suit shortly afterwards, and once there was just Rose and herself, she asked, 'Did you find what you were looking for?'

'No, Aunt Win has moved them. I've no idea why or where those papers are now. Do you think she's on to me?'

'You have to be prepared for that to be the case,' Jackson interjected as he appeared like a genie from a bottle, making both women jump. 'I apologise, I came for a glass of water.'

Mary shook her head. 'I doubt it. I suspect she shifts them around every so often just in case.'

'In case of what?'

'I don't know but clearly she's afraid they might be discovered. Are you sure you left everything as you found it?'

'I'm certain.'

'Then I'm at a loss. All you can do is keep looking every chance you get.'

Rose agreed with a nod before leaving to go to her bed.

Jackson and Mary discussed the situation for an hour or more, both wanting to help Rose but uncertain as to how to bring that about. Jackson retired, leaving Mary to check all was safe and the doors were bolted, then Mary climbed the back stairs wearily. All this cloak and dagger stuff was wearing on her nerves. The bickering and arguments between Rose and her aunt didn't help either. She'd be glad when the girl turned twenty-one and the whole sordid mess could be sorted out once and for all.

The following morning, over breakfast, Win informed Rose she would be having a small party for her birthday. 'I will discuss the menu with cook later before I to go Mrs Wincanton's whist drive.'

'I didn't know you were going out,' Rose said.

'Yes, she invited me last evening at the ball. I'm sure you can amuse yourself for a few hours.'

I certainly can! 'Yes, Aunt.'

Around mid-morning, Win sent for Mary to discuss the food for the party. 'Sit-down arrangements are difficult as I only have a maid to serve and I have no intentions of spending a fortune on hiring more staff.'

'Buffet then,' Mary said.

'Yes, now here is a list of what I think would go down well.' Mary took the paper and read it. 'Well?'

'I can't see any problems with this, madam.'

'Good. That will be all.' Win dismissed the cook with a wave of her hand.

Back in the kitchen, Mary read out the list to Katy. Jackson looked up from his newspaper as he listened.

'Best china then?' Katy asked.

'Yes and we'll need some centrepieces for the table, two should do.'

'Fresh flowers would be nice. I could do them the night before.'

'Good girl, you're a diamond, Katy.' The girl beamed at the compliment.

'Sit you down and study that paper while I make you a nice cup of tea,' Katy said.

* * *

Upstairs, Rose joined Win in the sitting room. 'Who have you invited to the party?'

'The Huntington-Phillipses, the Wincantons, some of my card-playing friends.'

'Mr Dean?' Rose asked after taking a breath.

'Certainly not! After last night I'm shocked you would even consider it.'

'So all of yours but not my one and only friend,' Rose said flatly.

'Charles Dean is not your friend, Rose. He is a scoundrel who should be avoided.'

'Why do you say that?'

'Because it's true. He will play with your affections then drop you like a hot potato when he tires of you.'

'Well, it's my party and I want him invited,' Rose said firmly.

'No, Rose.'

Rose shrugged, getting to her feet. 'Then cancel it because if Charles doesn't attend then neither will I!' With that she strode from the room, feeling full of confidence.

I'm standing on my own two feet at last, she thought as she went to the kitchen to tell Mary about her ultimatum.

22

Win fumed as she scratched out an invitation to Charles. She had to keep Rose sweet until she was married off and it galled her having to do so. Time was fast running out and Win felt panic begin to rise in her. Everything she'd worked for over the last few years could be gone in the blink of an eye if her plan failed. There had to be *someone* who Rose would accept as a husband, but Win was at a loss as to who that could be.

Addressing the envelope, she stared at the name – Charles Dean. *I'll bet he would marry her*, she thought, *if only to spite me*. Win weighed up the options; Rose and Charles wed would solve the problem of the will, house and money – Win would inherit the lot. However, the thought of it turned her stomach. She couldn't bear the idea of her love being with another woman, no matter what the reasons. And especially not her niece!

Taking the invite, she placed it on the tray on the hall table for posting. She would concede to Rose's wishes this one time, then a concerted effort would be needed to plan a wedding.

Pinning her hat in place, Win pulled her parasol from the umbrella stand before yelling for Jackson. 'I'm going out now, I'll be back for dinner, please tell cook. Oh, my bag...' Win retrieved the item from the sitting room and left the house, not waiting for Jackson's reply.

Rose noticed the invite on the table and smiled as she walked through the hall on her way to her room.

Jackson passed the message to Mary that the missus was out and would return for the evening meal.

Rose waited impatiently for half an hour before dashing into Win's bedroom. Hunting high and low, she eventually found what she was looking for – right back in the underwear drawer.

The will had been drawn up by Messrs Jones, Evans and Thompson based in Corporation Street. The bank in Stephenson Place held three hundred pounds of Rose's money, an amount too vast to contemplate. Assuring herself all was perfectly back in place, Rose rushed to her room to jot down the information. Now what?

Going downstairs, Rose went to Win's desk. There she wrote a letter to John Watts giving him the details she had discovered. She explained she was sending this communiqué by runner, and would appreciate him doing the same via Mary in the kitchen.

Seeing a small pot of coins at the back of the desk, she grabbed a threepenny bit then left the room. Out of the front door, she ran down the short drive and looked around.

'Cab, miss?' a fellow called out, standing next to his horse.

'No, thank you, I'm looking for a runner.' The man tipped his hat and whistled loudly. 'Thank you,' Rose said as a dirty boy came racing down the street, his bare feet slapping on the pavement.

'You called, miss?' he puffed.

'Yes, I need this delivered to...' Rose held out the letter and gaped in disbelief when the urchin read the address out loud.

'Right away, miss. Will I wait for a reply?'

'I'm not sure but if there is one, please deliver it to Mary the cook. This is for you with my thanks.' Rose handed over the twelve-sided coin.

'Ooh, ta, miss. Tarrar.' With that the boy set a blistering pace as he sped away.

With a wave to the kind cabbie, Rose went back to the house. She could do nothing more now except wait to hear from John Watts. Wandering into the kitchen, she smiled as she explained what she had done.

'A clever idea, Miss Rose,' Jackson said. 'I'll keep an eye out for any reply coming your way.'

Mary shook her head and rolled her eyes at the butler then said to Rose, 'That's what the missus wants doin' for your party.'

Rose glanced at the list Mary held out to her. 'That seems fine to me.'

'Anything you want to add?'

'Strawberries if you can get them, please.'

'There'll be some about but it'll cost.'

'Hang the expense, it's for my birthday,' Rose said with a carefree laugh.

Over dinner that evening, Rose informed Win of her addition to the party menu.

'Have you gone quite mad! They will cost a fortune!'

'Aunt Win, don't pretend we can't afford it. Besides, when do I ever ask for anything?'

'I suppose you're right and it would make the right impression on our guests. Very well, I'll tell cook.'

'I already have,' Rose said with a little smile.

'Rose, you really should communicate better with me.'

That's rich coming from someone with so many secrets! 'Yes, Aunt, I'm sorry.'

It was around ten o'clock when Rose went to say goodnight to her friends.

'Stay for cocoa?' Mary asked firmly.

'Yes, please.' Rose picked up on the question delivered like an order.

'Katy love, we need milk from the churn.'

The maid skipped off to the scullery and as she returned Mary passed a note to Rose. 'Came by runner earlier.'

'Yes, I saw him as he approached the kitchen door,' Jackson put in, not to be outdone by Mary.

Rose opened the letter, saying, 'Thank you, it's from John Watts. He has all the information now.'

Mary smiled widely. 'Katy, bring the cake as well, please,' she said then quietly added, 'this calls for a celebration.'

All four sat to enjoy their supper together, chatting about the forthcoming party.

23

The following couple of weeks passed fairly quietly. Most of the affluent families took their annual holiday by the seaside, to rest and recuperate in readiness for the next round of parties and balls.

Acceptances for Rose's birthday party arrived, including one from Charles Dean. Win had hoped he would have begged off due to another engagement, but in her heart she knew he would not have missed the opportunity to see Rose again. The man was very taken with her niece and the knowledge cut her to the quick. How many times had she asked herself *why couldn't that be me?*

Yanking the bell pull by the fireplace to summon the maid, Win sat in the sitting room.

A tap to the door and Katy walked in.

'How are things coming along for the party?' Win asked.

'Nicely, madam. All the best china and glassware is washed and ready. Mrs Winters is up to her eyeballs in food and I'm doing the flowers for the table.'

'Good. My guests will be arriving at eight o'clock sharp so

ensure Jackson is ready to answer the door, looking clean and tidy.'

'Yes, madam.' *Bloody cheek! We're always clean and tidy!*

'That will be all.'

Katy bobbed a knee and retreated back to the kitchen where she related Win's instructions.

'I take exception to that!' Jackson railed. 'When have any of us been anything but smartly turned out?'

'I thought the same, Mr Jackson,' Katy said.

'Well, much more of this and the missus will have a mutiny on her hands!' Jackson shook out his newspaper with a harrumph.

* * *

A little while later, Rose joined Win, saying, 'Katy is bringing tea.'

Win nodded. 'What have you chosen to wear for your party tomorrow?'

'My blue...'

'Certainly not!'

'I was about to say my blue and white striped dress!' Rose said sharply.

'Oh, yes, that would be appropriate,' Win mumbled as Katy brought in refreshments.

So would an apology, Rose thought, *but I doubt I'll get one.*

Katy disappeared and aunt and niece drank their tea in awkward silence. Then Rose asked, 'Has Charles replied yet?'

Win was tempted to lie and say no, but when he turned up on the doorstep she would look a fool. 'Yes, he will be coming.' Rose felt her heartbeat increase and she smiled widely. 'Now I'm sure I don't have to tell you...' Win began.

But you will anyway.

'That you must mingle. These people are helping you to celebrate your birthday, please remember that.'

'Yes, Aunt.'

'It's not as if you don't know them, you've met everyone at least once before.' Rose nodded. 'Good. Off you go.'

Rose left the sitting room feeling like a five-year-old being dismissed. She trundled down into the kitchen to see if she could help with the preparations. On asking the question, she was told all was in hand. Mary saw the look of disappointment on the girl's face and said, 'You can do the napkins. Katy will show you how to fold them.'

'We'll do flowers and lay them on that big tray then they can go up to the dining room,' Katy said.

Rose folded what seemed like a mountain of linen squares, happy with the results.

'They'm lovely, Miss Rose,' Katy praised.

'So are your flower centrepieces,' Rose returned the compliment.

'We got your strawberries, they're on the cold slab,' Mary put in.

'Thank you.'

'Is Mr Dean coming?'

'He is, Mary,' Rose answered excitedly.

'Right, we'll make the salmon and cucumber sandwiches tomorrow afternoon. The pork pies are done as well as the liver pâté. The trifle just needs cream. The pickles and chutneys are in the pantry along with a good selection of cheeses. Ham off the bone, beef slices, pheasant and salad all ready to serve.' Mary ticked off the items on her fingers. 'Oh, and there's wine, ginger beer, lemonade, and coffee and biscuits to finish.'

'Don't forget the little cakes for later in the evening,' Katy said.

'Oh yes, thanks, lovey.'

Napkins were carried upstairs by Rose and the flower arrangements by Katy.

'This all looks splendid!' Rose gushed as she saw sparkling glasses lined up on a table by the door. She placed the napkin tray on the sideboard next to the china and cutlery. On the table went the flowers next to cut-glass cruets.

'Posh, ain't it, miss?' Katy asked, stepping back to admire her handiwork.

'You've done an excellent job, Katy, well done and thank you all.'

The two girls tripped lightly back down to the kitchen.

'You'll have to have your dinner and breakfast on a tray as the dinner table is in use,' Mary said.

'I don't mind that at all.'

'Good, then I'll leave you to tell the missus,' Mary said with a laugh as Rose grimaced.

* * *

The following day, the kitchen was bustling and Rose went to lend a hand. She carried tray after tray of food up to the dining room, all of which was then covered with brand-new teacloths. Serving tongs and spoons were laid out on the table which groaned under the weight of so much food. The decanters of drink stood like sentries next to the glasses and around seven o'clock Mary went to check everything was at its best.

Pleased with their efforts, she retired to the kitchen, where she would spend the rest of the evening as usual. Opening the drawer set into the table, she pulled out a little gift that she, Katy and Jackson had bought between them. She hoped Rose would like it.

At seven thirty, Rose came to thank Mary, Katy and Jackson for all their hard work, and this was when she received her gift.

'A little summat from us three. Happy birthday, Miss Rose.' Mary passed over the gift.

Rose took off the paper to reveal a miniature book of poems. 'Oh, how beautiful! Thank you all so much, I'll treasure it always. I'll put it in my room for safekeeping.' Turning to go, she changed her mind and went instead to hug her friends, even Jackson, who blushed furiously.

When she'd gone, Katy said, 'She loves it, don't she?'

Mary nodded, unable to speak lest her emotions embarrass her by flooding their banks.

24

Jackson stood on duty by the front door as guests began to arrive, taking coats or wraps and hanging them in the hall closet. Win was on hand to lead them into the sitting room where Rose waited nervously. She was eager to see Charles again despite Win's misgivings.

'Clara, how lovely to see you,' Win said.

'Win, this is my nephew, John, I hope you don't mind that he has accompanied me.'

'Of course not. You are most welcome, John. Please come through.'

In the sitting room, Rose was introduced to Clara Billingham and her nephew. She was shocked to see the young man shaking her hand. 'John Watts at your service.' She worried that John was here and that something might be said that would show that they had already met.

'Welcome, Mr Watts,' Rose croaked, having found her tongue at last.

John saw his aunt to a seat and went to get drinks for them both from the glasses of wine set out on a table nearby.

'We meet again, Miss Hamilton.' The sultry voice brought Rose's attention back from watching her unexpected guest.

'Mr Dean! Welcome, thank you for coming.'

'Oh, I wouldn't have missed this for the world. Felicitations on your birthday.'

'Thank you. Please help yourself to wine.'

With all the guests now in attendance, Rose circulated to thank them for their gifts, much to Win's delight. The presents were placed on a table to be opened later. Seeing John Watts standing alone by the fireplace, Rose walked over to him.

'I'm sorry I gave you such a shock, Rose, but I had no idea your aunt was friends with mine.'

'What are the odds of that in such a big town? No matter, it's nice to see you,' Rose replied warmly.

'I'll be sending a runner with a note soon,' he whispered conspiratorially.

'With good news, I hope,' Rose said with a smile. She was totally unaware of Charles Dean watching her from the other side of the room, a frown on his face. He in turn had no idea Win was glaring at him; she, however, was grinning.

Rose and John Watts appeared to be getting along splendidly and Win couldn't be happier.

Jackson stood in the open doorway and hit a small gong, telling people the dining room was now open. Slowly, a few at a time, the guests moved to help themselves to the fine food on offer.

Jackson retreated back to the kitchen, saying, 'Everybody's tucking into the food like they've never been fed!'

'Good, that's what I like to hear. Now let me make sure we have enough replacements.' Checking the large table full of trays, Mary nodded. 'Right, Katy, up you go and behave yourself.'

Katy and Jackson went back to the dining room where he

poured more wine and she could keep an eye on any dishes that were running low.

Once all the guests had a drink and a plate, Katy nimbly took the near-empty trays to the kitchen and brought back full ones. Her coming and going was completely unnoticed by the people enjoying Mary's cooking. Standing or sitting, the food was devoured, the guests refilling their plates time after time. Katy listened keenly and smiled at the compliments given regarding the splendid fare prepared by Win's staff. These she passed on to Mary each time she fetched a replacement tray.

Rose sought out John Watts yet again, saying, 'I'm sorry to ask but do you have any news for me?'

'All in good time, dear lady. I can't explain here but what I can say is – your inheritance is safe provided you don't wed in the next twelve months.'

Rose beamed. 'Thank you.'

'Miss Hamilton, a splendid birthday party if I may say so.'

'Charles, have you met Mr Watts?' Rose introduced the two men.

'Pleased to meet you, sir,' Charles said. 'How do you know our charming birthday girl?'

'Our aunts play cards together, it would seem,' John replied, having chosen his words carefully. 'And yourself?'

'Miss Hamilton and I met at one of the many functions being held over the summer.'

Rose, breathing a sigh of relief, excused herself to replenish her wine glass.

'Going well, ain't it, Miss Rose?' Katy asked as Jackson refilled Rose's glass.

'Indeed, Katy, so far, so good.' Rose wandered away to join Win, who was talking with an older couple.

'Ah, there you are, dear. Mrs Huntington-Phillips was just

saying there's to be another ball very soon and we are to be invited,' Win said, a little louder than was necessary.

'I look forward to it, I did so enjoy the last one,' Rose answered with a smile.

'I'm glad to hear it. Now, Win, what entertainment do you have for us this evening?'

Rose's face drained of colour. Entertainment – this was something she hadn't thought of.

'We have music arranged; first, a string quartet and then I thought – some parlour games.' Rose was delighted that her aunt appeared to have thought of everything.

'Excellent! I shall go and find the best seat.'

Whilst everyone had been socialising and eating in the dining room, Mary had been dragging furniture around in the sitting room. The quartet had arrived and were now tuning their instruments, drawing the guests to their seats.

Charles pushed his way through to escort Rose and quickly sat down beside her. 'I have hardly had a chance to speak with you tonight,' he whispered.

Rose smiled and nodded as the music began.

Throughout the musical interlude, Katy refreshed wine glasses discreetly, and after an hour or so the musicians took a final bow to rapturous applause.

Jackson saw them out with his thanks and their payment.

Mary ensured the dining table was heaped with fresh food for those who might still be peckish.

Then it was time for the games to begin.

25

Win produced a bowl filled with little strips of paper. Rose, as the girl of honour, was tasked with the first game of charades.

Whilst everyone found a seat, she picked out a slip of paper and read what was written on it. Holding up one finger, she heard the calls, 'One word.' With a nod, she laid two fingers across her forearm. 'Two syllables.' Another nod. Rose pointed to her foot.

'Shoe!' She shook her head.

'Slipper!' Again she shook her head.

'Foot!' She nodded with a grin. She kicked out her leg and laughed when John Watts yelled, 'Football!' She then sat down as he took a turn.

On the game went with voices getting louder until Win called a halt. 'I think now we will play Forfeits.'

Mr Huntington-Phillips was chosen as the Judge and left the room. A large bowl was passed around into which each person dropped an object. An item of jewellery, a shoelace, a glove, a handkerchief... When completed, the Judge was invited back. Here he picked out a ring. Clara Billingham stepped forward and identified herself. The Judge then announced her forfeit – she had to make three people laugh or lose her ring.

Clara walked to her nephew and whispered in his ear, John Watts burst out laughing. One down, two to go. Moving to Win, she said, 'I *will* beat you at cards next week.' Of course Win tittered. Stepping to Charles, she leaned down to where he was sitting, saying, 'If only I was twenty years younger!' The whole congregation laughed loudly as Clara reclaimed her ring.

The Judge had a lady walking backwards in a circle, another yawn until someone else yawned, a gentleman hop around the room on one leg, and another pat his head whilst rubbing his tummy.

The games came to a halt whilst more food and drink was consumed.

'This is one fine party,' Charles said as he sidled up to Rose.

'I'm enjoying it enormously,' Rose said, still flushed with excitement.

'My God, but you're beautiful!'

'Charles, please...' Rose glanced around but no one spared them so much as a glance – except Win, who watched them avidly.

'I can't help it, every time we meet you are lovelier than before.'

Rose breathed with relief as Katy came to refill his glass. As the maid moved on, Charles said, 'Miss Hamilton, would you do me the honour of walking out with me?'

'No, she will not!' Win's harsh whisper took Charles by surprise. 'Come, Rose, your guests are waiting.' Win led her niece back to the sitting room where she had set up tables of tiddly-winks. Little coloured counters were soon flying everywhere with shouts of victory or moans of defeat.

Then each person was given a piece of paper to fold into a

boat. Katy carried in a flat tray of water and laid it on the table. Win crouched at one end of the tray and John Watts did the same at the other end. Both placed their small boats on the water and began to blow. The first paper craft to reach the other side would be the winner.

Eventually it was Rose's turn and immediately Charles laid down his boat. The blowing began and Rose was running out of puff. Seeing she was about to lose, she lifted her hand and slapped the water. Charles shot back as the water hit him full in the face; Rose nudged her boat across the pond to win.

Applause and laughter rang out as Charles mopped his face with his handkerchief. He bowed gracefully to Rose then kissed the back of her hand in gracious defeat.

Slowly the party began to wind down with people now content to chat and drink.

'That was a cheap trick,' Charles said.

'Maybe, but I won.'

'I didn't realise the girl with the violet eyes was a cheat.'

'I didn't cheat. There was nothing in the rules to say I couldn't do it,' Rose grinned.

'Fair enough. Now about my question of earlier.'

Rose looked into his eyes and her heart beat out a tattoo. 'There's nothing I'd like more but you know as well as I – Aunt Win would never allow it.'

Charles sighed. 'We would be chaperoned, and I promise to be a complete gentleman.'

'I know you would, but Charles – I can't. When I come of age next year, then I can choose my own path, but until then I'm bound by my aunt's wishes and rules.'

'Would you if you could?' he asked.

'Yes,' Rose whispered.

'Then I will wait. This time next year you can fulfil your promise to walk out with me.'

'I don't recall making any such promise...' Rose began.

'Do it now, so I have it to look forward to.' Charles saw Rose's eyes twinkle in the light of the gas lamps, her hair shining and her lips parted slightly, and he yearned to take her into his arms.

'We shall see. A lot can happen between now and then.' Seeing his mouth turn down, she went on, 'However, if we are still friends then I would be pleased to accompany you on a stroll to the park.'

Charles beamed. 'Now I'm satisfied, for the time being anyway.'

Win watched the interaction from across the room, wishing she could lip-read. What were they saying to each other? She prayed Rose had not agreed to his invitation to walk out because it was not going to happen, not as long as she could prevent it. Her attention was drawn to John Watts on hearing his laugh. Now there was a nice young man and Rose appeared to like him. Maybe it was time to find out if he was in the market for a wife. With a last glance at Rose and Charles, Win sauntered over to where Mr Watts was entertaining his aunt and her friends.

At last carriages were called forth and folk started to leave with their thanks for a thoroughly enjoyable evening.

When everyone had gone, Jackson, Katy and Mary began to clear away glasses, dishes and trays with bits of food left on them. Win joined them in the dining room, saying, 'Thank you all for your efforts, this evening was a huge success.' With that, she walked to where Rose was unwrapping her gifts.

'A silk scarf from Mrs Huntington-Phillips, and two tickets for the theatre from Mrs Billingham,' Rose said.

'How very thoughtful,' Win replied.

'This one is from Charles,' Rose said as she unwrapped a box, inside which was a diamond bracelet. 'Oh, my...!'

Win's teeth clenched hard enough to crack her jaw as she eyed the piece of jewellery.

'Aunt Win, look,' Rose said as she took out the bracelet and fastened it on her wrist.

'I can see, I have eyes, don't I?' Rose looked up at the sharp retort. 'I'm tired,' Win said by way of an excuse. 'I think I will retire.'

'Aunt Win – thank you for the lovely party, I've really enjoyed it.'

Win forced a smile and with a stiff back she left the room and climbed the stairs to bed.

Rose took the other stairs, down to the kitchen where butler, cook and maid were busy washing glassware, cutlery and dishes.

'What have you got there?' Mary asked, the diamonds catching her eye as they glittered in the light.

'A gift from Charles Dean.'

'Bloody hell, he must be rich!' Katy said as she stared at the bracelet.

Mary said nothing. She knew this was just one more thing to widen the rift between Rose and Win.

26

'Mary, there was virtually nothing left of the food you prepared!' Rose said.

'It's a nice compliment in itself for a cook, that is.'

'Katy, you were a marvel tonight, and you too, Jackson. Thank you all very much. Now I'll make us a nice cup of tea.' Rose set about the task, much to the astonishment of the staff, as the last of the washing up was finished.

A little later, Katy said, 'I'm for my bed.' Wishing them goodnight, she dragged her weary bones from the room.

Rose sat with Jackson and Mary chatting quietly, then Mary said, 'Miss Rose, I'm sure I caught a glimpse of John Watts as I came out of the sitting room.'

'You did, Mary, he came with his aunt and you could have knocked me down with a feather I was so surprised.'

'I'll bet.'

'He said he'll send a runner with more news soon.'

Mary nodded. 'Tell me about your party.'

Rose began to relate the goings on and they all laughed together regarding the paper boat game. Eventually she got to her feet and, giving her thanks once more, she also went to bed. Jackson retired, leaving the cook to finish her tea.

Mary lingered a while, her thoughts on how Win would have reacted to Rose's gift from Charles Dean. Her mind drifted back over the years to when she had been employed by Jenny and Miles Hamilton. Rose had been a babe in arms and the family happy. She recalled Win moving into the house she now sat in, and overhearing Miles objecting to it. Jenny had other ideas, saying it was only fair as Win was her sister and she wanted to be close to her. Miles had relented, and now Mary began to wonder why he had given in so easily. Was there more to this story, or was it simply that the sisters wanted to be near to each other? With Miles and Jenny dead, God rest their souls, Mary would probably never know, but the itch that she couldn't scratch persisted.

With a sigh, Mary doused the lights and negotiated the stairs and corridors in the dark as she had so many times before. As usual, Katy had lit the gas lamp in her room and Mary washed and changed into her nightdress. Turning off the lamp, she climbed into bed, thankful to be off her feet at last.

* * *

A couple of days later, Rose searched through her wardrobe for a dress for the Huntington-Phillipses' ball. Her fingers stroked the red gown longingly but she resisted the urge to wear it. Win would flatly refuse to go if she wore it, and Rose wanted to attend in the hope of seeing Charles again. She settled for the pale blue from which, at her request, Katy had removed the long sleeves and lowered the neckline a little. The full skirt would sit nicely over the small bustle and it fitted her really well.

Once she was ready, she glanced in the long mirror and smiled at the bracelet as it sparkled in the last rays of the sun.

Down in the hall, Win's curt nod said she approved of Rose's attire before leaving the house. Noticing the bracelet, Win didn't trust herself to speak for the whole of the journey.

The music had already begun when they arrived and the ball was in full swing. Going directly to the ballroom after being greeted by the hostess, Rose glanced around.

'Are you looking for someone?' Win asked snidely.

'No, I was admiring the gowns.' The little white lie tripped easily from Rose's tongue.

Win moved away to speak to a gaggle of her card cronies and Rose started as Olivia sidled up to her.

'I see you're in blue again.'

'I see you're in cream, just an in-between shade of lemon and white.'

Olivia stiffened. 'That's a pretty trinket on your arm.'

'Isn't it?' Rose touched her bracelet. 'A birthday gift from Charles Dean.'

'Oh.' Olivia swallowed noisily, knowing now that the 'trinket' must have cost a lot of money, having come from so rich a man. 'He doesn't appear to be here tonight so I'm guessing you won't be doing much dancing.'

'I wouldn't bet on that if I were you,' Rose said as a young man approached to sign her dance card, asking, 'May I book the next polka?'

'Indeed,' Rose answered with a beaming smile.

After the fellow had bowed and wandered away, Olivia spoke again. 'Well, you have at least one dance, I would make the most of it if I were you because it's unlikely your card will be signed again.'

Rose turned to face the spiteful young woman, saying, 'Have I wronged you somehow, Olivia?' Taken aback, the girl shook her head. 'Then why are you so venomous towards me?'

'I'm only speaking the truth!'

'No, you are not. You are being nasty because you're jealous of me. Now may I suggest you keep your forked tongue behind your teeth!'

Olivia stormed away, full of fury.

Rose heard a slow clapping behind her and turned to see Charles quietly applauding her. 'Well said, Rose. It was high time someone put that viper in her place.'

'Maybe I shouldn't have but I was so angry.'

'Rightly so, and yes, you did the right thing. Now may I?' Charles pulled out his pen and yet again filled her card. 'I'm a little late, I see,' he said noting the name already there, 'I must do better in the future.'

Rose smiled.

The small orchestra played the opening bars to a polka, letting the guests know which dance was coming next.

'Miss Hamilton.' The young man held out his hand to lead Rose to a place on the dance floor. The music began and Rose found herself whirling around at a brisk pace. She had no breath to speak but smiled broadly, relieved when the dance came to a close.

Charles watched closely, thinking, *You, Miss Rose Hamilton, will be mine one day, no matter how long it takes.*

27

Win had watched the contretemps between Rose and Olivia from across the room and sighed when Olivia had stamped back to her friends. She was hoping they were getting along but clearly it was not meant to be. Then she had spotted Charles signing Rose's card – again.

It was impossible to keep the two apart, it would seem, because to find a husband for Rose they had to attend any and all functions they were invited to. Win circulated, exchanging words with those people she knew, as well as being introduced to those she was meeting for the first time. She did, however, keep a keen eye on Rose and Charles.

For her part, Rose was enjoying being in Charles's company again, to say nothing about being in his arms as they swirled around the dance floor time after time.

'Aunt Win is watching us like a hawk again, ready to sweep down upon us,' Rose said.

'It's only natural, you are her ward, after all,' Charles replied.

'I suppose so but it's rather suffocating. Besides, we're in a room full of people, what does she think will happen other than dancing?'

'Oh, I could whisk you out of the door never to be seen again.'

Rose laughed at the preposterous suggestion and sighed inwardly as he drew her closer to him to negotiate between other dancers. The music drew to a close and he walked her back to where Win was standing. 'Thank you, Rose,' he said with a little bow. 'Win, how are you?'

'I'd be better for not seeing you!' she snapped before dragging Rose away. 'Come, Rose, we must say goodnight to our hosts.'

Once in the cab and on their way home, Rose said, 'I've had a lovely time, Aunt Win.'

'I'm sure,' was all the reply that came.

Jackson was in the hall to greet them and Win went straight to her bed. Rose followed the butler to the kitchen to enjoy a cup of tea as she did every night.

'A runner came earlier, Miss Rose, he said as how he had a message for you,' Katy said.

She handed over the note and her eyes widened when Rose read it, saying, 'It's from John Watts. He's asking if I will walk out with him. He's written to Aunt Win for permission.'

'Oooh, how smashing. Is he nice?' Katy asked.

'He is, yes,' Rose replied, feeling a little confused. She certainly liked the young man but as a life partner? She didn't think so.

'But he ain't Charles Dean, is he?' Mary asked.

Rose shook her head, knowing Mary had guessed correctly. 'No, he isn't.'

'The missus would never allow you and Mr Dean to...' Mary began.

'I know, Mary; I just wish I knew why. I realise he's older than me by a lot of years, but surely that can't be the reason, not if you saw the men she considered eligible!'

Mary studied her teacup and clamped her teeth together in an effort to not say any more on the subject. She cursed herself for bringing it up in the first place. If anyone should tell Rose the reasons, it should be Win.

Rose said goodnight and left her friends finishing their tea.

'It's nice that Miss Rose has a suitor, ain't it?' Katy asked.

'Yes, lovey, it is. Now you get yourself to bed while I lock up.'

Once Katy had gone, Mary and Jackson discussed the note from John Watts.

'He's up to something,' Mary said.

'It's not out of the realms of possibility that Mr Watts really does want to court Miss Rose,' Jackson said, but Mary didn't think so.

'I don't know why, but I can't believe it, so what does that leave?'

'The only other reason I can assume is – communication,' Jackson said. 'Maybe this is his way of talking to Miss Rose about her father's will without her having to find an excuse to leave the house.'

'It's a bit extreme, ain't it?'

'Maybe, but other than the fact that Mr Watts might genuinely like Miss Rose enough to want to walk out with her.' Jackson held out his hands palms upward.

Upstairs, Rose lay in her bed, thinking about the evening and being so close to Charles. She drew in a deep breath, still able to smell his cologne. They had chatted while they danced and then Win had insulted him. Why? What made her so vicious towards him? There had to be more to it and Rose determined she was going to find out one way or another.

* * *

The following morning at breakfast, Win said, 'Jackson, I'd like to see you, Katy and Mrs Winters in the sitting room when we've finished here.'

'Yes, madam.'

'You too, Rose,' Win added.

'Yes, Aunt Win.'

An hour later, Rose and Win sat, and Jackson, Mary and Katy stood in the sitting room. 'We have a new scullion arriving very shortly. She can have the little box room next to Katy. Her name is Dolly Pritchard.' Mary and Katy exchanged a quick glance as Win went on. 'Katy, you are to be promoted to lady's maid to Rose, although still helping Mrs Winters when required.'

'Thank you, madam.' Katy bobbed a knee.

'I think that's everything for now. You may go.'

Once the servants had left, Rose asked, 'Why do I need a maid to myself?'

'Because when you wed you will be expected to bring your own maid to your new husband's residence. Now I've received a letter from John Watts requesting my permission for you both to walk out.'

'Oh, Mr Watts – he's a nice man,' Rose said, hoping she'd injected enough surprise into her words that Win wouldn't guess she already knew.

'He is and for that reason I have replied, granting his request. Katy, as your maid, will chaperone.'

'Thank you, Aunt Win.' Rose left the room to join the staff in the kitchen to inform Katy she would be chaperoning, then she went up to her room.

That afternoon, Dolly Pritchard took everyone by surprise

when she banged on the back door and walked in like she owned the place.

'I'm Dolly, the new maid.'

'You are the new scullion, and when you knock you wait for an answer,' Jackson said sharply.

'Well, I'm in now,' the girl answered, dropping her bag on the floor.

'It would appear so. I am Mr Jackson, the butler. This is our cook, Mrs Winters, and this is the lady's maid, Katy.'

Dolly gave each a quick glance then asked, 'Where's my room?'

'Katy, would you be good enough to show Dolly to her quarters, please?' Jackson requested. Katy nodded.

Dolly strode forward, leaving Katy to pick up her bag.

'Dolly, Katy is not your servant. Carry your own bag!' Jackson's snapped words caused Dolly to snatch the bag and follow Katy out of the kitchen.

'Well, I never!' Mary said, aghast.

'A few lessons in manners will be needed there, I think,' Jackson said by way of agreement.

'That one's gonna be trouble, you mark my words.'

'I suggest any reference to Miss Rose's business be confined until our new scullion is in bed.'

'I concur,' Mary said.

Katy returned, saying Dolly was unpacking, and Jackson repeated his warning about any upstairs business. 'Yes, Mr Jackson. I wouldn't trust Dolly as far as I could throw her,' Katy said.

'Good girl. Any problems with our new recruit, bring them to me.'

Cook and lady's maid nodded their understanding.

28

'Katy, would you be so kind as to fetch Dolly? It's been half an hour since she arrived and I doubt she had so much to unpack that it would take this long.' Jackson checked his pocket watch before returning it to his waistcoat pocket.

Katy left the kitchen and ran up the back stairs to the servants' quarters. Knocking on Dolly's door, she waited and when no answer came she opened it and peeped inside. 'Oh, blimey!' she whispered as she saw the new girl lying on the bed, fast asleep. 'Dolly!' she called as she walked over and shook the prone girl.

'What you doin' in my room?'

'Mr Jackson sent me to get you, there's work to be done.' Katy shook her head and left the little room.

'Ah, there you are, Dolly. Had a nice rest, have you?' Jackson asked sarcastically. Dolly scowled at Katy for telling tales then sighed as Jackson went on. 'You can make a start by scrubbing Mrs Winters's table, then you can mop the floor.'

'She could do the floor,' Dolly pointed to Katy, 'while I do the table, then it would only take half the time,' came the retort.

'Katy is lady's maid as I've already told you, besides which – when does a scullion dictate to a butler?'

Mary stood at the range, her mouth open in astonishment at the girl's cheek.

Dolly looked around for a scrubbing brush.

'Scullery!' Jackson snapped. 'And be quick about it.' Sitting in his chair by the range, Jackson watched as Dolly found the brush, bucket of water and set about her task.

The bell on the wall tinkled and Katy rushed off upstairs to answer the call.

'Katy, has our new girl arrived yet?' Win asked as the maid entered the sitting room.

'Yes, madam, she's working as we speak.'

'Good. I'll have tea.'

Katy bobbed a knee and disappeared. Back in the kitchen, she began to prepare a tray for two in case Miss Rose might join her aunt.

'I've just cleaned that!' Dolly rasped as Katy placed the tray on the table.

'And?' Katy challenged.

'Well, I ain't doin' it again!'

'You will do as you're told, young lady, or you'll be back on the books of the Servants' Registry looking for another job!' Jackson jumped to his feet he was so angry.

Dolly threw the brush into the bucket, sploshing water all over Katy's work dress.

In a flash, Jackson was across the room, grabbing the scullion by the ear. 'Apologise – *now*!'

Wincing, Dolly muttered, 'Sorry.'

'Now then, Miss Pritchard, it seems to me that you have a chip on your shoulder the size of a mountain. You appear to think the world owes you something and I'm here to tell you that it doesn't.

There is a pecking order downstairs in this house, at the top of which is me. You, however, are at the bottom and the sooner you realise it the better we'll all get along.' Jackson let go of her ear and glared as she rubbed it. 'Do we understand each other?'

Dolly nodded and Jackson retook his seat, winking at Mary as he went.

The mopping of the floor was conducted without word or incident and Jackson breathed a sigh of relief. Then a hammering on the front door had him on his feet again.

'Good afternoon. My name is John Watts and I'm here to see the ladies of the house.'

'Please come in, sir. If you wouldn't mind waiting, I'll inform the mistress.' Jackson bowed his head and strode towards the sitting room, and a moment later he was back. 'If you will follow me, sir.'

Win was delighted to see John and asked for tea for her guest. 'Send Katy for Rose, please, Jackson.'

'Certainly, madam.'

Back in the kitchen, he explained who the caller was and Katy was despatched to fetch Rose.

Mary set the tray for three and brought out cake and plates. 'He's come a'courting,' she said.

'So it would seem,' Jackson replied.

'I never thought to see the day.'

'Indeed, Mrs Winters.' Jackson gave the cook a knowing look and she nodded. This wasn't missed by Dolly, who it appeared had all but been forgotten, and she wondered what was going on.

Katy carried the tray up and bobbed her thanks as John Watts took it from her and laid it on the table. Returning to the kitchen, she said, 'Ooh, Mr Watts is really nice!'

Upstairs, Rose poured as John and Win chatted amiably. 'What is it that you do for a living, Mr Watts?'

Rose's hand tightened on the teapot handle.

'I'm a solicitor, Miss Jacobs. I share a practice with my brother in town. I must apologise for calling unannounced, but when I received your letter I thought it would be prudent to visit you as a matter of etiquette. We had so little time to speak that last time we met.' He gave Win a disarming smile. 'I was delighted to have your permission to walk out with Miss Hamilton, provided, of course, that she is in agreement.' John inclined his head towards Rose, letting her know she was not being excluded from the conversation.

'I would insist on a chaperone, Mr Watts,' Win said.

'I agree, protocol must be observed.'

Turning to Rose, Win asked, 'Well, what do you say?'

'I would enjoy a stroll out with you, Mr Watts.'

Win beamed with pleasure. 'So be it.'

'Thank you, Miss Hamilton. If it pleases you, Miss Jacobs, I will call for your niece tomorrow at noon.'

Beneath Rose's sweet smile, she was wondering what news he had for her, but also if that was the only reason for his wanting to be with her. She wasn't sure how she felt about him possibly being a suitor.

'Is your brother a solicitor too?' Win asked.

'Indeed. We deal with a variety of clients from advice on business development to property disputes.'

Rose almost choked on her tea and to hide her discomfort she laid down her cup, asking, 'Would you care for some cake, Mr Watts?'

'No, thank you. I'm sorry but I really should be going. I have a mountain of work waiting for me which is, after all, what pays the bills and adds to my savings.'

Win nodded, clearly impressed with the conscientious young man.

'Miss Jacobs, Miss Hamilton – until tomorrow.' John took his leave as Jackson was summoned to see him out.

'What a thoroughly nice young fellow,' Win said once their guest had gone.

'Yes, he is very pleasant,' Rose admitted truthfully.

With a tap to the door, Katy appeared to remove the tray.

'Ah, Katy. You will chaperone Miss Rose tomorrow at noon when Mr Watts arrives.'

'Yes, madam.'

Down in the kitchen, Katy told the others about her assignment the following day.

'Very good, Katy,' Jackson acknowledged. 'That will mean that you, Dolly, will have to help Mrs Winters with the preparation of the evening meal.'

Dolly scowled. 'As well as cleaning this place up?'

'Yes, that is your job if I'm not mistaken.' Jackson raised an eyebrow as he towered over the kitchen maid.

'Do I get paid any more for helping her?'

'You cheeky little bugger!' Mary's outburst had everyone stare in amazement at the usually mild-mannered woman.

'No, you do not! And I'll thank you to use the lady's name in future.' Jackson gave a curt nod towards the cook.

Blowing out her cheeks, Dolly returned to her task of cleaning the range.

Mary smiled her thanks at the butler and silence descended on the kitchen once more.

29

That evening, when Rose and Win had eaten, the staff sat at the table for their meal. Ham off the bone, boiled potatoes, vegetables and rich gravy was served. Mary stared openly as Dolly devoured her food like a person starving. Mary closed her eyes as Dolly chewed with an open mouth, gravy running down her chin.

'Dolly, please close your mouth when you eat. Once the food goes in we don't want to see it again,' Jackson reprimanded.

Sighing audibly, Dolly banged her cutlery down on the table. 'Are you gonna do this all the time?'

'Do what?' Jackson asked.

'Pick on me. You ain't left me alone since I got here. Dolly do this, Dolly do that. Now I can't even eat in peace!'

'Now you listen to me, my girl! There is such a thing as etiquette. Table manners are important and while in this house you will observe them. Do you understand?' Jackson was struggling to keep his temper in check.

'All right, keep your hair on,' Dolly said.

'Dolly, you are lazy and rude, and if you wish to keep your job here you will change your attitude – as of this moment! Now eat your food – properly – then you will wash the dishes before going to your bed.' Jackson held up a finger, forestalling any backlash from the girl. 'Do not speak another word!'

Katy had watched with interest to see who would be the victor, although she knew it would be Jackson. She grinned at Mary, who was shaking her head in disgust.

Dolly picked up on the grin and glared at Katy in pure hatred. She continued to eat, making a great show of keeping her mouth closed. She was, however, completely ignored by the rest of the staff as they chatted excitedly about Miss Rose's new beau.

Jackson sat with his newspaper but kept an eye on Dolly as she washed, dried and put the dishes away. Mary was poring over recipes at the table and Katy had gone upstairs to help Rose choose an outfit for her outing with John Watts.

'I've finished,' Dolly said indignantly.

'Then you may retire to your room,' Jackson said as he turned the page.

'It's only eight o'clock!'

Jackson laid down the paper, giving the girl a look of *what of it?*

'It's too early to go to bed,' Dolly pursued.

'If you can behave yourself then you may remain here with us.'

Dolly took a seat at the table, thinking *round one to me!* Before long, boredom overcame her and she began to drum her fingers on the table. Jackson shook out the paper loudly and Dolly's fingers stilled. 'Ain't there anything to do around 'ere after tea?'

'Dinner, Dolly, and no – you will have to amuse yourself,' Jackson said.

'Bloody hell!' Dolly's reply was no more than a whisper.

'Don't you knit, Dolly?' Mary asked.

'Nah, knitting's for old ladies.'

'What do you like to do then?'

'Sing and dance. You can't beat kicking your heels up to a good tune.'

'Well, there's none of that here,' Jackson put in.

'So I see.'

Katy appeared, saying, 'Miss Rose is all set for tomorrow and the missus is almost bouncing with joy.'

'We know why too,' Mary said before clamping her teeth together at the sharp look from Jackson.

'Why?' Dolly asked, instantly picking up on the sudden tension.

Ignoring the question, Mary asked, 'Which dress is Miss Rose wearing tomorrow?'

Dolly rolled her eyes as Katy answered. 'The pink with her boater. I need to polish my shoes while I remember.' Grabbing the items needed from the scullery, Katy set about her task. 'Miss Rose is having an early night so I doubt she'll be down for a cuppa.'

Dolly eyed the servants one by one. They knew something she didn't, and she determined she would find out soon what they were keeping from her.

The evening wore on and eventually Katy and Dolly went to bed. Jackson and Mary sat to enjoy a cup of cocoa and a quiet chat.

'What do you make of it, Mr Jackson? Miss Rose and John Watts, I mean?'

'I can't help but wonder if it's a ruse so he can pass her information,' Jackson replied.

'I had the same thoughts. I don't think she would consider him as a husband, not while Charles Dean is on the scene.'

'I concur, Mrs Winters. That leaves our thoughts as the only reasonable conclusion to reach.'

Absorbed in their discussion, neither were aware of Dolly hovering at the top of the kitchen steps – a wicked smile on her face as she listened intently.

Slipping quietly back to her room, Dolly began to plan. If she was helpful and polite, maybe they would include her more and talk freely about the secret they were keeping. However, she doubted it, and it would take time to get them to trust her. She'd done herself no favours coming into this household as she had, which she realised had turned everyone against her from the offing. No, if she wanted to discover what was going on above stairs then sneaky was the way to go. She would have to nip down each night and hope to learn more until she knew the whole of it.

Smiling into the darkness, Dolly snuggled down. There was nothing she loved more than intrigue and she intended to enjoy it to its utmost.

***

'Are you looking forward to your outing?' Win asked over breakfast the following morning.

'Yes, the fresh air and exercise will do me good,' Rose replied.

'I was thinking more of...'

'I know what you were thinking, and yes, Mr Watts's company will be nice, I'm sure.'

'He's rather handsome, don't you agree?'

'I can't say I'd noticed.'

'Rose, really!'

'Aunt Win, I have said I will go out with him this once, so please don't read any more into it.' Rose drank her tea and got up from the table.

'Where are you going?'

'To prepare for my *outing* with the handsome Mr Watts.' With that, Rose stalked out of the dining room.

Jackson moved to clear Rose's plate.

'Oh, Jackson, that girl is becoming a handful. Where all this hostility is coming from I don't know.'

Don't you? Jackson thought but instead asked, 'Can I get you anything else, madam?'

'No. I'll be in the sitting room.' Win walked out, shaking her head.

Jackson smiled as he replaced the plate on the table. He strode to the kitchen, telling Katy that breakfast upstairs was finished. 'Right, I'll fetch the plates,' she said.

'There's hot water, Dolly, so you can wash them up,' Mary added.

With the dining room clean and tidy once more, Katy returned to the kitchen. 'I'm going to wash and change then help Miss Rose.'

'Very good,' Jackson acknowledged.

Dolly kept her mouth shut and her ears open for anything of interest. If she kept quiet, they might forget she was there and let slip a few things. She was, however, mistaken as Jackson and Mary were fully aware of her presence and were keeping upstairs business to themselves.

30

'Oh, Katy, why am I doing this?' Rose asked as she was helped into her dress.

'You want to know what he has to say, don't you?'

'Yes, of course, but he could send a note.'

'He might think it dangerous. What if the missus finds out? Then you'll be bugg... in trouble.'

'I suppose you're right. It's just that I don't want to give him any encouragement about... well, you know.'

'Then tell him that right from the off. Explain your aunt thinks he's a good catch and she has her eye on him as a husband to you.'

'I don't think I could...'

'Look, Miss Rose, he knows about the will. He's aware the missus needs you wed in the next twelve months. He ain't daft, he's a lawyer!'

'Yes, of course. I'm a little nervous, that's all.'

'Don't be. I'll be at the back of you every step of the way.'

'Katy, you're a treasure and I love you dearly.'

'I love you an' all, Miss Rose, as do the others, and that's why we're all on your side and will help in any way we can.'

The sound of the knocker had the two young women look at each other.

'He's here!' Rose gasped.

'Right. Chin up, deep breath. Lovely, let's go.' Katy followed Rose down the stairs as Jackson opened the door.

'Mr Watts, right on time. This is Katy, my maid.'

'Katy. You look lovely, Miss Hamilton.'

'I'll be back for dinner, Jackson,' Rose said as she swept through the open doorway, Katy on her heels.

John helped both ladies into the waiting cab, telling the driver to head to Park Street Gardens. Once the gentleman was settled inside, the cabbie clucked to his horse and set off.

Turning into Great Barr Street, the cab rattled along, passing dirty buildings squashed together. It turned right at the crossroads into Fazeley Street and picked up speed again. Passing under the viaduct, it slowed as it entered the Gardens then drew to a halt.

Very little had been said on the journey and Katy had felt uncomfortable; a bit like a spare part.

John helped them alight and the cabbie said he would be parked up in Bartholomew Street awaiting their return.

John and Rose walked onto the gravel path which would take them around the park, Katy a few feet behind them, feeling much more comfortable. She smiled to herself as she heard the two strike up a conversation.

'I must apologise if all this took you by surprise, but I thought it a good way for us to meet.' John kept his voice low in order not to be overheard by their chaperone. He had no idea that Katy had excellent hearing and wouldn't miss a word.

'I was rather taken aback, I have to admit,' Rose answered.

'I have a copy of your father's last will and testament.'

'Oh, I didn't think it would be possible.'

With a nod, John went on. 'I've read it thoroughly and the only reason I can come up with is that your father wanted his estate to stay in the family, i.e. you.'

'But why the age and marriage restriction?'

'Maybe he wanted you to come of age before inheriting because by then you would know your own mind and not be influenced by anyone else.'

'My aunt, you mean.'

'Yes, I expect so. As to the marriage clause, I'm fairly sure this is about keeping his hard-earned money and property in the family. As I told you previously, at the time the will was drawn up, should you have wed before you turned twenty-one then everything you owned would have transferred to your husband. This way, by naming your aunt, he tried to ensure that that wouldn't happen.'

'So Mary was right.' Seeing his frown, she clarified with, 'My friend who accompanied me to your office.'

'Ah, yes, Mrs Winters.'

'So where does that leave us, Mr Watts?'

'John, please. Exactly where we were before, I'm afraid. There's nothing to be done until you have your next birthday.'

'And then?'

'Then, my dear, you will become a very wealthy woman.'

'How?'

'On that day, the solicitor holding the will should visit you to inform you of your inheritance.'

'And if he doesn't?'

'Then I will visit him. You need only let me know.'

Rose smiled, feeling her cares fall away.

Katy, however, beneath her own smile, was wondering about

what would happen if Rose was to wed after her birthday. Would she keep her money and property then?

'John, you know my aunt thinks this outing is...'

'I do, Rose, if I may call you that?' At her nod, he continued. 'I can't deny that the idea is a pleasant one to me, but I must tell you my heart lies elsewhere. I hope you are not offended by my forthright honesty.'

'Not at all, John, I welcome it for my heart also is given to another.'

'Charles Dean is a lucky man,' he said with a grin.

'How did you know?'

'It's obvious to anyone with eyes to see. My counsel would be to wait should he propose to you though. Let's get your inheritance sorted out first, and then you can decide whether you would wish to wed.'

'John, I'll never be able to thank you enough for all your help.'

'You can by biding your time for twelve more months. Now I suggest we, including Katy back there, should go for afternoon tea.'

'Katy is my friend too and is on my side in all of this,' Rose admitted.

'I guessed as much.'

'How on earth...?'

'Because any closer and she would be walking on your skirt!'

The two burst out laughing as they turned to see Katy grinning like a Cheshire cat.

Settled in a tea shop, John ordered refreshments then turned to Katy. 'I'm aware you and Mrs Winters know all about Rose's inheritance...'

'And Mr Jackson the butler,' Katy added.

'Anyone else?' John asked.

'No,' Rose said with an embarrassed blush.

'Very well, let's keep it between the five of us. Katy, I'm relying on you all to help Rose in any way possible to keep her safe. By that I mean sheltered from her aunt's ploys to get her wed.'

'We'll do our best, Mr Watts,' Katy replied.

'Good. Now when you get home your aunt will want to know how we got on, so you will tell her this was all *my* aunt's idea. Say I agreed to keep her happy but you really don't think we are suited as a couple.'

'You'm a crafty one and no mistake,' Katy said.

'That's what makes me a good lawyer,' he said, wiggling his eyebrows.

The two young women laughed before all three clinked cups in a toast of 'success'.

31

'Really, Rose! Whatever did you do?' Win scolded after being told Rose and John were not compatible.

'Why must you always think it's something I've done?'

'I despair!'

'Aunt Win, this is the first time I've walked out with anyone. What did you expect – that I would come home engaged?'

I'd hoped. 'Of course not! I thought there might be a second outing, however.'

'Well, it's not going to happen. John Watts is a lovely man and I'm sure would be a true friend, but he has eyes for another.'

'Then why...?'

'Because his aunt pushed him into it just like you did with me!' Rose could feel her temper rising.

'I want you to be happy, Rose.'

'Then leave me to find my own husband!' Rose got to her feet and stormed from the sitting room in utter exasperation.

Meeting Katy in the hall, Rose was breathing hard.

'You all right, Miss Rose?'

'Yes, thanks, Katy. I've just had another row with Aunt Win.'

Katy nodded. 'Come and have a cuppa with us lot. You'll love our new scullion,' she said, pushing her tongue into her cheek.

Down in the kitchen, Rose was introduced to Dolly, who stood with the ever-present scowl on her face. 'I hope you'll like being here with us,' Rose said.

'That remains to be seen, don't it?'

'Dolly! Manners!' Jackson snapped. 'I'm sorry, Miss Rose...'

'Don't you apologise for me, I can do that myself,' Dolly cut across him.

'Then do it, and quickly!'

'Sorry, miss.'

'That's all right, Dolly, it must be strange for you coming into a household of new people.'

'Cup of tea, Miss Rose?' Mary asked in an effort to dispel the tension.

'Yes, thank you.' Rose sat at the table as Mary poured.

'Get on with your work, Dolly,' Jackson instructed as he took his seat next to the range.

'Aunt Win is in a foul mood again,' Rose said without thinking.

Mary shot a warning glance at Rose and then to Dolly who was peeling potatoes. Rose nodded and smiled her thanks at the reminder that the new girl would be all ears.

'We've got your favourite for dinner, faggots,' Mary informed her.

'Marvellous! I do so love your cooking, Mrs Winters.'

Jackson peeped over his paper at Dolly who, for once, appeared to be minding her own business.

'When are you and the missus out again?' Mary asked.

'Tomorrow night. We're attending a birthday party for somebody or other.'

'That'll be nice,' Katy put in, her eyes also going to the scullion.

Rose nodded. Clearly Dolly was not trusted by the rest of the staff so Rose would need to be careful what she said in the girl's hearing. Finishing her tea, Rose gave her thanks and left the kitchen to wander out into the garden.

'She didn't seem very happy about the party,' Dolly muttered.

'That's not your business,' Jackson replied.

'I'd love to go to a birthday party.' Dolly ignored the butler's remark.

'Wouldn't we all? Now are those potatoes done?' Mary asked.

'Yeah.' Dolly dried her hands on her apron.

'Thank you.' Mary set the pan on the range then asked, 'Can you bake, Dolly?'

'Yeah.'

'Good, you can make a cake for after our meal.'

Dolly sniffed loudly and went to fetch the butter from the cold slab, dragging her feet as she went.

'I can't see her working out,' Mary whispered.

'Nor can I, Mrs Winters,' Jackson concurred.

True to her word, Dolly could indeed bake, as everyone found as they enjoyed the cake she had made later that evening.

'This is lovely, Dolly,' Jackson said as he held out his plate for another slice.

'I agree, Mr Jackson, well done, Dolly,' Mary praised. 'Where did you learn?'

'My mother taught me before she left home to become a prostitute.' The shock of her statement had everyone freeze; Jackson choking on a crumb lodged at the back of his throat.

'Oh, Dolly, I'm sorry,' Katy said, breaking the hiatus.

'Don't be, I ain't. At least out on the street she was earning rather than giving it away for free.'

'Yes, well...' Jackson mumbled with embarrassment, having recovered from his coughing fit.

Unable to curb her curiosity, Katy asked, 'What about you?'

'I got chucked out of the house 'cos I couldn't pay the rent. My mother tried to get me onto the street as well but I signed on at the Servants' Registry instead.'

'A very wise move, Dolly,' Jackson said.

'I thought so an' all,' the girl replied.

'Do you have any siblings?' Mary asked.

'No, just me and Mother. Dad took off when I was little, God only knows what happened to him. He was a drunk so he could be dead now for all I know.'

'You've had a rough trot,' Mary said quietly.

'It could have been worse. At least here I have food and a bed.' Dolly smiled inwardly as she saw the looks of pity on the faces surrounding her. Now maybe these people might drop their guard a little and she could glean more information about the secret they were harbouring. With luck, the crusty butler wouldn't be so hard on her too. In fact, she could even come to quite like it here if she embellished the lies she was telling to garner more pity.

'Well, there's always plenty to eat in this house thanks to Mrs Winters,' Jackson said, actually feeling sorry for the girl.

'I ain't gone hungry yet,' Dolly replied, forcing a smile at the cook.

'Nor will you if I have anything to do with it.' Mary cut more cake and passed it to Dolly with a curt nod.

Dolly tucked in, pleased with herself at achieving her first goal of bringing the staff onside.

32

Dressing for the party, Rose wore a pale green brocade dress with matching teardrop hat.

'Are you looking forward to the party?' Katy asked as she carefully pinned the hat in place over Rose's piled-up hair.

'Not really, Katy, it will be another *let's find Rose a husband* evening, I'm sure.'

'Maybe Mr Dean will be there.'

'I can only hope.' Rose checked her look in the mirror. 'Thank you, Katy.'

Leaving her room, Rose descended the stairs with Katy behind her. Win was waiting in the hall. 'Very nice, my dear,' she said, looking her niece up and down.

'Cab is here, madam,' Jackson announced.

'Oh, the gift, I mustn't forget that. I bought a silk wrap in pale blue.' Win led the way to the cab and she and Rose got in.

'Where are we going again?' Rose asked as the cab pulled away.

'The Drummonds', their daughter is twenty years old today.'

Rose looked out of the window, wondering what was in store for them this evening.

On arrival they were greeted by Mrs Drummond, who was short and dumpy and dressed in pink silk. By contrast her husband was tall, thin and ramrod straight.

Rose sighed inwardly when presented to their daughter, Olivia. This was the spiteful girl Rose had put in her place at their last meeting. Wishing the girl a happy birthday, Win and Rose followed the line of people into the sitting room. The house, Rose thought, was similar in size to their own, although it was not so tastefully decorated. The upholstered furniture clashed with the green drapes and red carpet. The whole room was an assault to the senses; vases of flowers were everywhere, giving off a cloying scent. The massive chandelier threw out pools of yellow light, its weight threatening to bring down the ceiling. Rose skirted the room, afraid of being crushed should it fall. Gaudy cushions sat on chairs and pictures of ships on stormy waters adorned the walls, testament to Mr Drummond having been in the navy.

Rose grabbed a glass of wine from a passing maid's tray while Win took their present to the gift table. People nodded to her as they milled about but no one spoke. Glancing about, Rose saw only windows, no doors leading to the gardens to enable her to escape. A butler walked stiffly across the room and threw open the windows before retreating back to the hall. Rose immediately strode over to enjoy the cool air now coming into the room.

A moment later she was joined by Win and Mrs Drummond.

'I was just telling Win how I heard about your own party, Rose. Unfortunately we were away at the time and couldn't attend. I have, however, stolen Win's ideas for party games, I hope you don't mind.'

'Not at all, I'm very flattered,' Win replied as she puffed up with pride.

'Do excuse me, more guests arriving.' Mrs Drummond bustled away, leaving Win full of her own importance.

'Games,' Rose muttered, wanting nothing more than to be at home.

'Do join in, Rose, and at least look as if you're enjoying yourself.'

The gong sounded, telling everyone the buffet was open, and Rose tailed Win into the dining room. Standing in line, she felt like she was back at school. She smiled at a maid who collected her empty glass.

'All set for another evening of fun and frolics, are we?'

Rose turned abruptly, almost knocking the plate out of Charles Dean's hand.

'Not really. Nice to see you, Charles.' His deep voice had her heart beating faster as she looked into his eyes.

'You also, Rose.'

Win turned, an angry look on her face. 'I might have known you'd be here!'

'It would have been rude to refuse an invitation.' Lowering his voice, he went on, 'Besides, I think Mrs Drummond sees me as a future son-in-law.'

Rose paled visibly at the thought of Charles and Olivia becoming an item.

'I sincerely doubt that,' Win growled.

'Well, anyway, I couldn't even entertain the idea of wedding a viper like Olivia.'

'Careful, Charles, lest you be overheard and ostracised.' Win gave him a tight-lipped smile and turned back to fill her plate.

Rose grinned as Charles pulled a face behind Win's back,

which changed to surprise when Win said, 'I know what you're doing, Charles, do grow up.'

Unable to restrain herself, Rose giggled before she too turned back to the table of food. Her heart beat loudly, feeling Charles's eyes on her as she moved along in the queue.

'You look beautiful yet again, Rose,' he whispered in her ear and she caught a whiff of expensive cologne.

'I'll be over there, Rose, hurry up and join me,' Win said, pointing to a sofa.

'Don't go, join me and we'll find a way out into the garden,' he whispered again.

'Thank you but I'm not sure I could trust you,' Rose said teasingly.

'Very wise because I'm not sure *I* could trust me.'

With a laugh, Rose moved to sit with her aunt.

'That man is a menace!' Win said sharply.

'I like him, he makes me laugh.'

'Clearly, but I warn you, Rose, don't be taken in by his charm. It will lead to tears.'

The two ate their food in silence, happy to people-watch until the games began.

Eventually the guests were led to the music room which was devoid of furniture except for the piano in the corner and dining chairs around the perimeter.

Olivia, as the birthday girl, was escorted to the centre of the room by her father where he tied a silk scarf around her eyes. The gentlemen were then invited onto the floor, the ladies sitting down to watch. Olivia was spun around three times before being gently pushed forward. Calls and whistles rang out as Olivia stumbled forward with her arms outstretched. She turned abruptly on hearing her name called out, almost losing her footing. One daring young man shot across in front of her just as she stepped out and caught him by the arm. Taking off her blindfold to applause, she tied it onto the man she had tagged. It was then the turn of the women as the men took their seats. The game was played for quite a while before Mr Drummond called a halt.

Everyone sat down and the butler brought in a box which he handed to Mrs Drummond. A pianist settled himself on the stool and began to play. The box was passed along until the music stopped. The person holding it took off a layer of wrapping and the music struck up again. On it went with a maid scuttling to pick up the discarded paper until at last the box landed on Charles's lap. Taking off the last layer, he opened the box and drew out its contents. The pretty pendant necklace glittered in the lamplight as he held it up for all to see. Applause filled the room and the empty box was whisked away by the maid.

Mr Drummond announced there would be a break for further refreshments, after which there would be more games.

'You should give that trinket to Olivia,' Win said as she passed Charles in the hall.

'I should but I won't,' he replied. At the table where punch was being served, Charles sidled up to Rose. 'May I?' he asked, holding up the necklace.

'I don't think...' Rose began.

'It will match your bracelet,' he said, eyeing his gift to her.

'Thank you,' she said as he fastened the clasp at the nape of her neck, 'although really it should have...'

'Olivia has enough. Besides, she's not nearly pretty enough to wear it.'

Rose glanced around but they had not been overheard and she sighed with relief. 'People will talk,' she said softly.

'Let them. I think it's clear to everyone where my interest lies and it's not with Olivia Drummond.'

'I must find Aunt Win, I have her drink.' Rose turned away, a glass in each hand, a flush rising to her face. He had intimated that his interest lay with her and Rose was bursting with happiness, finding it hard to keep a check on her emotions.

'Until later,' Charles said.

'Oh, there you are, I'm dying of thirst,' Win said as Rose sat beside her. Spotting the necklace, she added, 'That's not very appropriate, is it? He should have given it to you to put in your bag.'

'Aunt Win, please...'

'I'm only saying it will be remarked upon.'

'Quite frankly I don't care. I'm tired of all this social etiquette. You *have* to wear this; you can't do that and God forbid you should cast a shadow over your family!'

'Rose!' Win's harsh whisper brought Rose's eyes to hers.

Rose's bluster melted away as she touched the necklace at her throat. 'If you want me to enjoy myself then please leave me alone.' Getting to her feet, Rose headed back to the punch bowl. Another drink was called for.

33

'Oh dear, is Win driving you to drink?' The honeyed tone in her ear had Rose turn.

'You have no idea,' she said with a smile.

'Actually I do, but never mind that now because the games are about to begin again.' Charles held out a hand but Rose shook her head.

'I think I'll stay here a while, but you should go and join in.'

'What, and leave a lady in distress? I wouldn't dream of doing such a thing. Come, let's find a seat and you can tell me all about it.' Once seated, Charles smiled. 'Now what's Win done this time that would put a frown on your beautiful face?'

Touching the necklace again, she said, 'She thinks this is inappropriate.'

'Ah. I won it and so it was mine to give to whom I wished. I did consider keeping it but I didn't think it would suit me.'

Rose laughed, her anger draining away as she looked into his brown eyes. 'I'm afraid my aunt has a knack of winding me as tight as a spring.'

'I recall the feeling very well and in my opinion you did the right thing by walking away.'

'Unfortunately she won't let this rest. As soon as we leave she will raise it again.'

'If you're not up to battling it out then the only other course of action is to ignore her.'

The applause from the other room drew their attention and Rose sighed deeply, seeing Win standing in the doorway watching them. 'Thank you for the advice. I'd best join my aunt.' Rose stood but all she wanted to do was stay here with Charles.

Charles inclined his head then gave Win a broad smile. He could practically see her hackles rise as she turned and strode away.

The evening drew to a close at last and cabs and carriages carried guests to their homes. No sooner was their cab on the move than Win began her barrage once more. 'I don't know what you were thinking, Rose, sitting with that man in full view of everyone there!'

'We were talking,' Rose protested.

'It's unseemly, Rose, don't you see that?'

'No, Aunt, I don't.'

'You are becoming unruly and rude, and I won't stand for it!'

'Except there's nothing much you can do about it, is there, Aunt?'

Win was surprised by Rose's outburst and it took a moment before she blustered, 'I could throw you out on the street!'

'You could – but you won't. How would you see me married off if you did that?' Rose couldn't see her aunt's face in the darkness of the cab, but she could imagine the look of shock that crossed Win's features. Then would come the frown; Win would wonder if Rose had discovered her intentions. After that the shake of the head as Win dismissed the idea.

'All I ask is that you conduct yourself in a manner befitting a young lady.'

Rose smiled at the grovelling note in Win's voice. 'All *I* ask is that you mind your own business and leave me to mine.'

Win harrumphed and nothing more was said.

Jackson had the door open as the cab rolled to a stop. He paid the cabbie while the missus and her ward stepped into the house.

'I'm going to bed,' Win snapped.

Jackson cast a glance at Rose, who just shook her head. 'Will you be taking tea, Miss Rose?'

'Yes, Jackson, thank you. Lead on.' Rose followed the butler into the kitchen where Mary welcomed her warmly. Over a hot drink, Rose related the events of the evening as the others listened eagerly. Dolly sat quietly, taking everything in and storing it away for possible future use.

After Rose retired, the staff began to muse about what they'd been told.

'Fancy threatening to throw Miss Rose out of her own home,' Mary said unthinkingly.

Her own home? The question rose in Dolly's mind. *I thought it was the missus's home.* However, she kept quiet and continued to listen.

'She would never do that, Mrs Winters, she couldn't bear the scandal,' Jackson said as he too picked up on the slip of the tongue.

'Well, I think Miss Rose is coming to the end of her tether. There's gonna be one almighty row there one day,' Mary said, shaking her head.

Katy appeared, saying, 'Miss Rose is settled for the night. She showed me her necklace, it's beautiful.'

'Worth a bob or two an' all I'll bet.'

'I expect so, Mrs Winters,' Jackson answered. 'You girls can get off to bed now.'

Katy and Dolly left the cook and butler to their discussions, but a short while later Dolly was again on the stairs, eavesdropping in the darkness.

'You really should be more careful about what you say in front of the new girl,' Jackson said.

'I know, I'm just so used to saying it like it is,' Mary acknowledged. 'Anyway, Dolly probably wouldn't even have noticed.'

That's where you're wrong, because I did! Dolly thought with a grin.

'I think you're right though, Mr Jackson, the missus would hate the scandal.'

'I'll tell you this, Mrs Winters, I'll be glad to see Miss Rose turn twenty-one years old.'

'Ar, me an' all. Let's just hope the missus doesn't get her own way before then.'

Dolly frowned, wondering what was meant by the cook's statement.

'Indeed. It won't just be Miss Rose who loses out, it could be us as well. Right, I'm going up.'

Dolly dashed away and headed for her room before the butler caught her. She had a lot to think about, and once in bed her mind began to try and fit the pieces of the puzzle together. What she didn't realise was that Jackson had seen her disappear up the back stairs by the light of the moon shining through the hall window.

As he ascended the same staircase, Jackson's mind was also wondering what the scullion could gain from her late-night sneaking about.

* * *

The following morning, Mary announced she was short of eggs and would need to go to the market.

'I'm sure Dolly would enjoy an outing, wouldn't you?' Jackson asked as he raised an eyebrow in Mary's direction.

'Yeah, I'll go.'

So with money, a list and a basket, Dolly was despatched on her errand. Once she'd gone, Mary asked, 'What's going on?'

'That little madam was on the stairs last night listening to our every word.'

'I never heard her get up. Her room is next to mine and you know how good my hearing is,' Katy put in.

'I only knew she was there because I saw her flit up the stairs,' Jackson said. 'We have to be extra careful now with what is said in and out of her hearing. Katy, I think it would be wise to have a quiet word with Miss Rose too when you are in her room helping her to dress.'

'I will, Mr Jackson,' Katy nodded.

'I wish she'd never come here, she's been nothing but trouble,' Mary muttered.

'We can't get rid of her unless she does something to warrant her dismissal,' Jackson advised.

'I know and on one hand I feel sorry for her, but I hate the thought of her sneaking around. I suggest we all lock our bedroom doors.'

'I agree, Mrs Winters, and late-night discussions to be kept to a minimum. In fact, Katy, nip up now and speak with Miss Rose while the going's good.'

Katy left the cook and butler both shaking their heads at the upset caused by one young scullion.

34

'Good grief, Katy, why would she do that?' Rose had listened patiently to what her maid had to tell her and was shocked at the revelation.

'I'm not sure, Miss Rose, maybe she feels left out with her being the new girl. Anyway, Mr Jackson thinks it a good idea for us to lock our bedroom doors.'

'You don't think she would go in your room, surely?'

'I don't know. I don't have much but I'm not risking it being pinched.'

'Oh, Lord, I hope she's not a thief.'

'We know very little about her other than what I've already told you. Miss Rose, can I make a suggestion?'

'Of course, Katy.'

'Lock your jewellery away just in case. You wouldn't want Mr Dean's gifts to go missing. Please understand I'm not saying Dolly would steal them, but until we know her better I think caution is called for.'

'Sound advice, Katy, which I'm glad to take. Please, keep me informed.'

'I will, miss.' Katy took her leave and bounded down the stairs to tell the others what had been said.

'Excellent. Now we must not let Dolly know we are on to her. Just remember to watch what you say.' Jackson looked from cook to maid and with a nod sat to read the morning newspaper.

A short while later, Dolly arrived back to a silent kitchen. She glanced around, saying, 'It's quiet in here, has something happened?'

'No, Dolly. We are just enjoying a little peace until the missus decides to disrupt it,' Jackson answered. Sure enough, Win's voice could be heard yelling from the sitting room. 'See what I mean?' Jackson asked.

Dolly nodded, laying the basket on the table along with the list and change. Mary checked it with an eagle eye and nodded, making the scullion scowl at the distrust shown her.

The bell tinkled and Katy sighed. 'She probably wants tea again. All she seems to do is drink tea, but I'll go and check.'

Mary prepared the tray and Katy returned, saying, 'Yes, tea for two.'

Upstairs in the sitting room, Rose had listened to Win railing on, yet again, about how important good behaviour was. She, in turn, had argued that she was not misbehaving. Once the tray was delivered, Win said, 'We are going to Owen Mason's birthday party tomorrow night.'

'Who?'

'The young man you thought was very rude and preferred the company of women.'

'Oh, him. There seems to be a lot of birthdays lately.'

'Everyone has one, Rose, it's just happenstance that they come together. Now, as I was saying...'

'I know... behave myself. Must I go, Aunt Win? I really can't stand that man.'

'Yes, because I've accepted on behalf of us both. I should imagine there will be a lot of Owen's friends there, all eligible bachelors.'

'I hope they're not all like him then.' Rose sipped her drink, recalling what a horrid boy Owen was.

'Wear something appropriate.'

'Aunt Win, I really don't think I can join in any more silly games.'

'For God's sake, Rose! Why must you be so selfish? Can't you put yourself out for someone else just for once?'

'For once? How many balls, soirées and parties have we attended over the last twelve months? All so you can weed out a worthy husband for me. What's the hurry, Aunt? Is it that you want me off your hands at last?'

'Don't be ridiculous!'

'I could always leave if that is the case. I'm sure I could manage on my savings.' Rose saw the horrified look cross Win's face and thought, *I have you now!*

'Rose, you misunderstand my intentions.' *I don't think I do, Aunt Win.* 'All I want is for you to be happy. I promised your parents I would take care of you and I'm doing my best to fulfil that pledge.'

'Does that include marrying me off to someone like Owen Mason, or a man old enough to be my grandfather?' Rose, feeling her temper rising, took a deep breath lest she say something she would regret.

'My dear girl, I've been on the lookout for someone with money and good social standing, so you would want for nothing.'

'Except love.'

'That could well come later.'

'Or not.' Rose placed her empty cup on the tray. 'I'll tell you again, Aunt, I will only marry for love or not at all.' Turning on her heel, Rose stamped from the room.

About to go out into the garden, Rose stopped as she heard the pitter-patter of rain against the windows. Instead she went to her room, intent on choosing a dress for the party. However, once there, she stood looking out of the rain-streaked pane onto the sun-baked lawns. It was almost like the trees sighed with relief at finally being able to drink. Then the heavens opened and the downpour came, heavy raindrops dislodging tiny gravel stones on the driveway. The already grey sky darkened and a silver streak of lightning flashed, followed by a deep rumble of thunder. Black clouds rolled overhead, split only by brilliant white forks of light. Then a crash so loud it made Rose jump before the sound gurgled away to nothing. She watched the storm as it passed over the land until it was barely discernible. Slowly the rain began to ease, and the sun came out, lighting up a beautiful arc of colour across the garden. Looking at each hue, Rose recalled the saying all school children attached to a rainbow. *Richard Of York Gave Battle In Vain*. Rose watched as the startling colours melted away into a clear blue sky, only then turning to her wardrobe, feeling enlivened by nature's beauty.

* * *

Downstairs, Dolly picked up on the tension in the kitchen as the staff chatted about the weather. It was as though they were guarding their words and as she prepared the vegetables she wondered. Could any of them be aware of her eavesdropping? No, she thought not; she had been very careful not to make a sound which would have alerted them to her presence. Then something else must be going on which she was not a party to, and Dolly determined she *would* find out what it was.

Once dinner had been served to the ladies upstairs, the staff sat to enjoy their own.

'The missus and Miss Rose are off to a party tomorrow night,' Katy informed them.

'Another one?' Mary asked.

'Yes, and Miss Rose is not looking forward to it.'

'Why?' Dolly asked pointedly.

'It's for a young man she met once before and he was rather rude. A bit of a mummy's boy from all accounts,' Katy replied.

'There'll be other folks there though so she could always talk to them, couldn't she?'

'Yes, Dolly, now eat your food before it gets cold,' Jackson intervened.

'What's she wearing?' Mary asked.

'The pale blue silk with the chiffon overlay.'

There they go again, small talk. Dolly chewed her food as she listened. *Come on, one of you, drop me a hint.*

'Well, the missus can't complain about that,' Mary said.

'Neither will...' Katy stopped before saying, 'Can I have some more gravy, please?'

Almost, Dolly thought, *you nearly said summat you shouldn't.* Pretending she hadn't noticed, she complimented the cook on her steak and kidney pie. The guilty looks on the faces around the table completely gave the game away, and Dolly was now convinced she was being shut out of something important.

35

That night, Rose shared her usual cup of cocoa with her friends before retiring with nothing much said other than that she was dreading attending the party. Shortly afterwards, everyone else went to bed, denying Dolly the chance to learn anything more, much to her disgust.

The following afternoon, Katy was helping Rose to get ready when Rose asked, 'How is Dolly settling in?'

'All right, I suppose, although we're all being careful about what we say in front of her. None of us trust her.'

'That must make for a strained atmosphere.'

'Yes, it's very wearing. Mr Jackson says, and we agree, that your business is your own despite you having shared it with us.'

'I'm glad.'

'He says we're not to let Dolly know anything because God only knows what she'd do with the information.'

'I'm sorry I've put you in this awkward position, Katy. I should never have bothered you with my problems.'

'It's no bother, Miss Rose! I'm sorry but it ain't like you have any friends to talk to. Besides, it was the missus who hired Dolly, not you.'

Rose sighed, watching in the mirror as Katy piled up her hair neatly. 'I swear if Owen Mason is rude again tonight I shall call him out on it.'

'Miss Rose, you can't! The missus would go mad.'

'Oh, Katy, I wish it was this time next year and that my twenty-first birthday had come and gone.'

'Have you thought about what you will do then?'

Rose's eyes moved to her maid without turning her head. 'No, I haven't. I've been too busy with trying to keep Aunt Win off my back.'

'Maybe you should, begging your pardon. You'll have lots of money and two houses. There'll be decisions to be made when the time comes.'

'Such as?'

'Well, it ain't my place...'

'Speak plainly, Katy, please.'

Taking a breath, Katy stepped to face her mistress. Holding out her hand, she ticked off each on her fingers as she spoke. 'Will you sell or keep the other house? And this one – would the missus stay here? She's in control of the money at present, would you take over from her?'

'I hadn't even thought about any of that!' Rose said, placing a hand on her chest.

'I thought not, but at least you have another year to make your mind up. I'm sure Mr Watts would be able to advise you nearer the time.'

'Katy, what would I do without you?'

'Just don't sack me when you become the missus.'

Rose burst out laughing. 'I would never do that to you,

Jackson or Mrs Winters, so you can assure them their jobs are safe.'

'And Dolly?' Katy asked as she helped Rose into her dress.

'Let's just see how things go on that front. What I will say is if her presence in the kitchen becomes untenable then she'll have to go.'

'Will you want a hat this evening?'

'No, it would hide the beautiful job you've done with my hair.' Rose stood to check her look in the long mirror and nodded. 'Right, let's go before Aunt Win starts yelling.'

Win was waiting in the hall with Jackson as Rose came down the stairs. Jackson opened the door and that of the cab, helping the ladies aboard.

On the journey, Win said, 'I think it's time for us to have our own carriage.'

'Won't that be expensive?'

'Yes, but think of the prestige.'

'It's not just the carriage though, we'd need a horse to pull it and a groom to take care of the animal. Besides, we don't have space enough to build a stable.' Rose was annoyed that Win was suddenly being frivolous with money – her money!

'Hmm. I'll think on it.'

'What gift did you buy for Owen?'

'Afternoon tea and two tickets to the Grand Theatre. Which reminds me, don't you have theatre tickets from Mrs Billingham to use?'

'Yes, I'd forgotten all about them.'

'Well, decide what you'd like to see and we shall go.'

Rather presumptuous of you, Aunt Win. What if I wanted to go with someone else? An image of Charles Dean jumped into her mind and she quickly pushed it aside. It would be totally out of the question; to be seen at such a prestigious venue with a man who was not her husband, and without a chaperone, would be inviting scandal.

'I thought Katy could accompany me, as a treat and by way of thanks for her hard work.'

'A maid! Rose, I don't think...'

'Yes, I've decided I will take Katy.'

Win fumed at being done out of a trip to a place where she could mingle with the nobs. Rose smiled to herself as she looked out of the window.

They arrived at the Masons' at the same time as Charles Dean, which only added to Win's ire. Indoors, Rose cringed at Owen's limp handshake as he and his parents welcomed their guests, then she and Win moved into the sitting room.

'You're looking as lovely as ever, Rose,' Charles said as he walked over to her. 'Good evening, Win.'

'Charles. Can't we go anywhere without seeing you?'

'It would appear not, but I do believe you secretly enjoy our meetings.'

You're not wrong there, my love, and it would be so much sweeter were Rose not here, Win thought but said instead, 'Charles, you live in a world of fantasy. Now if you will excuse us, there are people for Rose to meet.'

'More prospective husbands?' Charles asked quietly.

Win ignored the question and dragged Rose away towards a gaggle of women who were gossiping excitedly.

Charles watched them go, thinking, *You will never forgive me for not marrying you, will you, Win? I wonder how you will cope when I wed your niece.* His train of thought was broken as one of his friends clapped him on the back.

Rose glanced around, catching sight of Owen Mason in the

corner with his cronies, quaffing alcohol like he was dying of thirst.

'Rose, you know Mr and Mrs Drummond,' Win said, snapping her attention back.

'Yes, of course, good evening,' she answered politely.

'Do we know what's in store for us this evening?' Win asked.

'I'm afraid not,' Mr Drummond said, 'but if the boy continues to drink at that rate it could be rather interesting.' All eyes turned to Owen, who was guffawing loudly.

'Really!' his wife said, snapping open her fan to cool herself.

From another room came the sound of a piano playing and people began to drift in that direction. Suddenly Owen barged his way through the crowd, leaving folk nonplussed by his rudeness.

Rose followed the throng and stood just inside another massive room, watching as the dancing started.

'That boy needs a sound thrashing.' The whisper came from behind her.

Without turning, Rose said, 'I agree, Charles.'

'Dance with me, Rose, I need to feel you in my arms.'

'Aunt Win is watching.' There was nothing Rose wanted more than to be held by this handsome man. She ached to be in his arms and feel his strength surrounding her.

'When is she not? Please, Rose, come and dance.'

'Very well.' The whole conversation had taken place with Charles standing behind her, and Rose facing the dance floor.

Charles led her to the middle of the room and they began to waltz. All was going well until Owen staggered onto the dance area, glass in hand. Cavorting all by himself, he swung his arms around just as Rose and Charles passed him by. The drink shot out of his glass, hitting Rose full in the face. Owen didn't notice as he swirled around, barely staying on his feet. He didn't see the bunched fist coming towards him either as Charles threw the punch, which had the drunken boy measuring his length on the floor.

36

Rose stood with alcohol dripping from her face and hair as women screamed at the melee taking place. Owen's friends lifted him and dragged him away.

A maid brought a towel for Rose as she was led out of the room by Charles. Finding a small empty room, he sat her down and, taking the cloth, he dabbed her stricken face.

'My dress... ruined!' Rose managed.

'I'll buy you another,' Charles said.

'That awful, awful man!' Then Rose burst into tears. Without even realising, she folded into the arms suddenly wrapped around her.

'It's all right, I'm here,' Charles whispered comfortingly.

'And so am I!' Win growled as she stormed into the room. 'Unhand her this minute!' Charles let Rose go.

'Thank you, Charles, for saving me from humiliation out there,' Rose sobbed, feeling bereft that she was no longer being held.

'Rose, come! We're leaving.' Win held the door open and Rose got to her feet. On impulse she kissed Charles on the cheek, turned and hurried from the room. Win was flabbergasted at the display of affection and the pain in her heart stabbed yet again.

Charles's hand touched the place where she had kissed him then he felt the burning pain in his knuckles. It was worth hitting the boy for the reward it brought him.

Out in the hall, Mrs Mason was begging forgiveness for her son's disgraceful behaviour. Seeing Charles, she rounded on him. 'How dare you strike my son!'

'It would never have happened if you didn't mollycoddle him,' Charles replied.

'Now look here…' Mr Mason began.

'No, you look. That boy is spoilt rotten. He's given no discipline and so does exactly as he pleases.' The crowd in the hall muttered their agreement and Charles went on. 'His disgusting behaviour this evening has not only ruined a lady's dress, but has also humiliated her in front of all of your guests.' More mumblings sounded then halted as Charles continued. 'I only did what you should have done years ago. Maybe now your son might learn some manners, although in truth I doubt it!'

Spontaneous applause rang out. Charles saw Rose and Win to their cab, bidding them goodnight before stamping to his own carriage. Climbing aboard, he rubbed his hand absent-mindedly. *Well, that could see me not being invited to any more functions*, he thought. Closing his eyes, he felt again the touch of Rose's lips on his cheek and he smiled.

Inside the cab travelling in the opposite direction, Win was beside herself, her anger incandescent. 'What on earth did you think you were doing kissing him?' Rose sniffed, still feeling her embarrassment keenly. 'Thank God no one else was witness to it.'

'Aunt, please…'

'No, Rose, I will not leave it – not this time. When will you realise that Charles Dean is not for you?'

'Aunt Win, I'm wet and sticky and also angry so please let this drop or things may be said that cannot be taken back.'

'What do you mean?' Win was aghast at Rose's statement.

'Nothing, now please leave me be or I'll get out and walk home!'

Win closed her mouth, knowing that with the mood she was in, Rose would do exactly that.

At home, Jackson was shocked at the state of Rose as he welcomed them back. 'Miss Rose?'

'Send Katy up please, Jackson, and ask Mrs Winters for some hot water so I may wash.' Rose ran up to her room, leaving the butler to his errand.

'A mishap with a drink,' Win explained before going to her room.

Rose took off the dress and threw it on the floor. Sitting at her dressing table, she stared at her image in the mirror.

Katy kicked the door and Rose moved to open it. 'Oh, Miss Rose!' Katy exclaimed as she carried in a bowl of hot water and laid it on a table. 'Come on, let's get you cleaned up and you can tell me all about it.'

Katy helped Rose to wash, including her hair, then dried her off with a large soft towel. Feeling more herself, Rose related the events of the evening, including her daring kiss.

'You never did!'

Rose nodded. 'Aunt Win was furious.'

'I'll just bet she was but oh, how romantic, Mr Dean punching Owen's lights out.'

Unable to contain herself, Rose burst out laughing. 'Katy, you are such a tonic. Undoubtedly you'll tell the others and I don't mind, but not in front of Dolly, please.'

'I won't say anything if you don't want me to.'

'It's all right, lay their curiosity to rest but – discreetly.'

'I will. Tell me again about that punch that laid the drunk out.'

* * *

Later, Katy asked to see Jackson in the butler's pantry where she explained all that Rose had said and experienced.

'Thank you, Katy, I appreciate it. You can inform Mrs Winters the first chance you get out of Dolly's hearing.'

The two joined the others at the table and Katy gave Mary a sly wink, assuring the cook she would be in the know soon. What she didn't realise was that Dolly had caught the little message.

After supper, Dolly went to bed. Jackson stood guard on the stairs while Katy brought Mary up to date. Then maid and cook retired, leaving Jackson in the kitchen alone. It was only a few minutes later when he heard the faint slap of a bare foot on the top of the three steps.

'Come in here please, Dolly,' he called out. 'I know you're there.' Dolly came in sheepishly, a dressing gown covering her nightdress. 'Take a seat, Dolly, you and I have things to discuss.'

Dolly dropped onto a chair, asking, 'How did you know?'

'I heard you.'

'Ears like a shithouse rat, you have. It could have been Katy or Mary coming down again.'

'I knew it was you because I saw you a while ago when you had your ear pinned to that door.' He motioned to the door between the kitchen and hall. Dolly glowered at him. 'So what's all this about, Dolly?'

'What?'

'This sneaking around, listening in to other people's conversations.'

'Maybe I'm just nosy,' she said defiantly.

'Oh, you're definitely that, but why sneak? Why not just ask outright?'

"Cos you wouldn't tell me.'

'I expect you're right. You see, you didn't exactly start off very well when you arrived here, did you?' Dolly ignored him so he went on. 'What did you think – that you would be an upstairs maid?' Jackson shook his head. 'Your job is a scullion which means you work in the kitchen. As the butler, I am responsible for you and everything you do or say.' Dolly shrugged with disinterest. 'Now what were your intentions?'

'I don't know what you mean.' Dolly decided to play ignorant.

With a sigh, Jackson said, 'What were you going to do with the information you may have overheard?'

'Nothing.'

'Then why listen in the first place?'

Now Dolly turned angry. 'You lot have shut me out from the off! If I want to know anything, it's the only way I can find out!'

'Calm yourself, there's no need to get riled,' Jackson said quietly but firmly. 'There are, and will be, things that you have no business being privy to.'

'You are so why shouldn't I be?'

'Because I am the butler and you are the scullion. Social ranking, Dolly, which you must understand is vital for a house to run smoothly.'

'It's cracked if you ask me.'

'I didn't, and it's the way things work so you'd best get used to the idea.' Dolly folded her arms and dropped her chin. 'Don't sulk, it's childish. Now, I will overlook this provided I have your word it will not happen again.' Dolly lifted her head and glared at him. 'Well?' he asked and Dolly nodded. 'All right, you may go back to bed now, but remember, should I catch you again you will be out on your ear.'

Dolly scraped the chair on the floor and strode from the kitchen.

Jackson laid his hands on the table with a huge sigh, knowing full well the girl would be up to her tricks again as soon as she thought it was safe to do so.

37

The next morning, as Katy helped Rose to dress, she said, 'Katy, I have two tickets for the theatre and I would like you to come with me.'

'Me, Miss Rose? What about your aunt?'

Rose shook her head. 'No, just you and me.'

'I'll have to ask Mr Jackson for the time off; if he agrees then I'd love to come. Thank you.'

'Good. We'll go this evening. I'll mention it to Jackson. Now for breakfast.' Rose went downstairs, leaving Katy to quickly make the bed.

'Ah, Jackson, I've asked Katy to accompany me to the theatre this evening. I trust you can spare her for a few hours.'

'Of course, Miss Rose.'

Rose sat at the table with her food taken from the containers on the sideboard and Jackson poured her tea. 'The weather is on the turn, miss, so a warm wrap might be in order.'

'Good idea, Jackson. I take it Katy had a word about the party?'

'She did, miss,' he said with a wry smile.

Win bustled in and Jackson moved to fill her cup as she chose her food.

'Good morning, madam.'

'Hmm, that remains to be seen,' Win retorted. Jackson retreated to his usual place to wait quietly. 'Last night was a complete fiasco,' Win said, scraping butter over the toast vigorously. 'I've never seen the like.'

'It was Owen's own fault...'

'Regardless, Charles should not have struck him, Rose. It was bullish behaviour.'

'He was only trying to look after me. I thought it was very gallant of him.'

'Let us hope there's no more of his gallantry, otherwise people will refuse to invite him to their functions.'

'Oh, that reminds me, I'm out this evening.' Seeing Win's look, Rose clarified with, 'Katy and I are off to the theatre.'

'Be careful and don't be back late. In fact, I think I should come with you.'

'No, Aunt, this is for Katy and me. I'm twenty years old, surely I don't need a nanny any longer.'

'As you wish.' Win picked up the paper and buried her nose in it.

Rose rolled her eyes in Jackson's direction and he inclined his head, the shadow of a smile on his lips.

* * *

It was around mid-morning when Win heard the knock on the front door and a deep gentleman's voice speaking to Jackson. A moment later, there was a tap to the sitting room door and Jackson's head poked around it. 'Excuse me, madam, but a Mr John Watts is here to see you.'

'Show him in and ask Katy to fetch Rose. Oh, and ask Mrs Winters for coffee, please.'

'Very good, madam.' Standing aside, Jackson gestured for the guest to enter.

'Mr Watts, this is a nice surprise. Please have a seat, Rose will join us in a moment. You will take coffee?'

'Thank you, that would be most enjoyable.' John sat on a sofa, laying his hat and cane beside him.

Rose came in with a warm greeting, at which John got to his feet politely before sitting once more. Katy brought in the refreshments and left quietly.

'Aunt Clara has tasked me with delivering invitations to her afternoon tea party on Sunday next,' he said, handing an envelope to Win.

'How very nice,' Win said, opening it and scanning the page within. Rising, she went to her desk and quickly penned an acceptance, which she gave to John. 'We would be glad to attend, wouldn't we, Rose?'

'Yes, Aunt,' Rose said meekly, still trying to get over the surprise of their unannounced visitor.

Win and John chatted comfortably over their refreshments, then John rose to leave. 'Forgive my rushing off but I have more invites to deliver.' Picking up his hat and cane, he thanked Win for her hospitality and smiled when Rose offered to see him out.

John and Rose strolled down the drive and at the gateway he said, 'I have received a communiqué from your father's solicitor. Apparently he holds further papers and a letter addressed to you.'

Rose frowned. A letter from whom? 'When will I receive it?'

'Not until your birthday, I'm afraid. He's under strict instructions not to part with them until that time, when they will then be forwarded to you. I'm sorry, Rose, but again you will just have to be patient.'

'Thank you for letting me know. It's all very curious, though, don't you think?'

'I do, it's a real puzzle.' With a curt nod, he put on his bowler hat and shook her hand.

Rose watched him walk away, the tap of the metal ferrule on his cane echoing eerily as he disappeared into the mist that was settling over the town.

Win had watched from the window as the couple chatted before parting company, and Rose returned to the house with a thoughtful expression on her face. Had he asked her again to walk out with him, and more importantly, was her niece reconsidering it?

It was over lunch when Win raised the subject of the invitation once more, saying she was looking forward to attending. She was hoping Rose would divulge the contents of the discussion with John at the gateway, but she was to be disappointed when Rose kept tight-lipped.

When Jackson removed her empty plate, Rose gave him a meaningful look, saying, 'Would you ask Katy to come to my room when she has a moment, please? She can help me choose a dress for this evening.'

'Certainly, Miss Rose,' the butler replied, raising one eyebrow in answer to her look.

Rose stood as Jackson pulled back her chair and she quietly left the room.

'We are attending afternoon tea at the Billinghams' on Sunday if you would let Mrs Winters know,' Win said as she too stood to leave.

Helping with her chair also, Jackson said, 'Right away, madam.'

Alone in the dining room, Jackson wondered what was on Rose's mind but he knew that all would be revealed. Miss Rose would tell Katy, who would then tell the others, well out of earshot of Dolly, of course. Jackson strode from the room to carry the messages to the kitchen, itching to know whether there were further revelations in the Rose Hamilton saga.

Katy ran up the stairs to her mistress's room in eager anticipation of their evening out together. Tapping the door, she walked in, closing it behind her. 'Jackson said you wanted help with...' she began.

'Sit down, Katy, I have something to tell you.'

The maid's surprise at being offered a seat was written all over her face. 'I don't think it's proper, Miss Rose.'

'All right, but listen to this.' Rose related her conversation with John Watts of earlier in the day.

'What could it all mean?' Katy asked at last.

'I don't know, Katy.'

'Maybe Mr Jackson could shed some light on it.'

'Possibly, but Katy, discretion above all else, please. I can't risk Aunt Win finding out, especially now.'

'Of course, miss. Ooh, this is exciting, it's like one of them mystery books!'

'I find it more frustrating than anything else. I'm wishing my life away so I can reach my birthday and discover what all this is about,' Rose said on a sigh.

'The theatre will take your mind off things for a while at least.' Rose nodded at her maid's ever-cheerful words. 'Right, what do you fancy wearing?' Katy asked, opening the wardrobe door.

38

By the time Rose and Katy climbed into the cab Jackson had hailed, the mist had turned into a real pea-soup fog. The cab's candle lanterns had been lit and the cabbie was wrapped up against the damp. Very slowly they moved off down the gravel drive then halted, the cabbie listening for any other traffic. Happy there was none, he clucked to his horse and they set off again at walking pace.

'I can't believe this weather,' Rose mumbled.

'We're into autumn now, Miss Rose, and before you know, it will be snowing.'

Rose shivered at the thought.

The cabbie steered his horse up Lawley Street, through the tunnels beneath the railway junctions, knowing the streets like the back of his hand. Rather than risk the tramway on Curzon Street, he chose to follow the quieter Belmont Row and into Coleshill Street which ran parallel to the tramway. A few short streets later and they were there. Jumping down, the cabbie helped the ladies alight. 'I'll be 'ere when you come out, miss,' he said, tipping his battered top hat.

'Thank you,' Rose replied, glad not to have to find transport home at the end of the evening. The theatre doors were lit by gas lamps on either side and Rose and Katy went up the few steps before entering the bright foyer. It was bustling with people striding up the wide staircase to find their seats. The red and gold flocked wallpaper looked a little tired but the girls didn't notice. Rose rummaged in her bag for the tickets. A man in a uniform of bright red approached, asking, 'Tickets, please?' Rose held them out for him to see. With a click of his fingers, he summoned a young boy dressed in the same garb. 'Number two,' he said and the boy nodded. 'If you ladies will follow Andrew, he will show you to your seats.'

Rose and Katy did as they were bid, ascending a carpeted flight of stairs, and then went along a curved corridor.

Pulling aside a curtain, the boy said, 'Box number two. Enjoy your evening, ladies.'

'A box!' Katy gasped as they entered the space, which contained two chairs with a small table between. Katy leaned over to look down at people finding their own places in the stalls. 'Look at all these folk!' Katy's eyes roamed around the walls at the other boxes and their occupants.

A moment later, a tray was delivered containing a bottle of wine, two glasses and some pastries. 'Thank you,' Rose said, reaching for her bag.

'All included, miss,' Andrew said with a smile before stepping into the corridor and closing the curtain behind him.

Katy opened the wine and filled the glasses then sat down next to Rose. 'Thank you so much for this, Miss Rose.'

'You are most welcome, my friend,' Rose replied. Clinking glasses, they grinned at each other before taking a sip.

The orchestra filed into the pit and began to tune their instruments. Rose and Katy leaned over to watch with fascination.

Then the lights went down and a man walked on stage to applause.

'He must be the compère,' Rose whispered.

'Ladies and gentlemen, for your delight and delectation...' Oohs and ahhs sounded and he went on, 'we have a lady who has performed all across the country including the theatres of London...' More oohs. 'Tonight she will astound you with her voice as she sings a selection of songs just for you.' The man swung his arm from left to right across the audience. 'Please put your hands together and join me in welcoming back the one, the only – Vesta Tilley!' He threw out his arm and backed away into the wings as the curtains opened, revealing the star everyone had come to see. She smiled at the rapturous applause and, nodding to the conductor, she stepped forward. The music began and she burst into song, which prompted more clapping. After singing a verse, she invited the audience to join her in the chorus.

Rose and Katy sat in awed silence as the theatre was filled with voices. Vesta Tilley finished her set as flowers were thrown onto the stage by her admirers, who had left their seats to run down the aisles. After several curtain calls, the singer finally relinquished the stage to the compère once more.

'This is like the music hall I've heard about,' Rose said over the noise.

'It said on the poster it was an evening of variety tonight,' Katy replied.

Act after act performed: comedians, jugglers, mime artists, comedic pianists, a ventriloquist, a lion comique and a plate spinner. By the close of the show, Rose and Katy were buzzing with excitement as they made their way out to the waiting cab.

Neither had noticed the man in the box on the opposite wall watching Rose through his opera glasses. Charles Dean had seen them arrive, surprised to say the least. He had barely taken his eyes off Rose the whole evening, and he was convinced the fates were conspiring to bring them together.

True to his word, the cabbie was there waiting for them when they heard, 'Rose, I didn't expect to see you here.'

'Oh, Charles, how nice to see you. May I introduce Katy, my maid and my friend. Katy, meet Mr Charles Dean.'

'Pleased to meet you, Katy.'

'Likewise,' Katy said.

Charles had pushed his way through the crowds in order to catch up with Rose before she left.

'I take it you enjoyed the evening,' he said.

'It was wonderful!' Rose gushed.

Her violet eyes twinkled in the pools of yellow light cast by the gas lamps and Charles felt his heart beating like a drum. 'I won't keep you in the cold dampness,' he said. 'Goodnight, Rose, Katy.'

'Goodnight,' the girls chorused.

Charles stepped back as the cabbie helped the ladies aboard and only walked away once the cab disappeared into the fog.

'Miss Rose! That Mr Dean is so handsome!' Katy said once they were on the road.

'Isn't he?' Rose answered with a little giggle. 'It was a lovely surprise to see him here tonight.'

The journey was filled with lively chatter and laughter at what they had seen, which carried on in the kitchen over tea once they reached home. Jackson and Mary howled at the few jokes Katy could remember and eventually Rose left them to retire, saying she would ready herself for bed. Dolly had not even cracked a smile, which had not gone unnoticed.

'What's up with you?' Mary asked pointedly.

'Nothing, I just d'aint think it was funny, that's all.'

'No matter, you can go to bed now, Dolly,' Jackson instructed.

The scullion stamped from the kitchen, feeling like a five-year-old dismissed by her father.

Katy again began to tell them about the women's gowns she'd seen and the gentlemen in their top hats. After a while, she looked at Jackson, who put a finger to his lips as he walked quietly to the stairs. Seeing a movement in the shadows, he returned to his seat, nodding his head.

Dolly was, yet again, hovering in the darkness, listening to every word that was being said.

'I think I'll go up in a minute,' Mary spoke loudly, 'after I've washed these cups.'

Jackson hooked a finger and cook and maid followed him into his pantry. It was here that Katy whispered what John Watts had told Rose.

39

Rose spent the next couple of days indoors as the weather worsened. The rain was incessant, with only short bursts of sunshine here and there. By Sunday the land was drying out and it was bright and cheerful once more. Over the wet period, Rose had read, embroidered and wandered around like a lost child. Her thoughts had centred time after time on John Watts's words and what it could all mean. What were the other documents kept by her father's solicitor, and who had written her a letter? Rose knew she had to put it out of her mind, otherwise she'd go mad with frustration, but with so little to occupy her she was finding it increasingly difficult.

The afternoon would be spent with Clara Billingham, amongst others, including John Watts. It would be almost impossible for her not to discuss the situation with him again. She would just have to avoid him without it seeming as if she was being rude.

Katy joined Rose in her bedroom to assist with the preparations for the outing and it was then that Rose voiced her concerns.

'Maybe Mr Watts won't be there,' Katy said helpfully.

'I didn't think of that, but I suspect he will be,' Rose said as she watched Katy through the dressing-table mirror.

'Then let's hope Mr Dean will be in attendance because I'm sure he'll divert your attention.'

'I'm hoping so,' Rose said with a grin.

'Dolly was earwigging again the other night, Mr Jackson saw her. We went to his pantry so I could explain what you told me, but even Mr Jackson was at a loss, I'm afraid.'

'It appears we'll just have to wait then,' Rose replied, 'but another year is a long time.'

Katy fastened a small hat in place, saying, 'There you go, all ready.'

'Thank you, Katy, wish me luck.'

Going downstairs, Katy went to the kitchen and Rose waited in the hall with Jackson for Win.

Win rushed out of the sitting room as if she was late, despite being a stickler for always arriving early.

Jackson saw them into the waiting cab and closed the door.

'Have you any idea who will be there today?' Rose asked.

'How long is a piece of string?' Win replied sarcastically. Rose gazed out of the window with a sigh. 'I expect tea will be served indoors due to the uncertain weather,' Win went on.

'It is getting rather chilly now.'

'Don't forget to...'

'Mingle. I know.'

The streets were quiet and Rose suspected the parents of large families would be in bed, as was their wont on Sunday afternoons, their broods left to run wild for a few hours.

On arrival, Win and Rose were shown into the sitting room to be greeted by Clara and her nephew, John Watts. Rose smiled sweetly before wandering away to the window to look out on the gardens.

'I'm glad you're here.' The deep voice spoke behind her.

Rose turned, a beaming smile on her face. 'Charles. It's nice to see you again.'

'Another afternoon tea,' he said with a dramatic sigh.

'It helps to break the day,' Rose replied.

'Oh dear, that doesn't sound good.'

'I'm sorry, it's just that a person can only do so much embroidery before they want to scream from the rooftops.' Rose gave a little laugh but even to her own ears it sounded false.

'I see. Maybe you could join a committee or do some charity work. That would at least keep the boredom at bay.'

'Can you honestly see Aunt Win allowing it?'

'In truth – no. My apologies, I was trying to help.' Charles screwed up his mouth like a boy caught with his hand in the sweetie jar.

Rose's genuine laughter set his heart fluttering as he looked into her violet eyes. 'You really are beautiful, Rose Hamilton.'

Rose felt the blush flood to her cheeks and lowered her eyes daintily, the butterflies in her stomach going haywire.

'Don't you like me at all, not even just a teensy bit?' Charles asked.

'Yes! I mean of course I like you, Charles. Why ever would you think I don't?'

'I just wanted to hear you say it,' he teased.

'Oh, that was naughty,' Rose replied.

'Charles,' Win said curtly as she joined them.

'Good afternoon, Win. How are you?'

'Fine, thank you. I must insist that you do not monopolise Rose's time today.'

'That's a little unfair as I've only been here but a moment,' he said with a fake hurt look.

Win wanted to reach out and hold him to her, her love for him was still so strong.

'Charles suggested I might join a committee or...'

Rose's words were cut off sharply by Win. 'Certainly not!'

'But Aunt...'

'It's out of the question, Rose. I've seen what goes on at the so-called committee meetings, and before you know it they've poked their noses where they don't belong.'

'How so?' Charles asked.

'Supposedly to raise money for charities and the next thing is they've taken over the running of them.'

'It would find Rose something to do rather than her staying at home, bored out of her mind.'

'What happens in my house has nothing whatsoever to do with you.' *Your house?* Rose thought as she watched her aunt's anger begin to build. 'Therefore I'll thank you to keep your ideas and suggestions to yourself. Come, Rose, we should mingle.'

Rose was dragged away before she could say a word in Charles's defence. 'Why do you do that, Aunt?'

'What?'

'Interfere! Charles and I were talking and you came along and spoilt it.'

'Rose, don't be so silly. You are here to socialise with everyone, not just Charles Dean.'

'We had barely spoken before you came over like a galleon in full sail!'

'Stop this, right now!' Win's voice was low but held an underlying menace. 'I will not have you embarrass me again!'

'Again?'

'Yes. First the blue dress, then *him* filling your dance card, to say nothing of his striking Owen Mason!'

'How was that my fault? Anyway, it's clear no one is holding it against him, otherwise he wouldn't have been invited here today,' Rose returned in the same manner.

Win clamped her teeth together, screwing her eyes tight for a second. 'Can you not simply behave just for once?'

'I have done nothing to deserve your wrath, Aunt Win, and I feel you are being completely unfair.' Rose strode away to where tea was being served.

Win cast a glance in Charles's direction and bristled as he raised his cup as if in a toast.

Bloody man! How I wish I didn't love you so damned much!

40

Whilst Win was trying her best to keep Rose and Charles apart at the tea party, back at the house an almighty row was taking place.

Jackson had called Dolly out regarding her eavesdropping despite having said she would not do it again.

'You just don't like me, any of you!' Dolly shouted.

'Is it any wonder when you do these things?' Jackson asked.

'I wouldn't need to if you d'aint shut me out of everything!'

'Why do you feel you should be included in things that don't concern you?' Jackson kept his voice even in the face of Dolly's anger.

'Because, Mr High and Mighty Jackson, everybody else is in on stuff that I ain't privy to.'

'There's no need to be rude,' Mary put in.

'I wasn't talking to you!' Dolly shot back.

'That's quite enough!' Jackson's voice filled the kitchen, making everyone jump. 'This is your last chance, Dolly. Either you cease this dreadful behaviour, or I will need to bring it to the attention of the ladies upstairs.'

'Do what you like, I couldn't give a tinker's cuss.'

Katy and Mary exchanged an outraged glance at the scullion's statement.

'So be it. I'll be having a word with the missus on her return. I would suggest you prepare yourself, Miss Pritchard, for you may well find yourself dismissed.'

'You think I care? I'll go back to living on the streets and see how you like that.'

'It will not concern me one iota, Dolly,' Jackson said.

'You have brought this on yourself, Dolly,' Katy added.

'I ain't though, 'ave I? It's him,' Dolly pointed to the butler, 'who's causing all this bother. Never mind, if the missus chucks me out I hope you all sleep well while I'm freezing my arse off in a doorway somewhere.' Dolly saw her words hit the mark as Katy and Mary looked dejected.

'Don't come the *woe is me* attitude, Dolly, because it won't work,' Jackson said.

It already is working, look at your staff. 'I can look after meself, mate, don't you worry about that. Begging ain't so bad once you get the hang of it, and sleeping amongst the tramps teaches you a thing or two, like putting newspaper in your clothes to keep you warm at night.'

'Dolly, all we are asking is that you try to fit in with us,' Katy said, feeling wretched at the thought of the girl being pushed out onto the street.

'I would if *he'd* let me,' Dolly replied, shoving the onus onto the butler.

'I've had enough of this. I suggest everyone gets back to work. Katy, set the kettle to boil, Mrs Winters, our evening meal if you would be so kind, and Dolly, fetch the coal in and light the fires.' Jackson nodded as they all went about their tasks, even Dolly, and he breathed a sigh of relief.

***

In the meantime, over at the Billinghams', Rose and Win were saying their goodbyes before boarding the cab. Rose hadn't managed to have a word with John Watts, and in a way she was glad of it. In her heart, she knew he could tell her no more than she already knew.

'Well, that was quite pleasant – in the end,' Win said pointedly.

Rose ignored her aunt, choosing to stare out of the window. She watched a group of children running to surround the rag-and-bone man, and smiled at their innocent clamouring for his attention. She saw the beggars holding out tin cups, hoping some kind person would drop in a coin. Gents in their overcoats and top hats paraded with fine ladies on their arms. The ladies also wore their coats with their muffs hanging from their necks, ready for cold hands to be pushed inside them. The coal jagger with his cart passed in the opposite direction, reminding Rose that soon fires would be burning night and day in every hearth.

Jackson was waiting as they arrived home and Rose could tell instantly that he was not happy. Something had happened whilst she'd been out and she was eager to know what it was.

'I'll go and ask Mrs Winters what we're having for dinner,' Rose said, leaving Jackson to pay the cabbie.

'I'll be in the living room,' Win advised.

'Oh, you're back,' Mary said, instantly laying a tray.

'Yes, and I can see Jackson is out of sorts.'

'He and Dolly have had a fall-out,' Katy informed her.

'Oh dear. Where is she?' Rose asked, looking around.

'Dining room, lighting the fire,' Mary responded. 'There's brisket for dinner, by the way.'

'Miss Rose,' Jackson said as he entered the kitchen.

'I've heard. Would you like me to have a word?'

'If you think it would help, miss.'

'It wouldn't hurt, Mr Jackson,' Katy added.

'Very well.' Rose sat at the table, waiting for Dolly's return.

After a few minutes, Dolly came in, struggling with a bucket of coal. 'Fire's lit, scuttles are filled,' she said sharply.

'Miss Rose would like a chat with you, Dolly, so put that away and then sit down,' Jackson instructed.

Dolly did as she was bid then waited.

'I believe there is discord in the kitchen, Dolly, and it appears to stem from you...' Rose began.

'Oh, I knew it would be my fault!'

'Look at it this way. For years this house has been peaceful and now, after you joined us, that peace has been shattered.' Rose looked at the scullion and all she saw was defiance. 'Have you nothing to say?'

'No, because I've said it all before.'

'In that case...'

'It's *him*! He won't tell me anything! I know there's summat going on in this house, I just ain't allowed in on whatever it is!'

Rose glanced at Jackson, who raised his eyebrows as if to say, *you see what I have to put up with?*

'What business do you think you should be advised of?' Rose asked.

'They know yours and that of the missus...'

It took every ounce of Rose's composure not to look at the others. 'The butler knows only what we upstairs tell him, which filters down to the rest of you.'

'Well, summat ain't right 'cos they know more than I do!'

'What you have to understand, Dolly, is that as the last in the line of staff you will, by dint, be the last to know anything.'

Dolly harrumphed and Rose went on. 'Now, if there is any of

my business you wish to know, I suggest you ask me.' Rose waited and when Dolly said nothing she continued. 'Nothing? Good. May I suggest, in that case, that you stop wandering around the house in the middle of the night and do your job. I will consult with Mr Jackson on a regular basis to make sure all this nonsense has ceased. Should it prove that it has not, then I will be forced to let you go. Be warned, no amount of crying or making the others feel guilty at your plight will save you.'

Rose got to her feet. 'Tea in the sitting room, please, Mrs Winters.'

'Right away, Miss Rose.'

Rose left the kitchen, feeling she'd handled the situation rather well.

41

Over the next weeks, the leaves turned golden then brown, fluttering lazily to the ground. Slowly the temperature began to drop at night and with each new day the sun became weaker.

The endless rounds of parties would finally drop off as winter approached, much to Rose's relief. This was the time of the year that people usually visited Llandudno or Bournemouth for respite from their daily lives, and before the very cold weather set in. Win, however, grew more restless than ever, knowing that time was running out for her to find her niece a husband. She stood to lose everything should she fail and the thought terrified her. The only way she could think of to see Rose wed was to invite all the eligible bachelors to tea one by one and hope a husband could be found amongst them. And so invitations were sent out and Rose was informed in no uncertain terms that she would attend, she would behave like a lady, and make their visitors feel welcome.

Downstairs, life for the staff settled down, albeit with Dolly only speaking when she was spoken to. She had not been deterred from her night-time endeavours, however, and continued to roam the corridors in the darkness. Jackson, of course, was well aware of this but as the scullion caused no more upset he let it lie. Katy and Mary also knew and made sure nothing of import was said in her hearing. In short, very little had changed. The hope was when Dolly learned nothing new she would give up. Either that or the cold would see her stay in her bed.

Dolly, however, harboured an intense dislike of Jackson after he had told tales about her to Rose. This had prompted her to keep herself to herself, with the hope that if she melted into the background someone would slip up and say something they shouldn't. Only time would tell, so she kept her ear to the ground as she completed the tasks given to her.

There was no further communication between Rose and John Watts as she knew he would have nothing more to tell her until she came of age. The fewer functions being held meant, of course, that Rose saw less of Charles Dean, which only caused her to miss him more as time went on. At times she found herself staring into space, wondering where he was and what he was doing. Her stomach flipped each time she thought of him and, although relieved at not having to attend so many balls and soirées in the beginning, she now started to wish they were still taking place.

Rose wandered around the house, feeling lost and alone, having nothing to do but pester the staff.

One particularly boring morning, Rose decided on a shopping excursion, going to tell Win and expecting yet another battle before it would be allowed. She was surprised when Win agreed to her request without quibble.

'New winter gowns is a very good idea because I'm sure as Christmas approaches we'll be invited to yule parties.'

'I'll ask Jackson to hail a cab then,' Rose replied.

'I must change first...' Win began.

'Oh, I was thinking of taking Katy with me.'

'I see. Who, may I ask, will be paying for these new gowns?'

'Are you saying you won't pay if you don't come and, most likely, choose for me?' Rose was aghast at the hint of blackmail in Win's question, and was taken aback that her aunt could be so spiteful.

'We always go together, Rose, and now you don't want me but you do want my money!'

Whose money? The thought jumped into her mind but Rose pushed it away. 'Aunt Win, I'm perfectly capable of shopping for my own clothes. If that means you refuse to buy them for me – so be it! I have money; I'll pay for them myself!' Rose's temper flared. 'Of course that will mean you have no say over the designs I opt for.'

'Rose...'

'I'll be back for dinner,' Rose said as she turned to leave the sitting room.

'*Rose!*'

Halting, Rose faced her aunt with a look of triumph on her face at having stood up to the bossy woman.

'Have the invoices sent to me. Just be sensible when deciding what to purchase.'

With a curt nod, Rose hurried out to find Katy. In the kitchen, Rose explained what she had planned and Jackson, after giving Katy leave to go, went to whistle for a cab. Katy was excited about a trip into town, grabbing her hat and coat while Rose went to don her own, as well as get some money. She intended to treat Katy to lunch somewhere nice.

Once in the cab and on their way, Katy said, 'Mr Jackson said that the paper did a report saying that Birmingham might be awarded city status by Queen Victoria in January next year. The article said it was the first English town without a cathedral that would be given this status and it was chosen because of its size and reputation.'

'I saw the article as well. Birmingham will soon be on the world map, Katy, what a thing!'

'I was shocked that the missus is allowing you to shop without her,' Katy said sheepishly.

'She was all set to come but I wouldn't hear of it.'

'Good for you, Miss Rose.' Katy grinned as they continued to chat about gown designs, materials and colours.

Eventually arriving at the emporium where Rose had purchased her red dress, the cabbie was asked to wait. Knowing he was in for a long stint, he wrapped himself in a blanket and rolled a cigarette.

Rose and Katy were greeted like royalty and the shopping spree began. Rose tried on outfits, one after another, making her choices as she went. Some were boxed for her to take away, others to be made and delivered. Katy gave her opinions freely, much to Rose's delight, and finally Rose called a halt. The modiste, extremely happy with the sales, assured Rose the invoices would be sent to Win Jacobs.

The girls carried the boxes to the cab and Rose asked for the cabbie's advice as to a nice place for lunch.

'I know a bostin' restaurant, miss,' he said, knuckling his forehead as they boarded his cab. Then he took his seat and urged the horse forward.

'It's so busy!' Katy said as she looked out onto the throngs of people bustling about. 'There's hardly room to move.'

The pavements were crowded as folk pushed and shoved their way past each other. The roads were also packed with traffic, cabs, carts, trams and men riding horses, all making the going slow.

Reaching their destination, the cabbie helped his passengers onto the street. 'I'll sit inside with your packages, miss, to mek sure they don't get pinched,' he said, 'there's far too many light-fingered bugg... people about.'

Rose gave her thanks and she and Katy stepped into the restaurant. Taken to a table for two, a waiter brought menus. Katy ordered roast beef and Rose chose salmon. Wine was served and the girls clinked glasses.

'Thank you for this, Miss Rose,' Katy said quietly.

'Thank you for coming with me, Katy.'

The two talked in low voices over their meal, Rose explaining about the list of suitors invited by her aunt. Katy told of Dolly's continuing late-night escapades but that Jackson was keeping a keen eye on the girl.

It was when Rose confided that she missed seeing Charles that Katy came up with an idea. 'Why not suggest to the missus that she throw a party? It's her birthday soon if I remember correctly, and you can say it would be another opportunity for you to possibly meet a man to marry. And, of course, Mr Dean should be requested to attend also.'

'Katy, that's a splendid idea! Thank you, I'll mention it as soon as we get home. On that note, I think we should go in search of a birthday gift for Aunt Win.'

Paying the bill, Rose led Katy to the cab once more, asking the cabbie to take them to the nearest shoe shop. Win would be receiving a pair of the latest fashion in footwear from her niece when her birthday arrived.

42

The carriage ride home was filled with excited chatter, the girls looking again at the shoes Rose had bought for them both. Katy was ecstatic with her gift and stroked the fine brown leather lovingly.

'The missus will want to see your frocks and no doubt she'll have a reason why they're not suitable,' Katy said with a cheeky grin.

'I agree, but it's too late now.'

On their arrival, Jackson, as usual, paid the cabbie but it was Rose who gave him a handsome tip. Jackson raised an eyebrow but Rose said, 'The man was most helpful, waiting patiently for us while we shopped and had lunch.' He nodded as the boxes were piled into his arms, Katy carrying the rest, all of which were taken to Rose's room.

Katy couldn't wait to show off her new shoes, light brown leather with a large silver buckle on the front, a dainty heel beneath.

'Oh, lovey, they'm beautiful!' Mary exclaimed as she saw Katy's gift. 'You'm a lucky girl.'

'I know. We had lunch as well...' Katy rattled on about the outing with everyone listening avidly.

Dolly swept the floor, a scowl on her face, jealousy eating away at her as she looked at her own scuffed old boots.

In the meantime, Rose joined her aunt in the sitting room. 'How was your trip?' Win asked.

'Lovely, thank you. I'd like to show you what I've bought later.'

'Very well.' Win's short answer told Rose she was still unhappy at not having been asked to join her niece for the shopping trip.

Katy entered with the tea tray then disappeared again.

'Aunt Win, it's your birthday soon and I thought we could celebrate it with a party.'

Win was surprised that Rose had even remembered, let alone wanted to mark it as a special occasion. 'I don't think so, it would be expensive.'

'That's a shame because it would be an ideal opportunity to invite all the single men, as I'm sure you're still searching for my future husband.'

Win's eyes narrowed as she wondered what Rose was up to. The girl had dismissed every man put before her as a potential mate, and now suddenly she appeared all in favour of the idea. 'I suppose it would make sense...'

'You could ask all your card game friends, the Glendenings, the Drummonds...'

'It would be nice to share a birthday with everyone, I must admit. I'll have to speak with Mrs Winters about a menu.'

'I'll send her up before I unpack my purchases,' Rose said, going to the door. Over her shoulder, she called out, 'Don't forget to put Charles Dean on your list.'

So that's your game, is it? Win thought. *I've a good mind not to invite him!* By the same token, she knew Rose would refuse to attend if Charles didn't come, then the whole costly affair would be for nothing.

A quiet tap to the door before it was opened showed Mary asking, 'You wanted to see me, madam?'

'Yes, I've had an idea to hold a party for my birthday and need your input regarding the food to serve. Take a seat, Mrs Winters, I think this could take some time.' Win grabbed paper and pen, passing it to Mary to make notes as their discussion began.

Mary tentatively sat down. *This is the first time ever that my arse has touched one of her chairs!*

'We don't have enough room for all to sit so…' Win said.

'Buffet then, for how many?'

Win calculated. 'Around fifty or so, I would imagine, if all attend.'

'Hot, cold or both?'

'Both, I think, that way people have a choice.'

'Cold – I can do sandwiches of salmon and cucumber, pâté and crackers, the usual salad, pork pies, chicken, vol-au-vents, a selection of cheeses, cold meats, dips…'

'Very good.'

'Hot – beef stew, brown Windsor soup, pheasant with asparagus, venison in a rich sauce, fish, shoulder of lamb.' Mary reeled each off as she wrote.

Win nodded. 'Puddings?'

'Trifle, fruit tarts, egg custard, cakes and biscuits. Coffee and homemade sweeties to finish.'

'Excellent. Thank you, Mrs Winters, I'm sure I can leave all that in your capable hands.' Mary laid the pen on the table and rose. 'Oh, and can Jackson ensure we have plenty of wine,' Win added.

'I'll see to it, madam,' Mary assured her as she returned to the kitchen.

Win blew out her cheeks as she considered the expense, then thought it would all be worth it to get Rose married off. Then Win would never have to worry about money again; she would be one of the richest women in Birmingham.

* * *

Sitting at the large scrubbed table, Mary sighed at the amount of work awaiting her.

'Mrs Winters?' Jackson asked.

'The missus has had a notion to have a party for her birthday.'

'Bloody cheek! That was my idea, which I put to Miss Rose!' Katy blurted out.

'Regardless, we have a mountain of work ahead of us, and she asked to check we have enough wine, Mr Jackson.'

Jackson nodded as he scanned Mary's notes. 'How many attending, because there'll be enough to feed the five thousand judging by this!'

'She says fifty but that could change. I'll have to get to the butcher to order all this extra meat and the grocer an' all. Katy, you'll need to help me take an inventory of what's left in the pantry, please.'

'I could do that,' Dolly put in, taking everyone by surprise.

'All right, Dolly, I'm sure Katy has other things to do,' Mary said.

Mary and Dolly disappeared into the huge larder, leaving Katy to update Jackson on why she had given Rose the idea of the party.

'I wish this was Miss Rose's coming of age we were celebrating,' Katy said quietly.

'As do I, Katy. All this cloak and dagger stuff is very wearing on the nerves. Careful, they're coming back.'

Mary returned, shaking her head. 'I'll have to order a lot to cover this, Mr Jackson.'

'As you will, Mrs Winters, give the invoices to me as usual and I will ensure they are paid.'

'I'll do it tomorrow morning after breakfast because I'm up to my eyes making dinner just now. Thank you, Dolly, for your help.' The scullion nodded and went to the sink to prepare the vegetables.

While the staff were considering the complexities of the forthcoming event, Win had gone to Rose's room to view what she would be paying for. The dresses were laid out on the bed and Win was very surprised that she liked them.

'Very nice, Rose, you have chosen wisely. Shall I hang them up for you?'

'No! I'd like to try them on again first, then I'll get Katy to do it,' Rose said rather too quickly. Her red ball gown was still in the wardrobe and she didn't dare let Win see it.

'As you wish. Maybe I should buy myself a new dress for the party.'

'I agree. Something in the newest fashion, that will surely have all eyes on you.'

Not Charles's, though, if you're there, Win thought sadly.

'Your friends will be so envious when you greet them looking as though you've shopped in Paris!'

Win gave a tight-lipped smile and retreated back to the sitting room to make a list of invitees.

* * *

Over the next couple of days, Win sent out her invitations and the kitchen was a hive of activity. Orders were being delivered and food stacked in the pantry and on the cold slab. Jackson was checking the wine supply and Dolly was tasked with washing boxes full of wine glasses brought up from the cellar.

Win did indeed shop for a new gown, choosing emerald-green silk. She also arranged for a quartet to play for her guests.

The replies began to arrive and Win was not surprised to see Charles was the first to respond. She ran her finger over his writing, wishing he was attending for her, but knowing in her heart it was for Rose.

Why can't you understand I can't give my heart to anyone else because I still love you? Win wiped a tear from her eye as she placed his card on the growing attendance pile.

43

The day before the party, the staff rearranged the dining room, having carried large trestle tables up from the lumber room situated between the kitchen and the scullery.

'As if we ain't got enough to do,' Mary grumbled as she threw pristine white cloths over them, which reached to the floor, and under Jackson's keen eye Dolly laid out the wine glasses on another table. The dining table held trays of cutlery wrapped in napkins and piles of sparklingly clean plates. Bottles of white wine were stacked on the cold slab, their red counterparts stood next to the glasses. Serving tongs and spoons were placed in position, ready for the plates and dishes of food to be set next to them. The tantalising aromas of cooking filled the kitchen, drifting up to the rooms above.

Then the staff moved to the sitting room where space was made for the musicians. Chairs and sofas were dragged to the edges of the room, leaving a small area for dancing. Win watched, thinking it would be cramped but then not everyone would choose to dance; the men would most likely prefer to discuss business in the dining room.

'Excuse me, madam,' Jackson said, 'I took the liberty of ordering brandy and cigars for the gentlemen. I thought maybe we could open the parlour as a smoking room,' he added.

'Well done, Jackson, I wouldn't have thought of that,' Win praised, much to his surprise. 'Excellent idea. Some of these chairs could go in there too so we'll have more room.'

'Very good, madam.' Jackson went off to enlist the help of Katy and Dolly to shift even more furniture, beginning to wish he'd kept his mouth shut.

In the kitchen, it was all hands to the pump, helping Mary with the food, and by bedtime all were exhausted and ready for sleep.

In the morning, everyone was sluggish after their exertions the previous day but after strong tea, they rallied. Breakfast was served on trays before work in the kitchen began again in earnest. Mary toiled all day with the help of Katy and Dolly, even giving Jackson the odd job to do, and by the time the guests were due to arrive, everything was ready.

Win, in shimmering green silk, and Rose, in violet silk, waited in the sitting room; Jackson on alert by the front door and Katy on hand to take coats and wraps.

'My feet are killing me!' Katy whispered.

'We shall be glad to retire this evening,' Jackson replied in the same vein.

'Then tomorrow we will have to put everything back to normal,' Katy sighed.

The sound of wheels on the drive had Jackson open the door and in trooped the musicians with their instruments. Katy took them to their allotted area and left them to set up.

Cabs and personal carriages arrived one after the other, and folk in all their finery were shown into the sitting room.

Win was in her element, being the centre of attention, and

much was made of her new shoes given to her by Rose that morning. She had been surprised and delighted by the gift from her niece, and Rose had received the smallest of hugs in return.

Charles immediately strode across to Win on his arrival and, kissing the back of her hand, he presented her with a small box. Inside was a gold bracelet which he fastened on her arm.

'Charles, it's beautiful, thank you!'

'You look splendid tonight, Win.'

Win's pulse raced and she smiled broadly at the compliment.

The musicians were playing quietly in the background and Charles said, 'You really must dance with me later.' He smiled as Win inclined her head, agreeing to his request.

Taking a drink from the tray offered by Jackson, on waiter duty now that all of the guests had arrived, Charles moved away to converse with people he knew. As he mingled, he caught sight of Rose and he thought his heart had stopped. He watched her from across the room as she laughed at something a lady said to her. His eyes followed her as she walked as if floating on air. Unable to contain himself any longer, he strode to intercept her before she spoke with anyone else.

'Charles, I'm so glad you could come.'

'Rose, you look divine. Your dress matches your eyes perfectly.' She thanked him with a blush rising to her cheeks. 'I've missed seeing you over these last weeks, so I was delighted to be invited this evening.'

'Yes, it's gone rather quiet on the social side of life, but I'm sure it will pick up again nearer Christmas.' Rose's excitement at seeing him made her feel like she was babbling.

'All to the good; that way I will be in your company more often.'

'I should be circulating or, as Aunt Win would say, *don't forget to mingle, Rose.*'

Charles laughed and she saw the twinkle in his eye as he replied. 'Please don't leave me with these people, Rose, I swear I will die of boredom!'

It was Rose's turn to laugh, her eyes sparkling like diamonds in the light from the gas lamps.

Jackson banged a small gong and Rose said, 'The buffet, it seems, is now open.'

Slowly people meandered into the dining room where Katy was on hand to help serve. Win requested the musicians to partake of the food and wine, for which they were most grateful, as it was not a usual occurrence for them.

Mary's delicious fare was devoured, the guests returning to fill their plates time after time. Conversations and laughter grew louder as copious amounts of wine were drunk, and the parlour was put to good use by the gentlemen wishing to enjoy a cigar.

Having eaten their fill, the musicians struck up a chord, letting everyone know the dancing could now begin.

Win turned at the tap on her shoulder and nodded as Charles held out his hand. The love of her life was taking her for the first dance and on her birthday too. She felt his arm around her and wanted to melt into him. Everyone applauded as he waltzed her around the small space and Win's cares and worries disappeared. She was where she should be, in the arms of the man of her dreams. The tune ended and Charles walked her to a seat before bringing her a glass of wine.

As he turned, Charles saw Rose dancing with a young man and the green-eyed monster within him reared its ugly head. He wanted to snatch her away and hold her himself, keeping her from all harm. He was waiting when the next tune struck up, holding out his hand. Rose accepted and Charles was smiling once more.

'Thank you for dancing with Aunt Win for the first tune. I haven't seen her this happy for a very long time.'

'Now I can devote all my time to you,' he said mischievously.

Another couple bumped into them and both men stopped to apologise with a bow. The dance area was becoming crowded. 'Maybe we should move aside for others,' Rose said.

'Certainly not, I've waited weeks for this and I'm going to enjoy it to its fullest,' Charles said as he pulled her gently closer to him.

Win's heart sank as she watched them moving together as one, but at least she had the memory of his arms around her to keep her company in the lonely years ahead of her.

The evening wore on with more food and drink consumed, and taking a rest in the corner of the room, Charles asked, 'Rose, what are you doing to me?'

I could ask the same of you, she thought.

'I can think of nothing but you.'

'Charles...'

'You fill my waking hours and haunt my sleep.'

'Please, I...' Rose felt the heat rise from her bosom, her breath coming in little gasps.

'Tell me you feel the same, Rose, please. I have to know!'

Rose looked at the man she now knew she was in love with, the one she wanted to spend the rest of her life with despite the age difference. It was now or never and so, with a deep breath, Rose plunged in. 'Charles, there's nothing I'd like more than to be with you, but I can't until I come of age. There are things happening which I have no control over as yet, and until I do I cannot promise you anything.'

'On your birthday, I will ask you to be my wife.' Rose gasped, never expecting to hear those words. 'Be honest, Rose, is there a chance for me, or will my heart be broken forever?'

With a smile, Rose nodded, saying, 'Keep that proposal in your heart as a shield and look forward to that day, as will I.'

Charles closed his eyes, his sigh of relief long and steady.

Rose wanted to tell him about her plan to walk out with the fellows arranged by Win, all in an effort to keep her aunt under the illusion of her toeing the line. Not knowing how he would take it, she decided against the idea. He was sure to think her a hussy; just stringing him along. Nothing could be further from the truth but she couldn't risk losing him now.

'Then that is enough for me. If you should ever need my help with anything, send a runner and I will fly to your side.' Charles walked away as he noticed Win glaring in their direction.

Going to Win, he said, 'Now, birthday girl, would you dance with me once more?' He smiled when Win jumped to her feet eagerly.

'Whatever is going on in your family, Win, you need to get it sorted out because it's making Rose very unhappy,' he said.

The smile slipped from Win's face when she said, 'I don't know what you mean.'

'I think you do, Win. Maybe it's time you told her. Rose deserves to know but only you can enlighten her.' Seeing her look of sadness, he went on, 'Do it, Win, before it's too late.'

44

Charles's words had taken the shine off Win's good mood and even as the door closed on the last of her guests leaving, she rounded on Rose. 'What were you talking to Charles Dean about?'

'Nothing much, why?'

'He seems to think you are unhappy!'

Jackson stood back out of the way as Win paced the hall. Mary and Katy heard the row brewing from where they were clearing the plates in the dining room. Sharing a glance, they listened as they worked quietly.

'Well, I can't say I'm unhappy as such, but...' Rose began.

'But what?'

'I'm not full of the joys of spring either.'

'I keep telling you, a husband will keep you busy. You won't have time to dwell on your feelings once you're wed!'

'Not this again. How many times do we have to argue...?'

'Well, that's going to change as of right now, because be advised, young lady, I shall be arranging a wedding for you to the first man who will offer his hand!' Win held up her own hand

and went on, 'Don't say another word, I've made up my mind. Oh, and just so you know, your betrothal will not be to Charles Dean!' Win strode away, muttering under her breath.

Rose watched her aunt climb the stairs and enter her bedroom, slamming the door behind her.

'Miss Rose,' Katy called softly, 'are you all right?'

Rose nodded but she felt shocked at Win's outburst. 'I have no idea what all that was about.'

Mary clamped her teeth together lest what she knew should leak out. She so desperately wanted to tell Rose but felt it was not her place. Also, if the missus found out then Mary would find herself sacked for sure. On her recent trips out to do the ordering, Mary had called on friends working at other big houses. It was on these occasions she had learned more and more about Winifred Jacobs and the Hamilton family. She knew it was just gossip, for no one had any proof to back up their stories. However, it made for interesting listening and Mary had discussed it with Jackson whilst Dolly was not around. He, in his wisdom, had advised her to keep these speculations to herself. Now, after hearing Win's intentions, the cook was torn regarding the information she had gleaned from the gossipmongers of the town.

Jackson appeared with Dolly in tow just at that moment and shook his head at Mary as if reading her mind. He also had heard every word between aunt and niece as he'd stood by in the hall, and had guessed Mary's quandary. 'Come along, ladies, we have much to do. The furniture can wait until tomorrow, but dishes can't.' Jackson ushered the others back to their work, saying he would lend a hand.

Rose went upstairs and knocked on Win's door. Hearing the call to enter, she went in. 'May I have a word, Aunt?'

'Of course, take a seat.' Win motioned to the armchair by the bed.

'I know you're right, Aunt, and I'm sorry I've caused you so much trouble.' Win was shocked at the sudden change in Rose's demeanour. 'I'll try to be more accommodating with regard to suitors.' Rose didn't mean a word of it, but she had to appease her aunt somehow.

'I'm glad to hear it, because you will be having a visit the day after tomorrow from Giles Morton. He is twenty-two years old and his father is a manufacturer of mirrors. Very wealthy.'

'At least he's closer to my age,' Rose said meekly.

'Indeed, and it's my thinking he would make for a perfect match.'

'I look forward to meeting him.'

'Good. Was there anything else?' Rose shook her head. 'Very well, go and get some sleep.'

Rose met Katy on the landing as she went to her own room. Closing the door, Katy came to help Rose get ready for bed.

'Katy, I've just told Aunt Win I will walk out with a Giles Morton on Sunday.'

'Why? I thought...'

'I have to keep her sweet, Katy! You heard what she said; if I'm not careful I'll find myself in church with no way out. I need to reach my birthday unwed because...'

'What?'

'On that day, Charles Dean is going to propose and I'm going to say yes!'

'Bloody hellfire!' Katy's mouth hung open as she tried to digest what she'd been told. 'Beggin' your pardon, miss.'

'It's a lot to ask but I need you to help me, Katy.'

'O' course I will, whatever you want.'

'A chaperone. Aunt Win might ask you how Giles and I got along...'

'I'll say you hit it off well together.'

Rose sighed with relief. 'Thank you. The trouble is I don't want this Giles to think that we could become a couple.'

'I see your problem. Maybe you could tell your aunt he was very nice and all that, but you'd prefer to see someone else.'

'She has them lined up for me, Katy.'

'There you go then. This will sound a bit...'

'Just say it.'

'Right. Work your way through them, then you can do it again, saying you can't make up your mind as they were all so nice. With luck, that will bring us closer to your birthday.'

'Katy, you are a genius!'

'Am I to let the others know, miss?'

'Best had, otherwise they'll wonder what's going on.'

'Let's get you changed and you can forget it all and have a good night's sleep,' Katy said with a comforting smile.

'I'm so lucky to have you all as family, Katy,' Rose said while slipping out of her dress.

'And us, you.'

Katy retired to the kitchen, where again she asked for a private word with Jackson. She didn't miss the scowl thrown her way from Dolly and added, 'It's about Miss Rose's chaperone.'

'Come along then.' Jackson led the way to his pantry.

Katy quietly explained all that Rose had told her.

'Good grief, this is sounding more like one of those mystery novels on the market.' Katy raised an eyebrow and Jackson cleared his throat. 'Well, you can assure Miss Rose that she can depend on us. Just let me know when you're on chaperone duty.'

Returning to the kitchen, Jackson informed the others that Katy wouldn't be available at certain times and why.

Mary frowned and Jackson gave a barely perceptible shake of his head but the cook got the message.

Dolly smirked. At last she felt she was being included. Clearly keeping her mouth shut and her ears open was working.

Once the kitchen was clean and tidy again, it was the early hours and all went to their beds. Katy tapped Mary on the arm and tilted her head as Dolly disappeared into her room. Mary followed Katy and closed the door while Katy lit the lamp. Here, in whispers, Mary learned all there was to know.

Going to her own bed, Mary thought long and hard about what Katy had told her as well as what the gossips had said.

45

Mary was first up the next morning and when Jackson appeared she hooked a finger and went to his pantry.

'Mrs Winters?' Jackson asked, closing the door.

'I have summat to tell you and I need to know what to do with it.' Mary explained everything.

'It's all hearsay, Mrs Winters, and I would advise you to say nothing as I told you before. Keep your counsel until such time as it might be needed. Then you can reveal what you've heard.'

Mary nodded. 'I was just a bit worried when I found out about the missus lining up these men for Miss Rose to meet. They could just be after the money she stands to inherit.'

'No one has any evidence of this but the missus and the solicitors, none of whom, I'm certain, would divulge what they know. So, it stands to reason it's only gossip.'

'You'm right, o' course. I feel better having spoken to you about my concerns though.' Getting to her feet, Mary went to begin cooking breakfast.

Jackson remained where he was, rubbing his chin and

thinking about how these new bits of information could possibly fit into the puzzle that Rose was at the centre of.

After eating, the furniture was put back in place, and the rest of the day passed quietly enough.

Sunday arrived and with it came Giles Morton. Rose and Katy were introduced by Win and the haughty young man announced he would take Rose for afternoon tea.

The first sign that this outing would be unsuccessful was when Giles climbed into his personal carriage, leaving the ladies to get in by themselves. Jackson immediately came to the rescue, a look of disgust on his face.

'I know a very nice place for tea,' Giles said and Rose nodded. The rest of the short journey passed in silence, both girls feeling most uncomfortable.

Reaching their destination, Giles got out and Rose and Katy again had to alight by themselves. Sharing a glance, the women followed him into the beautiful old building. It was warm inside and Rose liked it instantly.

Shown to a table for two, Katy was placed at another which was close enough for her to hear their conversation. A waitress appeared, wearing a black dress covered by a pristine white apron, a frilly cap fixed to her hair.

'Good afternoon, Mr Morton, it's nice to see you again.'

'Good afternoon, Esme. Tea for two, please.'

The girl nodded and went to walk away.

'Excuse me,' Rose called and the waitress turned back. 'I'll take coffee instead, please.'

'Very good, madam.' Again the waitress turned.

'Also, can you take my friend's order, she's my chaperone.' Rose indicated Katy sitting alone. She was stunned at Giles's rudeness and at having to take matters into her own hands regarding the ordering of refreshments.

Katy ordered coffee too, a treat not often served at home because of the expense. The aroma of said drink had had her mouth watering the moment she had entered the large dining room. Looking around, Katy noticed another girl who sat alone, clearly serving the same role as herself. Locking eyes, Katy smiled as the other chaperone rolled her eyes with a smile of her own. Evidently they were thinking the same thing: *Why am I here doing this?*

Katy glanced at the arched doorway through which they had come. The large windows were set high in the walls on both sides, letting natural light flood the room. She wondered if the building had once been a little church.

The waitress delivered her orders which consisted of a three-tiered cake stand stacked with tiny sandwiches and cream cakes as well as a pot of coffee, sugar lumps and milk.

Katy suddenly realised that not a single word had been exchanged between Rose and her suitor. Just then, as she poured her drink, Giles spoke.

'I live out in the Ladywood area.' He watched Rose take a sandwich, placing it on her plate, then pour her coffee. 'P'pa is a very successful manufacturer of mirrors for business and private use. M'ma owns a string of racehorses which she treats as her pets. I receive a generous allowance which means I don't have to work.' He curled a lip at the very idea. 'I am looking for a wife who will run my household, keeping to a tight budget of course, and provide me with an heir who will eventually inherit the family fortune.'

Katy almost choked on her food and cast a glance at Rose, who was the model of decorum. She saw Giles then begin to shovel food into his mouth, and she turned away in disgust.

'How do you spend your time?' Rose asked.

Swallowing loudly, he replied, 'I'm at my club most of the time where I enjoy the company of my friends.'

Rose grimaced as he slurped his tea. Why did the nouveau riche always think it was acceptable to drink like they were drowning in the bath?

'M'ma is all in favour of this match; she thinks you might tame my wild streak.' He snorted and went on, 'I've told her there isn't a woman alive who could do that.'

Nibbling her sandwich, Rose's eyes sought Katy's from beneath her lashes and she smiled when her maid raised her eyebrow. The one-sided conversation went on; Giles talking and Rose murmuring the odd platitude.

Having drunk his tea, Giles snapped his fingers and the waitress came immediately. 'Put this on my account, Esme,' he said as he pulled out his wallet and gave her five shillings.

'Thank you very much, Mr Morton!'

Rose and Katy got to their feet simultaneously, evidently afternoon tea was finished.

The carriage ride home was again spent in silence, and Rose was glad to see Jackson waiting. 'Thank you for tea, Mr Morton,' Rose said as the butler helped her and Katy alight. Without waiting for a reply, Rose strode into the house.

'I will go and report to Aunt Win and then I'll join you in the kitchen,' Rose said, 'and thank you, Katy.'

'Well, how was it?' Win asked as Rose entered the sitting room.

'Absolutely dreadful!' Rose went on to explain and Win shook her head.

'Young men these days have no manners.'

'I'm sorry, Aunt, but Giles Morton is definitely not for me.'

Rose walked from the room to join the staff where she sat at the table. 'Where's Dolly?'

'Sweeping the scullery,' Mary said.

'Call her in, please, Jackson.' With a frown, Jackson stood up. 'She's always saying we don't tell her anything.' Rose smiled when the scullion came at Jackson's request.

'Have a seat, Dolly. Have I a tale to tell you all.'

Thrilled to be included, Dolly did as she was bid as Rose related the events of the afternoon. 'He never did!' Dolly exclaimed when Rose reached the part about providing an heir for the Morton family.

'He did, Dolly, I heard it plain as day,' Katy affirmed.

'I hope you told him to bugger right off!' Dolly's exclamation had the women burst out laughing and even Jackson cracked a smile.

'Miss Rose was a perfect lady throughout,' Katy assured them all.

'What did the missus say?' Mary asked.

'It appears she has lined up a few more gentlemen for me to meet. I feel like a piece of meat being auctioned off.'

'Well, let's hope they'm better than the last 'un then,' Dolly was quick to put in.

'I agree, Dolly. If I have to do this then I hope they at least have good table manners.'

Mary and Katy shared a quick glance, noticed only by Jackson, before the little gathering broke up; Rose going to her room while the kitchen began to bustle once more.

What no one knew was that Charles Dean had seen Rose and Katy enter the tea shop with Giles Morton. It had been happenstance that he had been walking down the street at that time, and the sight had stopped him dead in his tracks. Mortified, Charles had turned tail and hurried away with only one thought on his mind – Rose was walking out with another man!

46

It was a couple of days later when Charles Dean heard about Rose's outing with the rude Giles Morton, and it didn't come as a shock as he'd already seen it for himself. She had warned him previously that there were things going on in the family; was this what she meant? He had tried his best to fathom out what was happening but reached no conclusions. All he knew was his jealousy was eating away at him. He considered calling at the house in an effort to discover what Rose was up to, but decided against it for fear of upsetting her. He wondered how he could find out.

His eyes lit up as a thought struck. Going to the fireplace, he tugged on the bell pull. A few moments later, the maid arrived and bobbed a knee.

'Would you and Bess join me, please, and could I have tea?'

'Certainly, sir.'

It wasn't long before the cook and maid stood in the sitting room, the tea tray on a table next to Charles's chair.

'As you know, I attend a lot of functions and I thought it time I should reciprocate by holding a dinner party. I'd be grateful if you would draw up a menu, Bess, and hire whatever staff you think will be needed.'

The cook nodded. 'For how many, sir?'

'As many as will fit comfortably in the dining room. What are your thoughts?'

'I'd say we could fit twenty around the table. We have extra chairs in a spare bedroom, and plenty of glasses and crockery.'

'So be it. When should we plan it for?'

'I'll need a week to hire decent staff and order in the food. Daisy here can help with the cooking if needs be.'

'Very good, let's say the fifteenth then, shall we?'

'That's plenty of time. I'll let you have the menu as soon as possible.'

'Thank you. Oh, by the way...' he paused to pour his tea, 'have either of you heard any gossip about Rose Hamilton?' The cook and maid exchanged a glance. 'I need to keep up so I'm not taken by surprise or drop my big foot in somewhere it doesn't belong.'

'Well...'

'Please, tell me all.'

* * *

When Bess and Daisy had gone back to their duties, Charles mulled over what he'd heard. Somehow word had it that on her twenty-first birthday Rose stood to inherit a very substantial amount of money. Quite how this information had been leaked was a mystery, but it was said that Rose's father had set up a trust fund for her. However, that didn't explain Win's eagerness to get Rose married off so quickly, unless she stood to lose out on something.

Suddenly it all began to make sense, and Charles grinned. Winifred Jacobs was fearful of something, what it was he wasn't sure of yet, but it was tied into getting Rose wed, and her inheritance on her birthday. Was her walking out, with a chaperone, a ruse to keep Win happy until that time?

Clever girl! Charles's grin turned to a laugh as he was sure he'd hit the nail on the head, despite not knowing the all of it.

Later he wrote out nineteen invitations to his dinner party, Win and Rose first on his list, and put them on the hall tray for posting. The fifteenth of November couldn't come fast enough for him now as he was desperate to see Rose again. On impulse he wrote a note and went outside to find a runner.

* * *

Across town, Rose was ambling about, searching for something to do. Going to her room, she threw herself on the bed with a huge sigh. A moment later, Katy tapped the door and walked in. 'This has just come for you, Miss Rose, by runner.'

Rose took the envelope and tore it open, reading the contents out loud.

Meet me in the park by the bandstand at two o'clock.
  Charles.

'Are you going, Miss Rose?'

'I want to, Katy, with all my heart I do, but what about Aunt Win?'

'Tell her you're bored to the back teeth, which ain't a lie, so you're going shopping.'

'What a good idea!'

'Just don't forget to buy something, though, and please be careful.'

'I will, come and help me to get ready.' Rose was in a dither, unable to choose an outfit, so Katy made the decision for her.

'Right. Hat, coat, gloves, bag and – money.' Katy ticked off the list on her fingers.

'I wonder what he wants,' Rose said absent-mindedly as she tucked the note into her bag.

'Miss Rose, did you really just ask that?' Katy said with a grin.

Rose blushed. Then together they went downstairs, Rose to the sitting room and Katy to the kitchen. When Rose said where she was going, Win got to her feet with, 'I'll come with you.'

Rose hadn't accounted for this and in a panic she said sharply, 'Am I not old enough to go alone yet?'

'There's no need to snap. I thought you might like some company.'

'No, thank you.' Rose stamped from the room into the hall where Jackson was waiting, already having hailed a cab.

'Katy said you were going shopping, miss,' he said, wiggling his eyebrows, 'please take care.'

Rose grinned. Clearly Katy had told him about her note. 'Thank you, Jackson.' Before climbing into the cab, Rose quietly asked the driver to take her to the park bandstand. Her heart was banging out of her chest and her nerves were stretched taut at both meeting Charles and having kept the clandestine meeting from her aunt.

The journey was short and as the cab approached its destination she saw Charles pacing back and forth. The vehicle stopped and Charles saw Rose wave through the window. Rushing over, he instructed the cabbie to circle the park before climbing aboard.

'You came!' he said, taking the seat opposite her.

'Yes,' Rose replied on a breath.

'I was missing you terribly. Good grief, I feel like a schoolboy!'

Rose laughed. 'I can't believe I'm doing this.'

'Rose, my darling Rose. May I kiss you?'

Blushing to the roots of her hair, Rose nodded. As his lips touched hers, she felt the fire flow through her veins, and she melted into his arms as he held her across the interior of the carriage. Her eyes remained closed as he gently let her go.

'Rose Hamilton, I love you with all of my heart and soul, and will until the end of my days.'

'I love you too, Charles,' she whispered before his lips found hers once more.

47

As the cab rolled slowly around the park, Charles said, 'I've heard you will become a very rich woman on your birthday.' Seeing Rose's face fall, he quickly added, 'No, Rose, I'm not after your money. I have more than a man can spend in ten lifetimes. I only tell you this because I think Win is somehow tied into why you can't or won't marry before then. I don't know what her hold over you is, but know that I'm here to help if you need me.'

'It's all very complicated, Charles, and I wish I could share it with you but...'

'It's all right, you don't have to, but I do worry that you might need some support around you.'

'I have it and it's the very best I could ask for.'

'I saw you the other day with Giles Morton.'

Rose was shocked but recovered quickly, saying, 'Charles, it's not what it seems.'

'I know that now, but you can imagine what I thought at the time. Is this all tied into the business with Win?'

'Yes, but... all I can say is, whatever you see or hear, it is Aunt Win's doing, not mine.'

'I understand, I think. May I ask – will you be taking outings with any others?' Seeing her lower her head, he went on, 'I am of the belief that it's a ruse to play for time and keep Win happy, am I correct?'

Rose nodded. 'Everything is hinged on my birthday. Can you wait for me, though, Charles? It's many months away.'

'Yes, to the end of time. As long as I know you love me as I do you, then it doesn't matter. I told you that on your birthday I will propose to you, and I stand by this. My question is – would you consent to be my wife?'

Rose looked at the man she adored. 'Yes, Charles, I would.'

'Thank God! Now I can wait a happy man.'

'Forgive me, Charles, but I should be getting back. I told Aunt Win I was shopping so I had best do just that.'

'Of course.' Charles banged on the roof and the cab stopped. 'I will see you soon.' He climbed out as he asked where she needed to go next. Relaying the information to the cabbie, he reached in his pocket and pulled out a florin. He tossed it up and the driver caught it deftly. With a tip of his hat, he flicked the reins and the horse set off once more.

Charles went home happier than he had ever been in his life.

* * *

Rose bought herself a new pair of shoes with a bag to match then asked to be returned home. Jackson, as always, was there to pay the fare and the cabbie grinned when Rose said, 'Please give the gentleman a *huge* tip, he's been very kind.'

Indoors, Jackson asked quietly, 'Good trip, miss?'

'Excellent, thank you, Jackson.' The two shared a knowing smile before Rose went to show Win her purchases.

That night, as Katy helped her get ready for bed, Rose told her everything.

'How did he know about your money?' Katy asked, aghast.

'I have no idea but someone certainly has a big mouth.'

'Do you think it was John Watts?'

'No, definitely not. My father's solicitor, however, I cannot vouch for. It doesn't really matter because if Charles knows, then others will too.' Looking into the mirror, she said, 'I wonder if Mr Morton senior made that?'

Katy burst out laughing and Rose soon joined in. 'I was shocked when Charles said he'd seen us that day.'

'I'll bet, but he understands now, doesn't he?'

'To a degree, I think. Of course I couldn't tell him everything, which will have to wait.'

'Just think, in a matter of months you'll be Mrs Rose Dean!'

'It sounds nice, don't you think? Rose Dean.'

'Will you move into his house?'

'No. I've had an idea about that. I'd like to live in the house I grew up in. We'll have to see.'

'Well, it will be yours – legally, I mean.'

'Indeed and I'd like you, Mary and Jackson to come with me.'

'Not Dolly?' Katy asked with a wry grin.

'Definitely not as things stand now. Aunt Win hired her so she can keep her!' Again laughter filled the room. 'Katy, if Mary can send Dolly on an errand tomorrow I'll tell the others my plans.'

'I'll let her know.' Saying goodnight, Katy left Rose with a dreamy look on her face.

* * *

Down in the kitchen, Katy watched for her chance to pass Mary the message. Jackson was reading his paper as was his wont, and Mary was making cocoa. Placing a cup before Katy, Mary frowned. Katy's eyes went to Dolly then to the pantry.

'Anybody fancy pancakes?' Mary asked.

'Ooh, yes, please,' Dolly piped up.

'Be a love then and fetch the ingredients while I heat up the pan.'

No sooner had Dolly gone than Katy whispered the message. Mary nodded and Jackson peeped over the paper.

Seeing the scullion returning with her arms full, Katy moved to help. 'I love pancakes,' she said lightly.

'Me an' all,' Dolly replied happily.

After a good night's sleep on full bellies, it was around mid-morning when Mary asked Dolly to nip to the market.

'I can go,' Katy said.

'No, you have other things to be getting on with. Dolly can go if she doesn't mind.' Mary caught the look of triumph on the scullion's face but ignored it.

With a list and money in hand and a basket over her arm, Dolly set off, full of her own importance.

Katy immediately ran upstairs to summon Rose.

In hushed tones, Rose related what she had told Katy the night before.

With a look at Jackson, Mary admitted, 'That's what I'd heard as well – about the money, I mean.'

'Indeed, Mrs Winters spoke to me about it a while ago and I advised her to keep quiet,' Jackson added.

'Well, it seems it's out now,' Rose said.

'How, is my question?' Jackson said.

'Nobody knows,' Mary answered, 'but I must say you and Mr Dean will make a fine couple.'

'We cannot let Aunt Win hear about that.'

'Our lips are sealed, miss, you can rely on us.'

'Thank you, you are all very dear to me.'

Later that afternoon, Rose again popped into the kitchen, saying, 'Jackson, Aunt Win has arranged another outing for me on Sunday, so I'll need Katy again, please.'

'Of course, miss.'

Dolly, naturally, was all ears as Katy asked, 'Who is it this time, Miss Rose?'

'Someone called Edward Gerrard.'

'What, the undertakers?' Mary asked with surprise.

Rose stared. 'Oh, please don't tell me that!'

'It's the only Gerrards I know of,' Mary said.

Dolly sniggered and Jackson immediately scolded her. 'It's not funny, Dolly, the Gerrards are fine businessmen and very well-off.' With Dolly looking suitably chastised, he added, 'We'll all be meeting a Gerrard sooner or later and you'd do well to remember it.'

'This is getting ridiculous!' Rose shouted before fleeing the kitchen.

No more was said until later that night when Jackson and Mary had cocoa before bed. Dolly, as usual, crept downstairs to listen to their conversation. Jackson's ears pricked up and he tilted his head towards the stairs.

Mary nodded her understanding with a sigh. 'Poor Miss Rose, I feel sorry for her.'

'So do I, Mary. I wonder why the missus never married.'

'I have a theory about that,' Mary said, 'I'll tell you about it – one day.'

They both smiled at the sound of the gentlest of frustrated sighs coming from the stairs.

'Why not now?' Jackson asked.

'Because walls have ears, Mr Jackson.'

Dolly clamped her teeth together with a clack and, knowing she'd been rumbled yet again, she returned to her bed.

48

'We have received an invitation to dine with Charles Dean on the fifteenth,' Win said over breakfast a few days later.

'How nice,' Rose replied, trying her best to keep her excitement in check.

'I'm not sure it's a good idea.'

'Aunt Win, it would be rude to refuse, which would give rise to gossip, I'm sure.'

Win nodded. 'Very well, I'll send an acceptance today. You have your outing tomorrow with Edward Gerrard, don't forget.'

'I remember. Is he from the undertakers?' Rose gave Jackson a quick glance as he stood against the wall like a statue.

'Yes, he's the oldest son. He will be extremely wealthy when he inherits the business.' Rose grimaced at the thought of being wed to an undertaker. 'Don't look like that, Rose, I'm sure the young man is very nice.'

'I hope so,' Rose muttered. 'I'm going to town later with Mrs Winters.' Win nodded and buried her nose in the newspaper.

After lunch, Rose and Mary wrapped up warm and set out

with baskets in hand. 'Thank you, Mary, for letting me come with you, I was going mad cooped up in the house.'

'I guessed as much.' As they walked, they discussed Dolly's eavesdropping, Rose hardly able to believe the girl was still doing it. Rose told her friend about the invite from Charles, and Mary got caught up in the excitement as they talked about his proposing on Rose's birthday.

'You really love him, don't you?'

'Yes, Mary, I do.'

'In that case, I think there's summat you should know, and it's best told over a cup of tea.'

Finding a tea shop, they sat by the front window. Once refreshments were served, Mary began. 'Many years ago, before you were born, it was thought that Mr Dean and your aunt would marry.'

'Really?'

'Ar, now I don't know what happened but the wedding never took place as I'm sure you realise. The rumour at the time was that your aunt was devastated, so much so she went away for quite a while.'

'Where to?' Rose asked.

'The seaside somewhere, nobody knew for certain.'

'Then she came home?'

'Evidently, but she was never the same. She had turned bitter and nasty.'

'Do you think Charles had let her down?'

'I can't be sure, but that would be my guess for her to react as she did.'

Rose was shocked at the revelation but then she contemplated, 'And now you're worried he'll do the same to me?'

'I'm concerned, that's why I told you.'

Rose stared out of the window but all she saw was an image of Charles smiling back at her. 'What should I do, Mary?'

'Try not to worry because it will most likely be that he's true to you. Wait and see what your birthday brings.'

'Maybe I should avoid him.'

'Why? Nothing is certain, and from what you've told me it sounds like he's besotted with you. Don't risk losing the love of your life because of something that happened in the past...'

'If it was Charles who took the decision not to wed, then that would explain why Aunt Win is so angry with him each time they meet.'

'My thinking exactly,' Mary said, 'and she's never married because...'

'She's still in love with him!' Mary nodded. 'I have to speak with him, Mary, I need to find out the truth!'

'I can understand that, but don't do anything silly. I don't want you to end up like your aunt, all sour-faced and miserable. If you truly love him, and I think you do, then put whatever you learn behind you. Marry the man and have a good life.'

'What about Aunt Win?'

'She could have wed another, she didn't have to stay a spinster.'

'She would never have been happy though.'

'No, but she ain't exactly the life and soul of the party now, is she?'

'Thank you, Mary, for telling me all this, it was important for me to know.'

Finishing their refreshments, Rose paid the bill and they went about the shopping in a much more sombre mood.

That night, Rose told Katy of her discussion with Mary.

'Well, I agree that could be why the missus is such a misery,' Katy said, helping Rose out of her dress.

'I'm dreading meeting with Edward Gerrard tomorrow, Katy. I don't know how much longer I can do this just to keep Aunt Win happy.'

'As I see it, you have two options. Go along with it until it's too late to marry before your birthday, or tell her straight you ain't doing it no more.'

'I prefer the second.'

'Then you have your answer.'

'I'm scared she'll arrange a wedding anyway.'

'Even if she does, you wouldn't have to go through with it and then she'll look a fool. No, I suspect it's only a threat because I'm sure she couldn't handle the scandal.'

'That's true. All right, tomorrow will be the last time, Katy, and when we return I'll tell her not to arrange anything more.'

When Katy had gone, Rose lay in bed, her mind a whirl with all she'd learned. She woke some hours later in a sweat, having dreamed of a double wedding, Charles and Win and Edward Gerrard and herself.

Suddenly everything seemed too much to bear and she burst into tears. She cried like her heart was breaking until eventually she was exhausted. *You can't go on like this, my girl*, she told herself, *otherwise your meeting with Edward Gerrard will be for a completely different reason!*

It turned out the following day that young Mr Gerrard was a perfect gentleman. He took Rose and Katy to a matinee performance at the Gaiety Palace after a lovely afternoon tea. He insisted that Katy sat at their table and had regaled them with funny stories about his profession. Rose and Katy laughed until their sides ached when he described how two families had fought over a burial plot, after an administrative mistake had been made. He told them about a wife who hated her husband while he was alive suddenly turning into a 'casket crawler', crying and trying to get into the coffin with him.

All in all, Rose had enjoyed her time and told Edward so when he returned them home. Of course Rose and Katy spent time in the kitchen relating the tales they had heard, and everybody stared in silence when Katy said, 'That Edward is so dreamy.'

It appeared Edward had thought the same about Katy, as the next morning a note arrived from said gentleman inviting her to dinner!

49

A row ensued when Rose explained to Win in no uncertain terms that she would not be walking out with anyone else.

Jackson stood impassively next to the breakfast sideboard, his face a mask of disinterest.

'Mr Gerrard was very nice but not for me, and it appears I was not for him. His attention was more on Katy, as was evidenced by the note she received early this morning inviting her to dinner, and I say good luck to them both.'

'What? Damn the man!'

'You can't help who you like, Aunt Win, surely you understand that.'

'Never mind the paid help! This is about finding *you* a husband!'

Jackson's eyebrow lifted at Win's remark as Rose saw when she glanced at him.

'Aunt Win, that was rude. Nevertheless, be advised and arrange no more outings because I shall flatly refuse and it will be you left looking like an idiot.' Rose pushed back her chair as

Jackson moved to help. She swept from the room, her skirt rustling as she went.

Jackson returned to his place as Win shook out the newspaper so hard it tore down the centre. Throwing it on the table, she stormed out, leaving Jackson to chuckle as he pushed her chair back into place.

* * *

The days passed and the weather grew colder, keeping Rose indoors, so when the fifteenth arrived she was more than ready for a change of scenery.

Choosing a gown of midnight-blue velvet, Rose was excited to be seeing Charles again. Win wore dark green and, bundled up in coats, the two boarded the cab. No words were spoken on the journey, both women lost in their own thoughts.

They were greeted by a butler and their coats were taken by a maid. The house was warm and cosy, despite being so huge. Led into the sitting room, they saw they were not the first to arrive. Charles crossed the room to kiss their hands, welcoming them to his home, while a maid offered wine from her tray.

Win moved to speak with other guests and Rose saw her chance. 'I must talk to you in private,' she whispered.

'Win, I'm just taking Rose to the kitchen. She has a message for my cook from yours,' Charles called out so everyone could hear.

Win had no option but to nod her agreement as others looked at her.

Charles and Rose left the room and headed for the kitchen but stopped before they got there. Knowing time was short, Rose spoke in hushed tones. 'I've heard you and Aunt Win were to be married but...'

The Orphan's Promise

'No, Rose. Win thought so but I never did. When I told her that she disappeared for quite some time. I know she was hurt but I only ever saw her as a friend. It was never my intention to wed your aunt.'

'Oh, Charles, I'm sorry. I thought...'

'Badly of me, clearly.'

'No! I wanted to know what happened. Oh dear, I feel such a fool.' Rose lowered her head as her tears formed.

Charles lifted her chin and looked into her eyes. Liquid amethysts looked back at him and his heart flipped. He gathered her into his arms and kissed her. 'Come on, we'd best at least visit the kitchen.'

Rose was introduced to Bess Green and when she said Mary Winters was their cook, Bess laughed. 'Please give her my best, miss, if you wouldn't mind. Mary and I go way back but I ain't seen her in an age.'

'I will, in fact I'll suggest she calls on you for a good catch-up.'

'That would be grand,' Bess said, rubbing her hands together.

'We'll let you get on, Bess. Don't be long because I'm starving!' Charles said, making his cook laugh.

'Nowt new there then,' she countered.

'Careful, else I'll give you the sack.'

'You've been saying that for twenty years and – oh, look, I'm still here.'

Charles and Rose left the kitchen, Rose saying, 'You have a wonderful relationship with Bess.'

'Yes, she tells it as it is, and I love her dearly.'

Back in the sitting room, Rose went to Win. 'Well, it seems that Mrs Winters and Charles's cook, Bess, have been friends for years.'

'I remember Bess, I didn't know she was still here.'

The gong sounded and everyone meandered into the dining

room. Win smiled widely when she was seated in pride of place on Charles's right, Rose to his left.

The butler poured wine and the under-footmen brought in the first course, a choice between prawns or pâté. Quiet discussions began and gentle laughter filled the room.

'I didn't know you had electric lighting, Charles,' Win said.

'It was installed very recently, it's an absolute marvel. You should look into it, Win.'

'I doubt I could afford it,' Win said, making Rose look up sharply.

'I think we should, Aunt Win, it's the way of the future,' Rose said.

'I'm not so sure about that. I wonder if it's just a fad.'

'Not so, Win,' a man said from further along the table. 'Everyone who is anyone is having it put in. Even the shops are converting.'

'I see, well, maybe I should convert too in that case.'

The empty plates were cleared, the wine glasses refreshed and the main course of venison or pheasant was served.

'Bess is still an excellent cook, I see,' Win commented.

'Indeed she is,' Charles replied, giving Rose a crafty wink.

Rose declined a pudding, saying she'd eaten enough, sipping her wine instead.

Charles was asked how his business was doing, and he explained he was having another narrowboat built to cope with the demand of shifting goods from one town to another.

The ladies retired to the sitting room for coffee. The gentlemen went to the drawing room for brandy and cigars, after which they joined the ladies once more.

'Do you still have your piano, Charles?' a fellow asked.

'I do. Would you care to play it?'

'Rather!'

Charles led his guests into the music room, deftly flicking on the switch by the door which instantly filled the room with light. A baby grand sat in the corner and the guest positioned himself on the stool. He ran his fingers over the keys expertly before playing a tune which had everyone spellbound. Accepting applause graciously, he then continued with a modern song so all could join in and sing along.

Eventually the evening drew to a close and Rose was reluctant to leave. She'd had a wonderful time since Charles had set her mind to rest. She travelled home humming to herself, much to Win's annoyance.

50

Win went straight to bed and Rose followed Jackson to the kitchen where she related the events of the evening.

'Bess Green sends her regards to you, Mrs Winters, and I told her you would call on her soon.'

'Bess, blimey! Yes, I should go and see her.'

'She said to tell you that everything was fine and that she was still very happy with Mr Dean.'

Rose accepted the cocoa from Dolly, giving her thanks, then she asked Katy, 'So will you accept Mr Gerrard's invitation?'

'Yes, Mr Jackson has given me leave to go.'

'I wouldn't, not with an undertaker!' Dolly said nastily.

'It's just as well you weren't asked then, Dolly,' Jackson retorted.

Rose left the staff to their chatter and retired to bed, still humming to herself.

* * *

Over the coming weeks, the weather worsened and snow fell, blanketing the city in white.

Rose and Katy spent time together as Rose readied for bed, and it was then that Katy revealed how well she was getting on with Edward Gerrard. They had been out together quite a few times which, of course, Rose was aware of. Katy was deliriously happy and Rose was delighted for her.

'Do you think he might propose, Katy?' Rose asked.

'I hope so,' Katy replied a little timidly.

'Just think, before long we could both be married women,' Rose mused. Katy grinned at the idea, Mrs Katy Gerrard, she liked the sound of that.

Preparations began for Christmas and excitement was in the air, the only one not to join in was Win. Her mood had soured even more than usual as time passed because she was no nearer to getting Rose wed. She could see her inheritance slipping away and it galled her. She knew it was selfish but she wanted that money and the two houses that went along with it. She just couldn't find a way out of the predicament she felt Rose had placed her in.

She realised then that there were festive functions to attend, so there might still be a chance for Rose to meet someone who she could take to. The thought rallied her and her spirits rose once more.

Sure enough, requests for their attendance came in thick and fast; yuletide balls, dinners, soirées and parties. It was going to be a busy time so new gowns would be needed. Win asked Rose to accompany her on her shopping trip but Rose declined, saying she didn't want to go out in the snow. Win didn't believe it for a moment. She knew Rose wanted to shop alone to choose her own outfits, and Win grudgingly had to allow it. So, Win went alone.

It was a couple of days later that Rose did her buying, and

Christmas gifts for the staff came first. For Mary, leather side-button boots and bag to match, Dolly a new skirt and blouse, Katy a winter coat and for Jackson a bowler hat and walking cane. Win was more difficult to buy for but Rose settled on the latest-style hat with a feather on the side. Then it was on to the gown shop, where she bought a gown in russet velvet, another in burgundy silk and a ball gown in shimmering emerald green.

Arriving home, Jackson unloaded the cab as the first snowflakes began to fall. Rose and Katy carried the packages to Rose's room.

'Oh, my!' Katy said, holding up the green gown once Rose had unpacked it. 'Ooh, this is lovely!' The burgundy followed into the wardrobe, as did the russet with, 'I love this!'

'You can leave those, they're Christmas gifts,' Rose said as Katy moved towards the pile on the chair.

With a nod, Katy left to return to the kitchen. 'Wait 'til you see what Miss Rose has bought,' she said but would say no more.

The festive season was a succession of balls and gatherings despite the heavy snowfall and Rose revelled in Charles's attention at each and every one. Of course, the gossip began; it was unseemly that a man who was old enough to be Rose's father should be showing such an interest in her. The quiet remarks to Win on the subject only served to fuel her anger, thus causing arguments between Rose and herself.

On Christmas Eve, before dinner, Rose went to her favourite room in the house – the kitchen – her arms full of packages. One by one, the gifts were given out and gratefully received. It was the custom in this house that gifts were exchanged the night before as the big day was usually too busy.

Dolly couldn't believe she had a new skirt and blouse, and holding them against her she whirled around. Katy's coat fit perfectly and Jackson tried on his bowler, which he tipped with his cane, a broad grin on his face. Mary wept with joy at her bag and boots.

Rose's present from the staff took her breath away. On a silver chain hung a heart-shaped locket and as she snapped it open, her tears fell. Inside was a tiny picture of her parents.

'How did you manage to...?' she sobbed.

'The photograph was in amongst your mum's things so I took it to a place in town. I don't know how they do it but – well, there's the result,' Mary said.

'Thank you all so very much, I love it!'

'May I, Miss Rose?' Jackson asked and at her nod he fastened it around her neck.

'It looks lovely,' Katy said.

'It's the nicest thing I've ever had,' Rose said as she laid her hand over it.

'What about your bracelet from Mr Dean?' Katy asked.

'Beautiful, yes, but this – this is very special indeed,' Rose replied.

Leaving them, Rose went to the sitting room, hat box in hand.

'That's a pretty necklace, Rose,' Win said, eyeing the locket.

'It's from the staff. Look, Aunt Win.' Rose opened it up once more and Win's face fell as she looked at the tiny picture.

'Isn't it beautiful?' Rose asked.

'Very nice,' Win said, trying to control her emotions. The faces of her sister and her husband had taken Win by surprise and she fought to regain her composure.

'I have something for you.' Presenting Win with her gift, Rose waited.

Win took out the hat and gasped. 'Rose, it's... stunning! Thank you.'

Rose's present from Win was a pair of over-the-elbow gloves the same shade of green as her ball gown. 'These are lovely, Aunt

Win, thank you.' After a moment, Rose said, 'Aunt, let's do something different tomorrow.'

'Like what?'

'Let's ask the staff to eat with us. I'm sure they would love it.'

'It's rather unconventional...'

'Please, Aunt Win!'

With a glance at her new hat, Win relented. 'Very well, but only because it's Christmas Day.'

Rose rushed from the room and skipped down to the kitchen once more. 'Jackson, may we have six places set for dinner tomorrow evening, please?'

'Of course, Miss Rose. Are we expecting guests?'

'No, Jackson, you are all invited to dine upstairs with us.' Rose smiled at the shocked faces. 'It's Christmas and I want to spend it with my friends.'

'Thank you, Miss Rose, I'll see to it,' Jackson replied with a croak.

Rose left them and Mary dropped onto a chair. 'I never thought to see the day!'

'Indeed, Mrs Winters, that young lady is one in a million,' Jackson added.

'Sunday best clothes then,' Katy put in. 'Dolly, you can wear your new outfit.'

Dolly grinned. Now she truly felt part of the household.

* * *

Dinner on Christmas Day began rather awkwardly, the staff never having eaten upstairs before. Mary, Katy and Dolly brought up the dishes of hot food and Jackson carved a goose. Rose took it upon herself to pour wine and gradually the atmosphere lightened. Everyone began to enjoy themselves, even Win's constant scowl disappeared. Mary and Katy fetched the Christmas pudding and custard jug. Win won the silver sixpence which was placed in the pudding mixture before it was steamed to perfection. She beamed as everyone applauded and she called for more wine. The whole evening was a huge success and one the staff would remember all of their lives.

51

Dolly's night-time eavesdropping ceased after the delights of Christmas as she considered herself now to be one of the family. She joined in more and scowled hardly at all. Jackson was convinced it was down to Rose for involving the girl more in the goings on of the house. However, they remained guarded in what was said in front of the scullion; Dolly could still not be truly trusted as far as they were concerned.

The New Year saw further snowfalls and people stayed indoors as much as possible. The poorer folk didn't have that luxury, still having to go to work wrapped up against the freezing temperatures. The children, of course, couldn't get out in the snow quick enough. They threw snowballs, built snowmen and broke off the long icicles, wherever they could reach them, sucking on the icy treats like lollies. The thick snow caused problems with the trams and cabs, and in some areas only the draymen could get through to deliver their beer barrels.

Soon enough, however, the thaw began and the white blanket turned to dirty slush before disappearing altogether, leaving puddles in its wake. February held onto the cold and the sky was filled with smoke from thousands of chimneys, industrial and domestic alike.

Jackson, as usual, delighted in informing the other staff of snippets of interest he found in the newspaper, such as the re-introduction of birching. 'That,' he said, 'will keep the juveniles in order.'

Mary nodded her agreement.

'Another brothel keeper has been to court and fined five pounds,' Jackson went on.

'I should think so too! It's a disgrace, the amount of these places springing up everywhere,' Mary blustered.

March came in like a lion with howling winds tossing street detritus high in the air before whipping it away. Some of the trees in the park were uprooted, their roots snapping like twigs as they fell victim to the gales. Then suddenly everything changed; the winds dropped and the sun appeared, albeit weakly. Spring had sprung and the clean-up began. Wrecked chimneys were re-pointed, their pots renewed, fences were mended and the streets were swept. Buds appeared as nature came to life again after her long sleep, and with it Win's anxieties rose yet again.

Time was marching on and she still hadn't managed to get Rose any nearer to the altar. The dreadful weather over the last months had given her no opportunities to further her cause and Win's grumpy demeanour returned in full force.

Rose had missed being able to meet up with Charles, and as she roamed the garden wrapped in a thick shawl, she had a sad air about her. She too was aware of the passage of time, and began to feel nervous about what her birthday would bring.

She confided more and more in Katy when getting ready for bed, about how Win would be affected when Rose was given a copy of her father's will.

'Of course she'll be upset,' Katy said, 'but there will be nothing she can do about it.'

There had been many occasions when Rose just wanted to tell her aunt she knew about the will, but recalling John Watts's advice she had remained silent. The whole sorry mess was eating away at both of them, and Rose didn't know how much longer she could keep her countenance. Had it not been for Katy, Mary and Jackson, Rose felt she might have gone mad with it all. Her love for Charles also helped enormously, and knowing he felt the same way had been her saving grace.

Now, as she pottered around the garden in the chill that still lingered, Rose smiled to think that one day soon she and Charles would be married. She wondered if he would be happy to move into her childhood home with her, or whether he would expect her to live at his home. Rose couldn't bear the thought of being without her friends, and that only added to her worries. Maybe it was something to broach with Charles on the next meeting. Would that seem too forward of her? She realised there would be time enough to decide once her birthday had passed and he had proposed.

One bright morning, Win said she was going out but would be back for lunch. The cab Jackson had whistled for carried her away from the house and Win felt her nerves twang. She had given the cabbie the address quietly and now she was on her way. She wondered how she would be received at her destination, calling on spec rather than having sent a note, but it had been a spur-of-the-moment decision. The nearer she got, the more her anxiety grew because she knew in her heart the meeting would not be a pleasant one.

On arrival, the cabbie was instructed to wait and Win yanked on the bell pull. Momentarily the maid opened the door and Win was invited inside. She was taken to the sitting room where the maid retreated to prepare a tea tray.

'Win! This is a surprise.'

'Charles.' She noted he had not said *nice* surprise.

'Take a seat, tea will be along shortly.'

Win sat in the chair next to a roaring fire and eyed the man sitting opposite her. This was the only man in the whole world she would have wed, but finally she was beginning to accept it would never be.

The tea tray was delivered and Charles poured. 'Now tell me – what can I do for you?'

'You know the answer to that, Charles,' Win said tartly.

'I'm sorry, you have me at a disadvantage.'

'Don't play the innocent with me, Charles, I know you too well.'

'Then please give me a clue?'

'Rose.'

'Ah.'

'Indeed. I want you to leave her alone, Charles.'

'I'm afraid I can't do that, Win. You see, Rose and I are in love.'

His words cut Win like a knife and the pain almost stopped her breathing. 'Charles, you know I can't allow it,' she managed.

'The thing is, Win, it's none of your business and before long you'll have no more say in the matter.'

'Why are you doing this to me? You are torturing me!' Win banged her cup and saucer on the table next to her.

'Win, I'm not trying to hurt you, please believe me. I can't help what I feel for Rose.'

Win's eyes filled with tears. 'It should have been me!'

Charles sighed. 'It could never have been you, especially after what happened.'

'You could have forgiven me.' Win knew she was begging and hated herself for it.

'Maybe, but it would have made no difference. I'm sorry, Win, truly I am.'

The anger bubbled up inside her again and Win got to her feet.

'Win, I think you should know, I intend to make Rose my wife.'

'And you should know, I'll see you in hell before I'll let that happen!' Win ran from the room, tears of despair and hurt rolling down her cheeks. She cried all the way home, her heart having finally broken, knowing now that Charles would never be hers.

Rushing straight to her room on reaching home, Win chose to stay there. Katy took a lunch tray up to her but later she removed it, the food untouched.

'I wonder what's up with the missus,' Mary mused.

'I saw she'd been crying when she got back,' Jackson put in.

'What, the missus?'

He nodded. 'Whatever has happened, it has upset her greatly.'

Not having seen her aunt since she got home, Rose went to Win's bedroom and knocked tentatively on the door before walking in. 'Aunt, are you unwell?'

'No.'

'Katy said you haven't eaten.'

'I wasn't hungry.' Win was sitting in the armchair by the window.

'What's wrong? Can I help in any way?' Rose asked as she walked across the room.

Win looked up at the beautiful girl standing before her, Rose's violet eyes sparkling with concern.

'Unless you can stop seeing Charles Dean, then no, you can't.'

'Charles...? Aunt Win, tell me what the matter is.'

Win took a breath. 'Get out, Rose! Leave me be!'

The venom behind the words had Rose step back a pace. 'Aunt Win, please, you're scaring me!'

Win was on her feet in a second and slapped Rose's face so hard it rocked her head on her neck.

With a hand on her stinging cheek, Rose gasped.

'You keep away from him, do you hear me? I warn you, Rose, you stay well away from him or you'll be sorry. Now *get out*!'

Rose fled from the room, passing Katy on the landing bearing a tea tray. Delivering it to Win, Katy rushed to Rose's room to find her crying. Between sobs, Rose revealed all.

52

Win knew she had gone too far by slapping her niece but she was so angry. Now she sat simmering, her fury still bubbling enough to make her shake. She picked up the cup from the tray and threw it at the door, where it shattered; shortly afterwards the saucer followed it. Her hands bunched into tight fists and she hammered them on the dressing table, making all her little pots jump about. She kept on until the pain made her stop. Covering her face, she wept bitterly.

Rose and Katy heard the crash and came running. There was a grinding sound as Rose pushed open the door and stepped onto the broken crockery. They exchanged a look before Rose went to her aunt.

'Whatever has happened to bring you to this?'

Win looked up and Katy gasped at the hatred in the woman's wide, staring eyes. 'This is your fault!' Win growled. 'Everything is going wrong because of you!'

'Aunt Win, please – just talk to me.'

'I don't want to talk to you – ever again!' With that, she launched herself from the chair, catching Rose by the hair. Rose screamed but Win would not let go, instead pushing hard against the girl, causing them to crash to the floor.

Katy ran over to them and tried to pull Win away, but Win held on for dear life. Katy ran from the room, yelling for help, then dashed back to try and help Rose.

Win was yelling at the top of her voice, 'He's mine! You stole him from me!' She pulled hard at Rose's hair with one hand and hit out with the other, catching Rose a glancing blow to her cheek.

Rose was screaming and struggling to free herself.

Jackson was through the door first and, seeing the melee, he raced across the room. He dragged Win off Rose and spun her around, slapping her face hard, the shock of which made Win stop and stare.

Mary and Dolly had followed and stood in stunned silence at what they saw. Katy helped Rose to her feet and led her away from her furious aunt.

'Dolly, fetch the doctor – and hurry!' Jackson said. He sat Win down and waited for her anger to dissipate, but he was mistaken. Again she jumped up and this time she went for him, her fists flying in all directions. Grabbing her arms, Jackson twisted them behind her back.

'Katy, find me a binding, quickly!'

Katy pulled the belt from Win's dressing gown and passed it to the butler, just dodging a kick from Win.

Jackson secured her hands and pushed her onto the chair, then he stepped back, blowing out his cheeks.

Win was growling like a dog, spittle dripping down her chin in strings. Her eyes were focused totally on Rose, who was being held by Mary.

'You! You! You!' Win screamed loud enough to wake the dead. 'He's mine! Do you hear me? He's *mine*!'

Jackson was astounded that Win had not yet tired herself out.

Win was still yelling when Dr Hughes arrived. It was Katy who explained what had happened as far as they knew it, but what the initial cause was remained a mystery.

The doctor tried to approach Win, talking quietly to her, but Win, yet again, shot out of the seat, trying to knock the man over. Jackson came to the rescue once more.

'Something traumatic has happened to cause this. I'm going to need help getting her to the hospital.'

'Why? Won't she calm down soon?' Rose asked.

'Miss Hamilton, Win is sick. Not in the usual sense, you understand, she's very poorly in her mind.'

'Has she gone mad?' Rose asked, her voice cracking.

'It's looking that way, but my hope is that it's only temporary. We'll know more when we get her to the hospital.' The doctor nodded, a sad look on his face.

Win was muttering now. 'It's her fault! He's mine! *Mine!*'

'I'll give you a hand with Miss Jacobs,' Jackson said.

'I'm coming too,' Rose said, 'you'll need her details for your records, won't you?'

'Yes, of course, but I warn you it won't be easy for you.'

Jackson and Dr Hughes manhandled Win down the stairs and into his carriage. Jackson and Rose climbed inside and the doctor took the driving seat. Win seemed content to sit and mutter as they rolled along. Her eyes were cast down as she rocked back and forth, mumbling the same words, 'He's mine!'

Mary, Katy and Dolly watched as they disappeared down the drive, then went inside for tea to calm their nerves and discuss the whole debacle.

'She just turned on Miss Rose!' Katy explained while Mary poured tea. 'Spitting and clawing and pulling her hair, I couldn't believe what I was seeing!'

Mary listened. She knew things would come to a head eventually but she'd never expected this.

'She smashed the crockery and she kept shouting, "He's mine!" over and over again.'

'Who's hers?' Dolly asked.

'I don't know, Dolly, but I think I can guess,' Katy answered.

'Who?' Dolly asked again, getting frustrated.

Mary provided the answer. 'Charles Dean.' With a sigh, she went on, 'This isn't over by a long stretch of the imagination, especially if the missus gets out of that bloody awful place.'

All three shivered at the thought of being taken to the asylum.

* * *

Across town, Dr Hughes drew the carriage to a halt outside All Saints Hospital in Winson Green. It was known as Birmingham City Asylum and was an imposing building.

Jackson and Rose helped a still-muttering Win out of the carriage and in through the hospital door.

'We need some help here with Miss Winifred Jacobs,' the doctor said, having been recognised by the receptionist. Pressing a buzzer, she gave Rose an understanding smile.

Two burly men in grey uniforms came through a door and relieved Jackson and Rose of the now-struggling woman, taking her back the way they had come. 'Her name is Win Jacobs, treat her gently,' Dr Hughes said.

Watching her aunt being taken away, Rose gave a little whimper, and Jackson placed an arm around her. *Protocol be damned*, he thought.

Turning to Rose and Jackson, the doctor hooked a finger. 'Come with me, please.'

They followed him to his office where Rose gave Win's details, name, date of birth, address, and so on. 'How long will she be here?'

'It all depends, Miss Hamilton. An illness of the mind is very difficult to deal with. It's not something we can put a bandage on.'

Just then, a series of screams and banging sounded, making Rose and Jackson jump.

Dr Hughes smiled. 'That will be Lucas, he wants his meal. Lucas is one of three people.'

Rose and Jackson exchanged a puzzled frown.

'One minute he is Lucas, the next he is a woman called Geraldine and then he becomes Jordan, who is a little boy.' Seeing their looks of disbelief, he went on, 'We have many different mental disorders in here. For instance, we have a lady who lost her baby to pneumonia and it tipped her over the edge. We gave her a doll when she came to us and she cares for it like she would a living child. She feeds it, changes it, and sings it to sleep. She never puts it down for fear of losing it again, and that loss is what keeps her in a world of her own. She has loved that doll for thirty years.'

'Thirty...!' Rose gasped. 'Will she not get better?'

'No, I'm afraid not. You have to be prepared, Miss Hamilton, that your aunt may be with us for some time to come, if not for the rest of her life.'

Rose burst into tears and Jackson again placed a comforting arm around the girl. 'Will she be allowed visitors?' he asked.

'Of course. All our patients have visitors – at the beginning. After a while, they stop coming as the stress is too much for them. It would be my advice, Mr Jackson, to leave Win in our care, and should there be an improvement we will let you know.'

Jackson nodded and led Rose out of the building to find a cab to return them home.

53

Once home, Rose and Jackson went to the kitchen to join the others.

'Thank you all for your help,' Rose said. 'Dr Hughes can't tell us how long she will be in the... hospital, or even if she will ever come out.'

'How are you feeling, Miss Rose?' Mary asked.

'Other than shocked, I feel fine.'

'I wonder what brought it on?' Katy mused.

'She seemed her usual self when she went out, but on her return she was – changed somehow.' Jackson shook his head.

'Where did she go?' Rose asked.

'I...' Jackson began.

'What, Jackson, tell me, please,' Rose begged.

'She went to see Mr Dean.'

'Bloody hell!' Mary gasped.

Rose got to her feet. 'I need to see Charles. I have to find out what was said between them to turn Aunt Win into a raving lunatic!'

'You can't ago to a man's house alone, Miss Rose!' Katy said.

'I will accompany Miss Rose while you get dinner ready,' Jackson said, taking control.

Again, mistress and butler set out on yet another cab ride.

'Thank you, Jackson.'

'I will wait in the foyer while you talk with Mr Dean,' he said, inclining his head.

On arrival, the maid showed them in. Charles was surprised to see them both and Jackson explained he would be in the hall.

'Rose, how delightful to see you...' Charles began.

'Aunt Win came to see you this morning.' At his nod, Rose went on, 'What happened between the two of you?'

'I'm not sure I can discuss your aunt's business...'

Rose cut across him again. 'I have to know, Charles! Whatever it was put my aunt in the asylum this afternoon!'

'Oh my God!' Charles rubbed his forehead. 'Rose, I'm so sorry. She came to ask me to stop seeing you, and I said no. I told her I wanted to marry you and she stormed out.'

Rose explained about Win attacking her and shrieking *He's mine! You stole him from me!*

'Rose, please sit. There's something you should know.' Rose obliged and he continued. 'Years ago, everyone thought Win and I would marry. We had been close friends for a long time, but something happened which changed everything, even our friendship.'

'What was it?'

'I can't tell you. Please understand it's not my place; it should be Win who explains it to you.'

'She can't, Charles! She's incarcerated, probably for the rest of her life!'

'I told her back then that I couldn't marry her and she's hated me ever since.'

'She doesn't, though, Charles, she's still in love with you even after all this time.'

'This is such a mess. Rose, please forgive me but I cannot give you the reason. I will say I loved her like a sister. I told her that, all those years ago.'

'Would you have wed if this *reason* hadn't happened?'

'No, Rose, I wouldn't. I explained to her that I didn't love her in that way.'

Rose burst into tears and Charles was at her side in an instant. 'Oh, my darling girl, please don't cry.'

'It was so awful,' Rose sobbed, 'she was like a demon, spitting and screaming!'

'I'm so very sorry you are having to deal with all this.'

Rose got to her feet. 'I must go, I'm very tired.'

'Of course. Come.' Charles led her out of the room to where Jackson was waiting with the maid. 'Take care of her, Jackson, please.'

Jackson inclined his head. 'I will, sir.'

Charles watched the cab roll away and returned to his seat by the fire. Staring into the flames, he wondered again about Rose's question. Would he have married Win had she not told him what she had? He shook his head, no. What he had said about loving Win as a sister was true, but more than that…? It would never have worked; he could never have felt for Win what he felt for Rose.

Thinking of Win now being kept in that most dreadful of places, Charles felt a pang of guilt. Had he wronged her back then? No, he had been honest about his feelings despite the hurt it caused. Win went away, to the seaside somewhere, and she didn't come back for twelve months. When she returned, she was a different person. Gone was her gaiety, replaced by a sourness.

She didn't laugh any more, just scowled every time they came into contact with each other.

From what he'd learned from Rose, it appeared Win had never forgiven him, but neither had she lost her love for him. Clearly his telling her he would marry Rose had pushed her further than her mind could cope with. That was where his guilt lay, he should never have said a word, but it could not be undone now, and because of it Win had ended up in the asylum.

Dropping his head into his hands, Charles muttered, 'Oh, Win, why couldn't you have lied to me all those years ago!' He knew in his heart, however, that it would have made no difference.

* * *

In the cab on the way home, Jackson exceeded his remit of butler by holding Rose close as she cried. He, as had Mary, had watched Rose grow into the sweetest of young ladies. He and Mary had joined the family when Rose was about six months old and both had doted on the child. When Rose lost her parents and moved to live with her aunt, Jackson and Mary had gone with her. Win was quite happy to employ them both as it added to her prestige. Katy, of course, had come to the household much later.

On reaching home, they went to the kitchen, Rose saying she wanted to be with her friends. Over tea, Rose explained what Charles had told her, despite Dolly being there with her ears pricked up. Now was not the time to be concerned over a scullion.

'If Aunt Win won't be coming home, I'll have to sort out the money situation with the bank.'

'Don't worry about that now,' Mary said, raising an eyebrow, 'there's plenty of time to sort it all out.'

'Miss Rose, let's get you to bed. I know it's early but you need the rest.' Katy helped her mistress up the stairs to her room. 'Mr Watts should be able to help with the bank situation,' she said, aiding Rose with undressing.

'Why, yes, of course! I'll go and see him tomorrow,' Rose said.

'Take Mr Jackson or Mrs Winters with you because they might have questions you might not think of.'

'I will, thank you, Katy.'

Rose lay in bed, watching the darkness deepen. Her mind whirled with everything that had taken place, her head aching with trying to make sense of it all.

Not realising she had slept, Rose woke to sunshine filling her room. She dragged herself out of bed and dressed, feeling the weight of the world on her shoulders as she remembered the events of the previous day.

With only a cup of tea for breakfast, Rose said, 'I have to go out and would like you to accompany me, Jackson. We must see the bank manager in order that I have access to the accounts.'

'Certainly, Miss Rose.'

Jackson went outdoors and waved to the cabbie, who always seemed to be in the same spot waiting for a fare. As it drew up, Rose gave the address of her solicitor, and once inside she explained Katy's idea of seeing John Watts first.

'A very sound notion, if I may say so,' Jackson said.

At Messrs Watts & Watts, John greeted them warmly. He had heard of Rose's unfortunate circumstances, for gossip travelled like wildfire, and instantly agreed to accompany them to the bank.

'I'm so sorry to hear about your aunt, Rose,' John said.

'Thank you, John. Jackson has been such a great help.'

Arriving at the Midland Bank on Stephenson Place, the three alighted. John took the lead by introducing himself and asking to see the manager. They were kept waiting only a moment before being shown into his office. Here John related what had happened regarding Win Jacobs, and asked for Rose to have access to the accounts.

When the manager blustered about it being a most unusual request, John produced the copy of Miles Hamilton's will. He had brought it in case there was any dispute concerning Rose being able to draw household funds.

'Miss Hamilton will have to sign a form to become the signatory before the specified date,' the manager said, having read the will.

'Mr Jackson and I will both witness it and Miss Hamilton and I would insist on having a copy,' John said.

'Very well.' Opening a drawer in his desk, the manager pulled out three forms, all of which were signed, dated and witnessed. Shaking hands with the manager, they left the bank.

'Thank you, John, I would never have thought to ask for a copy,' Rose said, holding up the paper.

'Mr Jackson would have, I'm sure,' John said with a smile.

'Indeed, Mr Watts.'

Having dropped John off at his office, Rose and Jackson went home.

'How did you get on?' Mary asked as they entered the kitchen.

'It's all sorted,' Rose answered, giving Katy a knowing smile, which her maid returned. 'It's going to be very strange here without Aunt Win.'

'It will take some getting used to, I'm sure,' Mary agreed.

'Miss Rose, might I suggest that you decide what to do about any forthcoming engagements,' Jackson put in.

'Thank you, Jackson, something else I wouldn't have thought of. I'll check Aunt Win's diary and cancel whatever she had planned.'

'Shall I bring tea up, Miss Rose?'

'Yes, please. I hope all this doesn't mean you will all be calling me the *missus* from now on.' Rose gave a small smile as the staff assured her they wouldn't.

54

Rose cancelled the parties Win had accepted, saying her aunt had been taken ill, and she had no idea when Win would recover.

Slowly Rose adjusted to becoming the head of the household, and over the next few months her only visitor was Charles.

Their meetings at first were a little strained because of the secret Charles held, but as time passed Rose came to rise above it.

Charles had wanted to go and see Win but Rose said it would only make matters worse. There had been no updates from the asylum on Win's condition or progress, and Rose often wondered if her aunt was getting better.

As spring gave way to summer, Rose was very aware of her upcoming birthday. The staff suggested she hold a party but Rose refused. It was not appropriate, she thought, with Win being in what she continued to refer to as the *hospital*.

As usual, Jackson kept the staff up to date with the news reported in the papers.

'Another murder in Whitechapel,' he said, shaking his head.

'Oh my God! How many is that now?' Mary asked.

'Twelve, I believe.'

'It's odd that the murderer only targets women in that area.'

'Indeed, Mrs Winters. All desperate and destitute women having to ply their trade on the streets.'

'Who was it this time?'

'Alice McKenzie, so the paper says. Murdered on 17 July. It seems the constabulary are no nearer to catching the killer.'

'It's terrible. I hope they get him soon 'cos folk are scared out of their minds,' Mary said sadly.

'I concur. This Jack the Ripper is a very dangerous man and needs to be apprehended as soon as possible.'

* * *

On the morning of Rose's birthday, the sun shone brightly and she received Charles in the sitting room.

'Good morning and the happiest of days to you. I have come to fulfil my pledge.' Charles dropped to one knee, holding out a tiny box. 'Rose Hamilton, please say you will marry me.'

Rose stared at the diamond ring being held out to her. So much had happened over the last months and there was still the secret hanging over her. She looked at the man she loved with all her heart, his eyes begging her to say yes.

'Ch...' she began and her heart hammered in her chest. If she were to marry him, would his secret come between them?

'Rose?' Charles looked up into the violet eyes he adored, praying she would not refuse him.

'Charles...' she began again. Then, taking a deep breath, she said, 'Yes, Charles, I will!'

Standing up, he placed the ring on her finger and kissed her passionately. 'I vow to take care of you and to love you until death takes me.'

They were kissing again when Katy brought in the tea tray. She smiled as she placed it down.

'Katy, please ask everyone to join us and bring some wine and glasses.'

When all were gathered, Rose nodded to Charles.

'I am delighted to announce that Rose has consented to become my wife.'

Applause filled the room and the staff congratulated the happy couple with a toast.

Jackson heard the front door knocker and slipped out of the room to answer it. He returned to say a Mr Thompson of Jones, Evans & Thompson was requesting to see Rose.

'Show him in, please, Jackson,' Rose said as the staff left to go about their business.

'I think I should retire also,' Charles said, 'I'll be in the kitchen with your friends.'

Rose smiled. 'Mr Thompson, please take a seat. Would you care for tea – coffee?'

'Miss Hamilton,' he said with a little bow, 'coffee would be a rare treat for me, thank you.'

Rose yanked on the bell pull and when Katy arrived asked for coffee for them both. Once refreshments were served, Mr Thompson pulled out some papers from his briefcase. He passed them to Rose with a smile before he sipped his delicious drink. Then he said, 'Happy birthday, Miss Hamilton, everything you need to know is contained in those documents.'

Giving her thanks, Rose scanned the will, then the deeds for the house she now sat in and the one she had lived in with her parents. There were deeds for six further houses which were rented out, thus providing a monthly income. As well as this there was documentation stating she was now company director of a large import/export business.

Rose gasped as she read. Clearly Win had not been a party to all this, otherwise wouldn't she have had copies to keep with the will Rose had found?

'Mr Thompson – I'm – I can't believe it!'

The solicitor merely nodded as he savoured his drink.

Rose continued her reading. She discovered various bank accounts, both personal and business, and her mouth hung open at the fortune amassed on the pages.

Mr Thompson placed his empty cup on the table. 'You are now a very wealthy young lady, Miss Hamilton, and engaged to boot, I see,' he said, nodding to her sparkling ring.

'Yes, as of this morning,' Rose said, as if in a trance.

'Congratulations. I have one more item for you and then I'll be on my way.' He retrieved an envelope and handed it to her. 'Thank you for your hospitality and good day to you.'

'Thank you, Mr Thompson,' Rose said, pulling the bell pull once more after laying the papers aside.

Jackson saw the gentleman out and returned to the kitchen.

Rose opened the envelope and retrieved its contents.

Dearest Rose,

If you are reading this then it means I am beyond the world of the living. I have so much to tell you I hardly know where to begin.

When your father and I married we both longed for children to fill our happy home. However, it was not to be. Soon enough, the doctors told me I could never become a mother. After the initial shock and upset, we resigned ourselves to the fact it would only ever be us two.

At that time, Win came to live close to us and I persuaded your father to let her move into one of our houses. She was my sister and I wanted her near, as you can imagine. Win and I never really saw eye to eye, I'm afraid. She's a very selfish person, Rose, so be aware in your dealings with her.

Win was very great friends with a man called Charles Dean, and we all thought they would wed before too long. However, it was not to be. One fateful day Win had to tell him a secret she had been harbouring, before it was too late to hide any more – Win was pregnant.

Rose's hand shot to her mouth in disbelief and shock.

The trouble was, Charles was not the father.

Rose blew out her cheeks. Now she knew what Charles had refused to tell her, and she read on eagerly.

Charles had already told her they would not be married and her pregnancy now had shattered their friendship. Win went away to have the child, a baby girl.

Rose had a very uncomfortable feeling at this but she had to continue reading.

Win brought her daughter home and asked – no, begged – us to look after her, to raise her as our own. So Rose, my darling, you became our daughter and I was extremely happy.

Rose laid the letter on her lap when Katy came for the tray. 'Mr Dean is asking…'

'No, Katy, not yet. Ask him to give me some time alone, please. I won't be long.'

Katy nodded and took the tray away.

Rose's heart beat like a drum. The woman she'd known as her aunt all these years was actually her mother! She realised that had Win kept her baby, the scandal would have been horrendous for the family. So where was her real father, and why had he not made an honest woman of Win? Going back to the letter, she hoped to find out.

Until, that is, I found out why Win would not disclose the name of the father of her child. Imagine my shock to learn it was my very own husband!

'Dear God!' Rose exclaimed. Her father and Win? She tried to take it all in but her mind was doing somersaults. Her eyes on the letter once more, she read on.

I should have left him but I couldn't, Rose. Despite everything I still loved him. I forgave him on the understanding I could keep you as my own.

Charles and Win became estranged, understandably, considering the circumstances and to my knowledge he never learned who the father of Win's baby was.

Again Rose paused. Did Charles know now or was he still in the dark? Rose knew she would have to tell him, she wanted no more secrets in their relationship.

With regards to your father's will, he chose the clauses carefully, Rose. He didn't want you to wed before your time and thereby lose your fortune to an unworthy husband. He knew also that Win would never sell the business – should she discover its existence along with the other houses. This way, he said, the estate would stay in the family and provide you with a life without financial burden.

I'm sorry if this has come as a shock to you, my darling girl; I feel sure Win would not have breathed a word of it.

'You are right there,' Rose muttered.

Always remember, I loved you the most. If I am correct, you will be very wealthy now. I wrote this letter, Rose, so you would be aware of your parentage.

I tried my best for you, Rose, and I loved you with all my heart.

Jenny

Rose folded the letter and pushed it back in the envelope, tears streaming down her cheeks. She took some time to bring her emotions under control before summoning Katy. When the maid appeared, she asked that Charles join her.

Charles came bustling in, saying, 'Mrs Winters has been keeping me amused with tales of your childhood...' Seeing Rose's face, he asked, 'Rose?'

'Please sit and read this...' Rose handed him the letter.

Seeing her name on the envelope, he said, 'It's addressed to you.'

'Read it, Charles, it's important.'

When he finished, he exclaimed, 'Bloody hell!'

'Eloquently put, Charles.'

Despite the gravity of the situation, they both smiled.

'So now we both know,' Rose said as she retook the letter handed to her.

'I had no idea it was your father,' he said in all honesty.

Rose passed him the will and after scanning it, he said, 'So this is why you couldn't marry me before your birthday.'

Rose nodded. 'My solicitor informs me I will be able to keep the properties and business.'

'And rightly so,' he added quickly.

'I will, however, need some help with them.'

'Then I'm your man.'

'I think it's time the staff are aware of all this, don't you?'

'Do they need to...?'

'Yes, Charles, they are my friends and they have supported me throughout.'

Once again, everyone was gathered in the sitting room and Rose related what she had learned. All were shocked at the revelations and were about to be dismissed when another knock came to the door.

With a sigh, Jackson went to answer and a moment later led Dr Hughes into the room.

With a nod, he said, 'I'm sorry to intrude, Miss Hamilton, but I have some bad news, I'm afraid. Your Aunt Win was found dead this morning in her room. She had hung herself.'

Rose dropped to her seat, turning pale in an instant. Mary and Katy gasped and Jackson went to them to comfort them, as Charles did with Rose.

'Last night she asked for pencil and paper and this was left for you.'

Rose took the slip of paper and read out loud.

Happy birthday, Rose. You are my daughter and I did love you.
Tell Charles I'm sorry.

'Oh my God!' Rose gasped. 'I can't believe...' She looked into Charles's eyes as he wrapped his arms around her.

Jackson saw the doctor out, assuring him the funeral would be arranged.

Giving their condolences, the staff filed out, leaving Charles to look after their new mistress.

55

'Poor Aunt Win,' Rose said, amid sobs.

Charles held her gently. 'She was an unhappy woman for many years. She wanted something she could not have which, over time, clearly over-stressed her mind. I'm so sorry, Rose.'

'She waited until my birthday before she...'

'Darling, don't think on it. She's gone to a better place now.'

'All these years she was my mother and I didn't know.'

'No one did except Jenny and Miles, it seems.'

'How could my father have...?'

'These things happen, my love. We don't know the circumstances and I would say – don't let this spoil the fond memories you have of him. Besides, had it not happened then you wouldn't be here and I would never have married.'

Rose nodded, knowing he was right. 'I'll have to arrange a funeral.' Then Rose began to cry again.

'You are in no fit state to be thinking about that just now.' Charles rang the bell pull and a moment later Katy appeared.

'Katy, could we have some tea, please. A universal remedy is sorely needed here.'

'Yes, sir.' Katy made no effort to move and when the couple looked up she said, 'Beggin' your pardon, Miss Rose, but would you like me to have a word with Edward?'

'Oh, Katy, of course! Yes, please.' Then to Charles she said, 'Katy's sweetheart is Edward Gerrard.'

'Ah, that's fortunate.'

'If he could call as soon as possible I would be grateful, thank you, Katy.'

Down in the kitchen, Katy told the others what Rose had said.

'Take the tea up then go and fetch him, because the sooner it's done, the happier we'll all be,' Jackson said.

An hour later, Edward sat with Rose and Charles, delicately discussing Win's funeral.

'She took her own life, Edward,' Rose said sadly. 'Doesn't the law state that she can only be buried at night between nine o'clock and midnight?'

Edward shook his head with a little smile. 'The law was changed in 1882. It's my guess that the coroner will find your aunt to be insane, by dint of her being in the asylum. This means she can be interred in consecrated ground during daylight hours with relevant prayers. I'm sorry if this is upsetting you, Rose, it's always a difficult time for the family.'

'Thank you, at least it's laid my mind to rest.' Rose had not corrected him when he referred to Win as her aunt; there seemed little point now.

'What do we have to do now?' Rose asked.

'I will contact Dr Hughes and let him know we are taking care of Miss Jacobs. When the coroner's report comes through I will contact you regarding a date and time for the interment. For now, it would help me if you could choose a burial package.' He passed her a brochure he'd pulled from his briefcase.

Charles sat in quiet support while Rose made her choice of casket and flowers.

Edward made notes and took back the brochure. 'Be assured we will collect Miss Jacobs at the appropriate time and carry her to our chapel of rest. She will go to her final resting place from there.'

Rose heaved a sigh of relief. She had dreaded the thought of the cortege having to leave from the hospital.

When Edward had gone, Rose seemed a little happier, saying how reverent and caring the young man had been.

'Once we have the details of the funeral I will place an obituary in the newspaper for those wishing to attend.'

'Rose, you can't do anything more for now, and you have to remember it's your birthday.'

'And what a birthday it is!'

'Don't let Win spoil it for you.' Charles held up a hand and went on. 'I know you are terribly sad just now, but without sounding callous, life must go on.'

'I know but I don't feel much like celebrating.'

'I can see that, my love. Come with me.' Charles helped her to her feet.

'Where are we going?'

'The kitchen. Mrs Winters informed me you spend most of your time there, and you need your friends around you now.'

The atmosphere downstairs was subdued when the couple entered until Mary threw her arms around Rose. In turn, each of the staff hugged her, even Dolly, and Rose smiled her thanks.

Katy made tea and Mary brought out cake as all sat around the huge table. Over the next hours they discussed the funeral, the will and Rose's inheritance, as well as the engagement, then finally they began to reminisce about Rose's childhood.

Eventually Charles rose to leave, saying he would be back the following day. Rose saw him out with a kiss before returning to the kitchen. Talk then moved on to the wedding, which would take place after a suitable mourning period had been observed.

The days seemed to pass slowly and it was a week later when Edward called at the house again. 'Dr Hughes informed me that he had received the coroner's report, and you'll be glad to know Miss Jacobs now lies in our chapel of rest.'

'That was quick, I thought it would take longer,' Rose admitted.

'Normally, yes, maybe the coroner is short of work.' Edward saw the surprise on Rose's face and immediately said, 'I'm sorry, that was insensitive.'

'No, it's all right.'

'Rose, please understand that in my line of business there have to be light-hearted moments to prevent us from being immersed in the sadness of death. I do apologise.'

'There's no need, Edward. I'm amazed that you can still laugh, to be honest. I recall you telling Katy and me about the "casket crawlers".'

His hand shot up to cover his mouth and Rose laughed, the heaviness of the situation lifting from her, leaving her feeling light again. 'You know, you are perfect for this profession, Edward Gerrard. Thank you for making all of this so easy to deal with, Edward, I appreciate it.'

Giving a little bow, he said, 'At your service. Now if we might choose a time and date...'

'Of course.'

When Edward had gone, Rose told the staff the details of the funeral. Then she went to write Win's obituary.

56

On the day of the funeral, Rose, Charles and the staff gathered to walk behind the carriage carrying Win's coffin. Each of them held a single yellow rose to be placed on the grave. As they traversed the streets, people stood still; men removed their hats or caps, and women quieted their noisy children as a mark of respect. Black horses, with their plumes bobbing, walked sedately along pulling the carriage, and the conductor strode out in front.

Arriving at the cemetery, pallbearers hefted the casket onto their shoulders and, all in step, carried it to the gravesite. There they lowered it to the ground, bowed their heads and stepped back.

There was a good turn-out, Rose noted, as she stood next to the vicar.

Rose's eyes brimmed with tears as the portly man spoke the relevant prayers. The coffin was then lowered into the ground and Rose let her emotions free. She cried for the loss of her father and Jenny, who for many years she'd thought of as her mother. She wept for Win, her birth mother, and the time they had wasted with bickering and secrets. Life could have been so much better for them both if Win had only told her the truth before this.

Stepping forward, Rose dropped her flower into the hole and saw it land on the casket. She had thought to put it on the soil once the grave was filled in, but her distress was too great to wait. She thanked the vicar and walked away with Charles at her side. At the church gate, Rose fought to bring her emotions under control. As each mourner departed with a kind word, she shook their hand, giving her thanks for their attendance. The Glendenings, the Huntington-Phillipses, Clara Billingham and her nephew, John Watts, as well as Win's card-playing friends and many more drifted away, leaving Rose, Charles and the staff alone.

They walked slowly back to the house for a private wake. Mary had provided a small buffet and Katy set the kettle to boil.

Quiet chatter filled the kitchen about the funeral and Rose listened, realising she had no blood relatives left now Win was gone. She was, however, very grateful to have her good friends around her.

Accepting a plate of food, Charles said, 'I've never spent so much time in a kitchen – until I met Rose, that is.'

'It's my favourite room in the whole house,' Rose answered, 'I've always felt welcome here.'

'That's 'cos you are, Miss Rose,' Mary said.

After their funeral tea, Rose and Charles heard tales of the missus which made them smile. 'I remember her throwing a blue fit over summat you'd done,' Mary said. 'She was all dressed up to go out and she got so riled up she spilt her tea on her skirt. Having to go and get changed made her late and you know how she hated that.'

The following hours were spent reminiscing, then Charles rose to take his leave. Jackson whistled for a cab then retreated back to the kitchen while Rose and Charles said goodnight in the hall.

'Sleep well, my love. I will come tomorrow,' Charles said before he kissed her tenderly.

'Thank you, Charles, I couldn't have got through today without you.' Waving him off, Rose went to say goodnight to her friends, then she went to bed, telling Katy she could manage by herself.

For the next week, Charles spent part of the day with Rose before going on to his work. Rose, for her part, wandered around the house with nothing to do. So it came as a surprise one day when John Watts came to call. He suggested Rose should visit her father's office and introduce herself.

'I know nothing about business, John,' she said. 'Would you come with me?'

Assuring her he would be happy to do so, they set off in the waiting cab. Eventually arriving at a massive building, they asked a fellow where they could find the manager.

'You want the foreman, Geordie, he's in there.' The man pointed to a door and with thanks they knocked and walked in.

'We're looking for the foreman,' John said.

'That's me. Tim Dibley, otherwise known as Geordie on account of me hailing from Newcastle in the north-east.'

'John Watts, solicitor, and this lady is Miss Rose Hamilton.'

'Gerraway! Miss Hamilton, I'm pleased to meet you. Please take a seat.' Once his visitors were sitting down, he went on. 'You were nobbut a bairn the last time I saw you. Eeh, we were all so sorry to hear of your father's passing. He was a good gaffer.'

Rose nodded her thanks, liking the musical way he spoke, the lilt rising at the end of the sentences. 'Can you tell me, Mr Dibley, who has been in charge since then?'

'Call me Geordie, miss. As to your question – I have. After the gaffer died, we had no instructions as to who would take over. It was a worrying time but we had a meeting and decided to go on as we were. There was plenty of work so I stepped into Mr Hamilton's shoes, as best as I could, regarding the buying and selling.'

'What about the finances?' John asked.

'I worked closely with the gaffer so I know about invoicing, banking and the like. Each Friday morning I fetch the wages from the bank and pay everybody on a Friday night. So far it seems to have worked fine.'

'Mr Di... Geordie, does this mean you and the other workers are still on the same rate of pay since my father died?' Rose asked.

'Wey aye. It's not in my remit to adjust the wages, everybody knows that. We're all just glad to be in work and still have money coming in.'

'I think it would be a good idea for Miss Hamilton to see the books, if you don't mind,' John said.

'Right away. Excuse me a minute.' Geordie left the office and yelled across the warehouse. 'Ezra! Fetch the books!' Back in the office, he said, 'Can I offer you tea?'

'No, thank you,' Rose said and John shook his head.

The office door flew open and the man they had spoken to earlier walked in carrying a huge ledger.

'Ezra Darlington, meet Miss Rose Hamilton and Mr John Watts, her lawyer. Miss Rose, this is your accounts manager.'

'Well, I'll goo to the foot of our stairs! I'm pleased to meet you, miss.' Ezra's Black Country accent was in stark contrast to that of the foreman. 'I've bin keepin' the books up to date 'til such time as we... well, we d'aint rightly know when.'

'Thank you, Mr Darlington, would you be kind enough to show me, please?' Rose asked, not at all sure she would understand what she was looking at.

'O' course, miss. I ain't a qualified accountant, you understand, but I've done me best,' Ezra explained. 'This side is what comes in moneywise, and that side is what goes out. That there is the running total of what's in the bank once the wages come out.'

Rose was aghast at the amount amassed in the company account at the bank. 'Mr Darlington, you've done splendid work here, I have to say.' She was pleased he'd kept it all so simple and she could see at a glance how everything worked.

'Ta, miss. It ain't my proper job though, I'm in charge of warehouse one.'

Rose frowned and it was Geordie who explained. 'Every warehouse has a manager, miss, and in each is a different commodity. Ezra's is silk from China. Another is coffee beans from Columbia, one for tea from India and so on.'

'May I see yours, Mr Darli...'

'Ezra, miss, and ar, if you'll come along o' me I'd be glad to show you.'

Rose and John followed as Ezra led them to a separate building. Inside were racks of bolts of brightly coloured silk.

'Oh, my!' Rose gasped. 'Ezra, could I buy some of this?'

'Rose, you don't need to buy it, the company belongs to you now,' John reminded her.

'Which colours am you after, miss? I'll 'ave 'em sent to your 'ouse this after.'

'One bolt of each, please, Ezra, and thank you! I have an idea which will see them put to very good use.'

Rose and John were shown around the numerous other warehouses by Geordie, and by the time they returned to the office Rose was amazed to say the least.

'I'd rather like that tea now, if it's all the same to you, Geordie,' Rose said, taking a seat once more.

'Mr Watts?' Geordie asked, and when John nodded he went

on, 'Right away.' He set the kettle to boil on a pot-bellied stove in the corner of the room which kept the office warm.

'Rose, I think it's probably time to employ an accountant, thereby relieving Ezra of the burden,' John suggested, 'despite the excellent work he's been doing.'

Rose looked at the men, asking, 'Would you both be happy with that?'

'I would certainly,' Ezra said without preamble.

'Me an' all, miss,' Geordie concurred.

'Would you like me to get on to that for you, Rose?' John asked.

'Yes, please, John. Now, Ezra, according to your immaculate book-keeping no one has had a raise in salary since my father died.'

'Ar, miss, that's correct.'

'Well, we are about to change that right now.' Picking up a pen and headed notepaper, Rose wrote a letter to the bank authorising the rise of funds collected each Friday by Mr Tim Dibley. 'Produce this at the bank the next time you go,' she said, handing the letter to Geordie. 'Ezra, please show me the workers' salary page in the ledger.' Against each name, she had him increase the wage by one pound per month, and Geordie's by two pounds, befitting his station as foreman; the men were delighted, of course. Rose explained where she was living and had been since her parents' demise, and that her door was always open. 'I don't foresee any problems, given you gentlemen have run this place perfectly well for years. I would, however, like to pop in now and then if only to say hello.'

'You'd be most welcome, pet... erm, miss,' Geordie said as he poured the tea.

'Thank you,' Rose said with a grin at the slip of the tongue.

With refreshments finished, Rose said, 'I'll leave you to your work now. Thank you, gentlemen, for all you have done over the past years, and continue to do.'

'I'll get the silks to you right away, miss,' Ezra said.

Bidding them farewell, John returned Rose home, congratulating her on her first business dealing.

Later that afternoon, a horse pulling an old cart rolled up the drive and Jackson, in a huff, went out to see what was happening, all ready to berate the man he thought was a tinker.

'Delivery for Miss Hamilton,' the driver said as he and another man jumped down.

Rose came running out, saying, 'It's all right, Jackson, I'm aware of this. Can you direct them to the sitting room, please?'

Jackson nodded. 'Follow me.'

The men carried the packages, which were tightly wrapped in brown paper and each stamped with the name of the colour, following behind the butler.

Rose tipped the men before they left. Then she asked for Mary, Katy and Dolly to join her. Jackson stood silently by once everyone was assembled and Rose unwrapped each parcel.

'Oh, Miss Rose!' Mary gasped as she saw the beautiful bolts of silk set out on the chairs and sofas.

'Now I want each of you to choose one to be made into a ball gown.'

'What?' Katy croaked.

'Can I 'ave this 'un?' Dolly asked quickly, pointing to the bright orange, clearly afraid one of the others would beat her to it.

Rose nodded. 'Mary?'

'I love the lilac, Miss Rose.'

Another nod. 'Katy?'

The maid chose a shade sitting between sky and royal blue.

'What about you, Miss Rose?' Mary asked, hardly able to believe her eyes.

'I have mine already,' Rose said with a little smile as she thought of her red gown hanging in the wardrobe. 'Jackson, would you please send a runner to Mr Dean, asking him to call on me and to bring his cook and maid.'

Inclining his head, Jackson left the room.

'Ladies, please take your material to your rooms for safekeeping. Then tea, I think.' Rose smiled at the excited chatter as the staff did as they were bid.

Jackson returned, saying the runner had been despatched.

'Good. Now tomorrow I would like you to go to town and have yourself a new dinner suit made, the invoice to be sent to me.'

'Thank you, Miss Rose. May I ask what all this is about?'

'I want to hold a ball, Jackson, so I'll need some help finding a venue large enough to hold about – I don't know – lots of people!'

'Very good, miss. May I suggest the Town Hall? It will cost, of course, but it should be more than sufficient for your needs. It's often used for such events.'

'Excellent. We will need to hire staff to provide and serve food and drinks.'

'We are avail...' Jackson began.

'No, Jackson, hire, please, because you, Mary, Katy and Dolly will be in attendance as guests of honour, as will Mr Dean's cook and maid.'

Jackson's eyes filled with tears and he inclined his head to hide them from Rose.

'Jackson, you are all very dear to me. There have been times, often, when I have looked on you as a father figure.' Rose heard her butler sniff and went to him. 'Would you forget etiquette for a moment and give me a hug?'

Jackson looked at the girl he loved like a daughter and

nodded, holding out his arms. Rose stepped forward and felt those arms fold around her and his gentle kiss to her hair. Reluctantly Jackson let her go and wiped away the tears rolling down his face. 'My little Rosie,' he whispered.

Rose was surprised then said, 'You haven't called me that in a very long while.'

'Times change, miss, and you're a grown woman now.'

'Maybe, but promise me I can always be that to you.'

'I promise until my dying day you always will be.'

'In that case, Arnold...' Jackson's mouth dropped open; this was the first time ever that Rose had used his Christian name. 'Would you walk me down the aisle on my wedding day?'

'I'd be honoured, my little Rosie.'

57

Charles arrived an hour later with Bess and Daisy in tow, wondering what was going on.

Rose greeted them warmly and explained her idea about the ball. Given the choice of silks, Bess opted for bright green and Daisy went for egg-yolk yellow. Charles said he would hire the Town Hall on her behalf.

Katy brought tea and cake and took Bess and Daisy to the kitchen to visit the other staff and have their refreshments there.

Rose brought Charles up to date on her trip to Hamilton's to meet with the workers along with John Watts.

'Now that you have everything in hand regarding the business and organising a ball, might we consider a date for the wedding?' Charles asked.

'How about three months from now? That will give us plenty of time to make plans.' Despite everything that had happened, Rose was happier than she had ever been.

'Perfect. I shall see the vicar first thing in the morning.'

'Charles, have you given any thought to where we will live once we're wed?'

'I have and I suspect you won't want to move in with me and leave your staff behind.' Rose nodded with a sad look on her face. 'Then what say we look for a larger house together? One that can accommodate both your staff and mine.'

'That would be ideal, but what about our houses?'

'We could rent them out. It seems to make perfect sense to me. A new life – a new house!'

'Oh, Charles, yes! Let's do it!' Rose said, getting caught up in Charles's enthusiasm.

And so it was settled, they would go house hunting once the visit to the vicar was completed.

The following day, Charles arrived to tell Rose the date for their wedding would be 12 November. Not only that but he had booked the Town Hall for 1 October for the ball.

'Then we must get everyone's silks made into dresses, as well as invites to the ball and the wedding sent out! Oh dear, it will all be such a rush!' Rose fretted as she rang for Jackson.

'Jackson, our wedding is set for 12 November, so please inform the others. Oh, and Mr Dean and I will be out for most of the day.'

Giving his congratulations, Jackson went to the hall to see Charles and Rose out. Then he returned to the kitchen with the good news and the message for Mary.

'Blimey, I'd best get a move on then,' Mary said, 'if we want our frocks ready for the ball.'

'I will accompany you as I need to hire staff from the Servants' Registry as, it seems, we are all to be Miss Rose's guests of honour.'

'Bloody hell!' Dolly exclaimed.

'I second that, Dolly,' Katy added.

'Also, I have to be fitted for a new suit, Miss Rose says,' Jackson said.

Whilst the butler and cook went about their business, the two maids chatted quietly.

'I never thought I'd be accepted here,' Dolly said.

'You almost weren't,' Katy answered. 'Mr Jackson was all set to sack you because of your eavesdropping.'

'I know, it was daft of me.'

'Yes, it was, but it's in the past now so time to forget it.'

Dolly nodded and, as she did every day now, she thanked her lucky stars to be a member of this wonderful family at last.

* * *

Over the next week, it was chaos in the house, with women being fitted for new ball gowns, as well as doing their work. Bess and Daisy were also going through the same over at Charles's residence. Annie, the dressmaker, was indeed delighted with the work, which enabled her to take on workers to fulfil the orders.

Charles and Rose searched for a property which would suit them both. They began to despair as nothing seemed to fit their requirements, until one fine morning they found exactly what they were looking for. The massive house boasted a large hall, sitting room, parlour, music room, day room, orangery, huge kitchen, scullery, butler's pantry, lumber room, eight bedrooms, indoor bathroom and sweeping staircase. Back stairs led to eight rooms for servants, and their own bathroom. All were lit by electricity and Rose fell in love with the place the moment she saw it. Outside were stables, tack room, and at the bottom of the short lane was a beautiful three-bedroomed cottage, which Rose thought would be ideal for Katy and Edward were they ever to marry.

The owners, they learned, were moving abroad and the money from the sale of their beloved house would prove very useful when buying their new home. Without preamble, Rose and Charles bought the property that very day. Going to the bank to arrange bankers' drafts, Rose insisted that she and Charles pay half each, much to the manager's amusement.

Arriving home, Charles left Rose with a kiss, he needed to inform his cook and maid they would be moving house just before Christmas. Rose went to the kitchen to do the same thing.

'What, move in alongside Bess and Daisy?' Mary asked.

'Yes,' Rose enthused. 'We'll be tog… Mary, what's wrong?'

'Two cooks in one kitchen, Miss Rose. I can't see that working, despite Bess and me being friends.'

'Oh, Mary, I didn't think about that!' Rose said. She had been so caught up in the excitement of it all, clearly she hadn't thought it through enough.

Again Jackson rescued the situation, saying, 'It could work well if you have one week on and one off. A rota would need to be drawn up as to who is on duty and who is at rest.'

Mary nodded. 'It's about the only way it could work.'

'Miss Rose?' Jackson asked and at her smile he went on, 'So be it. I will see to the rota so it's fair.'

'Good. Now Charles and I would like you all to visit the new house with us next week. We would like your opinions and Jackson, you can allocate bedrooms in the servants' quarters. I'm sure you will all be happy because the rooms are huge.'

The sale of the house was pushed through quickly as the sellers had passages booked on a ship sailing five days hence. With keys in hand, Rose and her staff, and Charles with his, went to see their new abode.

Bess, having been told about the rota system to which she wholeheartedly agreed, went with Mary immediately to seek out the kitchen. Jackson, with pen and paper, went to inspect and allocate the rooms up the back stairs. The maids ambled around downstairs, oohing and ahhing as they went.

Eventually everyone congregated in the sitting room, denuded of its furniture now. 'Well?' Rose asked and all spoke at once. Holding up her hand, she asked one by one for their opinions. It was unanimous – everybody was happy.

'Jackson,' Charles said, 'the logistics of all this is monumental. Have you any ideas on how to get us all moved in?'

Thrilled to be asked, the butler nodded. 'I would suggest, sir, ground-floor furniture first. Then bedroom furniture, leaving the beds until last, of course. Erm...'

'Yes?' Rose asked.

'Begging your pardon, miss, but you and Mr Dean may want to order a new bed for when you are married.'

'Yes, of course,' Rose said, blushing uncontrollably.

'Then,' Jackson went on, 'kitchens also to be emptied save for enough utensils, and so on, to see us through until after the wedding, when the rest can be transported.'

'That's a sound plan,' Charles said. 'Well done, Jackson, I'm impressed. When would you propose we begin?'

'As soon as possible, sir. It might be advisable for Miss Rose or yourself to be here,' he swung an arm out, 'to decide what should go where.'

'Rose, that will be up to you, darling, because I have nothing to bring. I will leave everything where it is, so it will only be Bess and Daisy's rooms to clear.'

'Charles, surely...' Rose started to say.

Shaking his head, he cut across, 'If we need more we can buy it. I'm not attached to anything in my house, it's only – stuff.'

'If you're sure,' Rose said and smiled at his nod.

'I have taken the liberty of allocating our rooms, sir, so with your permission I will show the ladies to their quarters.'

'Thank you, Jackson,' Charles said.

Once they were alone, Charles gathered Rose into his arms and kissed her gently. 'What shall we call this place?'

'Dean Manor,' Rose said without pause.

'So be it.' They shared another kiss before pulling apart as the staff joined them again.

'Welcome one and all to Dean Manor,' Rose said and smiled when everyone applauded. She knew she would be happy at last here with Charles and their friends.

58

Jackson, with Charles's and Rose's approval, took on the role of supervisor for the move. He hired a reliable firm of men to do the heavy work, and the maids began to pack up the kitchen under Mary's watchful eye.

Rose, in the meantime, sent out invitations to the ball, requesting all ladies to be in bright gowns, as was the new fashion coming in from Paris. She wondered how many of her female guests would comply, once the invites had been posted. Rose smiled, knowing this would probably be the only chance she would get to wear her red dress at last.

Jackson had hired an army of cooks, maids, footmen and under-footmen for the occasion and asked they attend him for interview. Mary and the cooks drew up a menu for the buffet and Jackson instructed the others in their duties. Satisfied, all were sent on their way with a warning not to be late on the day of the ball.

Over the next weeks, furniture was taken to Dean Manor and Rose went with it to ensure it was put where she wanted it. Also acceptances to the ball came in thick and fast and Rose began to feel her spirits lift.

Annie, the dressmaker, delivered the finished ball gowns and the excitement grew as they were tried on. Rose was so impressed she requested Annie make her wedding gown.

Eventually, 1 October rolled around and the weather was cold but dry. Charles arrived with Bess and Daisy. Jackson had booked cabs and looked splendid in his new suit. The ladies gathered in the hall in their new gowns, looking like a rainbow. Rose descended the stairs and everyone gasped at how beautiful she looked.

In warm coats, the ladies were helped into the transport by Jackson. Rose and Charles travelled together and he said, 'You look divine, Rose, red is definitely your colour.'

A footman was waiting at the entrance of the Town Hall and all were ushered inside out of the cold. In the huge room a small orchestra was set up and ready. Another room held tables laden with food and drink. Maids and under-footmen took their outdoor clothing, and Charles and Jackson led the ladies through to the ballroom to await the guests.

Rose couldn't have been happier when she saw all the brightly coloured gowns. The musicians played softly in the background until everyone had arrived. They were fed in the kitchen while the guests enjoyed their buffet.

Rose and Charles were congratulated on their upcoming wedding and then the dancing began. Jackson and Mary waltzed around the room, as did Katy and Edward. Dolly and Daisy were sought out by the young men who had attended with their parents. Jackson then danced with Bess, sharing his time between the two cooks.

The whole evening was a great success and Rose was complimented on her idea of bright and colourful gowns, and made to promise to share any new Paris fashions she learned about. Everyone went home happy, having enjoyed a thoroughly pleasant evening.

* * *

After a couple of days, Rose knew it was time to concentrate on planning for the wedding, as well as getting as much as possible moved into the new house.

Before they knew it, 12 November was upon them. Katy helped Rose into her gown: champagne silk with a covering of Nottingham's finest lace. She wore the locket given to her by her friends, the one containing the picture of her parents, for she still thought of Jenny as her mother, and the bracelet Charles had given her for her birthday.

Everyone left for the church, leaving Rose and Jackson in the hall. 'You look beautiful, my little Rosie,' Jackson said, tears clouding his eyes.

Rose smiled, her own tears threatening. 'Today is the day, Arnold.'

'Miss Rose, are you certain about this?'

'Yes, I've never been more sure of anything in my life.'

'Then let us go.' Jackson helped Rose into the cab then went back to lock the front door. Climbing in beside her, he banged on the roof and the cab set off.

Rose and Jackson walked down the aisle arm in arm and she smiled, seeing Charles waiting for her. The church was filled with people who gasped at her loveliness.

The ceremony took place and Mr and Mrs Dean led the congregation out to the transport which would take them to the reception, again at the Town Hall.

Jackson had, once more, organised the music, food, drinks,

and servants and when champagne flowed like water everyone agreed the wedding was the highlight of the year.

Rose and Charles only had eyes for each other and it was clear to all that the match was perfect. The happy couple left the reception for a honeymoon in Paris, waved off by all their guests. Both were bursting with happiness at the thought of spending the rest of their lives together.

* * *

Over the next couple of weeks, Jackson and the staff had their work cut out making sure everything was finally transported to Dean Manor.

Daisy, Charles's maid, fit in well with Katy and Dolly. The scullion was surprised and delighted to be promoted to maid and another couple of girls were taken on as scullions. Jackson, of course, continued to enjoy his position as butler over them all.

By the time the newlyweds returned from honeymoon, Katy and Edward were engaged and already planning their own wedding.

Rose was very happy with the news and offered them the cottage at the end of the lane as their home once they were married, which they accepted gratefully.

* * *

For months, Rose and Charles were deliriously happy until one day Rose took sick.

Dr Hughes was summoned immediately and after a quick examination he informed Rose she was going to be a mother. Charles was beside himself with joy at the news and shouted it all over the house. The staff, naturally, were delighted and Rose and Charles could hear the celebrations taking place in the kitchen.

'Shall we?' Charles asked.

Rose nodded and they made their way downstairs where they joined in the jubilation by drinking a toast to the safe arrival of baby Dean. Looking back over the years, Rose never thought she would be blessed with such happiness. She thought now she would never feel sad again. She prayed the house would be filled with children, light, love and laughter in the years to come.

* * *

MORE FROM LINDSEY HUTCHINSON

Another book from Lindsey Hutchinson, *The Pick-Pocket Orphans*, is available to order now here:

https://mybook.to/PocketOrphansBackAd

ABOUT THE AUTHOR

Lindsey Hutchinson is a bestselling saga author whose novels include *The Workhouse Children*. She was born and raised in Wednesbury, and was always destined to follow in the footsteps of her mother, the multi-million selling Meg Hutchinson.

Sign up to Lindsey Hutchinson's mailing list for news, competitions and updates on future books.

Follow Lindsey on social media:

- facebook.com/Lindsey-Hutchinson-1781901985422852
- x.com/LHutchAuthor
- bookbub.com/authors/lindsey-hutchinson

ALSO BY LINDSEY HUTCHINSON

The Children from Gin Barrel Lane

Minnie's Orphans

The Hat Girl From Silver Street

A Winter Baby for Gin Barrel Lane

The Runaway Children

The Hat Girl's Heartbreak

The Ragged Orphan

The Bad Penny

The Orphan's Promise

The Pick-Pocket Series

The Pick-Pocket Orphans

The Pick-Pocket's Plight

The Pick-Pocket's Return

Sixpence Stories

Introducing Sixpence Stories!

Discover page-turning historical novels from your favourite authors, meet new friends and be transported back in time.

Join our book club Facebook group

https://bit.ly/SixpenceGroup

Sign up to our newsletter

https://bit.ly/SixpenceNews

Boldwood

Boldwood Books is an award-winning fiction publishing company seeking out the best stories from around the world.

Find out more at www.boldwoodbooks.com

Join our reader community for brilliant books, competitions and offers!

Follow us
@BoldwoodBooks
@TheBoldBookClub

Sign up to our weekly deals newsletter

https://bit.ly/BoldwoodBNewsletter